This book is for Ryan, forever the good king of my heart.

"Colleen Oakes creates a fantastic, dark backstory for the Queen of Hearts from *Alice's Adventures in Wonderland* in her novel *Queen of Hearts*."

"I highly recommend baking some celebratory tarts and settling down with *Queen of Hearts*, though I warn you that when you finish it, you're going to be gnashing your teeth to find out what happens next."

— xoJane.com

"The Queen of Hearts series is darker and more twisted than Carroll's version, and Wonderland is less whimsical and more dangerous than most of the other incarnations we have seen. Filled with deadly politics, monstrous creatures, and bloody beheadings, *The Crown* is just the beginning of a longer tale about how a princess became a queen, and an innocent girl became a menacing villain."

— Hypable

Queen of Hearts

Volume Two:
The Wonder

Colleen Oakes

SparkPress, a BookSparks imprint
A division of SparkPoint Studio, LLC

Published by SparkPress, a BookSparks imprint,
A division of SparkPoint Studio, LLC
Tempe, Arizona, USA, 85281
www.sparkpointstudio.com

Printed in the United States of America.

ISBN: 978-1-940716-21-3 (pbk)
ISBN: 978-1-940716-20-6 (ebk)

Cover design © Julie Metz, Ltd/metzdesign.com
Cover photo © Malgorzata Maj/arcangel-images.com
Cover silhouette illustration of Queen by Monica Gurevich, based on
previous art by Truenotdreams Design
Formatting by Polgarus Studio

"The cat only grinned when it saw Alice. It looked good-natured, she thought; still it had very long claws and a great many teeth, so she felt that it ought to be treated with respect."

— *Alice's Adventures in Wonderland*
by Lewis Carroll

CHAPTER ONE

Leaves crunched loudly beneath Dinah's back as she turned over in the Twisted Wood, her eyes weaving through the maze of living trees. Yes, the trees in the Twisted Wood were alive. Not alive in that they spoke or walked or had faces, but that they *saw* her; of this Dinah had no doubt. It was strange and unnerving, these eyes without eyes. She lay on her back, blinking in the midafternoon light, watching the tree branches as they swayed in the wind, so far above she had to squint to make out their budding leaves. The trees of the Twisted Wood were taller than the Black Towers, and sometimes just as wide. Their thick, gnarled trunks of pine and oak choked her passage, and the night before Dinah had found herself not so much walking as maneuvering through them. Each tree was so different—some had bountiful blossoms of pink that swirled through their branches and up their trunks, some had velvety ferns that draped from weeping branches, and some were barren, with only their branches to shelter them. There were trees that grew sideways—they were long and low. Others were spindly towers of wavy bark, their branches shooting straight into the heavens. Some trees looked as though they had been burned; they were as black as night and their trunks gave off a faint aroma of ash. They were alive and thriving, however, as evidenced by the black and white swirled flowers that danced on the tips of their branches. It was incredible—and terrifying.

As Dinah lay still, she considered how the trees knew everything—they knew where she had been and what had happened; they knew that she had once been the Princess of Wonderland Palace. They knew that her father, the brutal King of Hearts, had betrayed her mere days before her coronation to the throne and murdered her beloved brother, the Mad Hatter, by throwing him out a window. They knew of the stranger who had sent her on her way, fleeing the palace on Morte, the devil steed, a Hornhoov whose bloodthirst was legendary. They knew Wardley, the love of her life, had promised to come for her. And they knew that her father was probably tracking her now as she lay motionless under a pile of leaves. She closed her eyes for just a moment more. It wasn't just Dinah's history that these trees knew—she could feel their keen awareness in her bones. These trees of the Twisted Wood knew who drew the location of the stars night after night, and who formed the Todren. They knew each Yurkei and Wonderlander, those who embraced the dark and those who chose the light. Yes, the colossal trees of the Twisted Wood were aware, and that fact had both frightened and comforted her as she trekked into the wood that previous evening, with Morte following her, always at a distance of at least twelve paces. Farther and farther they wove their way into the wood, as the trees groaned and cracked around them, always knowing.

It wasn't until Dinah collapsed in a particularly thick tuft of muddy leaves that they stopped. With her last bit of effort, she pulled her wool cloak over her and closed her eyes. Sleep took her immediately. The slumber was dreamless, a black nothingness, and she was grateful upon waking that she had not been visited by any night terrors. Now, blinking her eyes in the morning light, Dinah marveled at how much clearer her mind was after a night of rest. Morte slept nearby—Dinah could hear his loud breathing. She prayed it would warn away any other wildlife in this corner of the wood. He sounded terrifying, a creature of nightmares.

She rubbed her eyes gently, grimacing as her broken fingers ached with a sharp pain. Her back rattled in protest, as it felt like she had been sleeping on a stone slab rather than a bed of leaves. Her stomach gave a loud growl and Dinah reached for her bag, but not before she settled Wardley's sword close beside her. She untied the brown straps attached to the muslin and slowly laid out its contents, taking a full inventory of what she had: two white linen tunics, a belt, one heavy black dress—so odd!, eight full loaves of bread, twelve large pieces of dried bird meat, a bag of rapidly rotting berries, an ancient rolled map of Wonderland, the remnants of her bloody nightgown, and a sharp dagger. She pulled the dagger out of the bag. It was obviously expensive, the hilt inlaid with dozens of amethysts, interspersed with rich swirls of silver and gold. The black gown beside it was heavy and completely devoid of color—it was the kind of thing that Dinah would wear, but Vittiore would never let such a thing be draped on her shoulders.

Vittiore.

Dinah ground her teeth together, gripping the dagger. No doubt Vittiore would soon be crowned Queen, taking Dinah's place on the throne next to her father. She had always been part of the plot, always waiting in the wings to get her hands on Dinah's crown. She had always suspected that Vittiore wasn't exactly the poor child found in a sack that she claimed to be. Vittiore had been in on it from the start, the plot to frame Dinah, the plot to kill her brother Charles. Dinah angrily closed her fists around the dagger hilt before forcing herself to calm down. She turned the dagger over in the sunlight. *Maybe I can exchange it to buy food*, Dinah thought, before she realized how silly that sounded. She would be going to no villages, no towns. Her father and Cheshire expected her to be weak, to look for help amongst Wonderlanders. She wouldn't. She would just disappear into these woods, forever. *I will learn to survive*, she thought, *I will wait for Wardley and then we will find a boat and sail to the Other Worlds.* The thought made her weary and morose. Heavy despair seemed to hover around her, waiting for the perfect opportunity to overwhelm. If Dinah didn't keep moving, then it would come for her swiftly. Her legs were sore when she pushed herself up onto her feet, strapping the sword firmly across her back. Morte slumbered on, and Dinah thought it best not to wake him. He no doubt needed the rest as much as she did, and waking an angry Hornhoov might lead to being crushed to death. Better to let him sleep.

Making note of the path behind her, Dinah began wandering through the trees as she finished the rest of the berries. The wood seemed to go on forever in every direction. Tiny clusters of flowers brushed her face as she pushed past a tree that spiraled in on itself, its trunk circling into the sky. The tree was weeping a frosty milk that dripped down its branches and formed a white moat around the base of the trunk. Dinah knelt beside the tree and peered into the milky substance. Tiny pink insects with gossamer wings skated over the surface, dipping their long noses into the liquid. The milk was sucked up into their bodies and distributed into their veiny, transparent wings. The white substance then gave their wings a crumbly texture, like toasted bread. At this transformation, the insects tucked their wings back and walked away, looking more like tiny lizards than the butterflies they had resembled at the start. They looked at Dinah with indifference as they strolled away into the forest, a trail of white bread slices marching in sync.

"Incredible," murmured Dinah. She stood. The sun flashed on something hard and metal as Dinah raised her eyes. She leapt backwards, stumbling on a wide root, and the sword fell to the ground. She scrambled for her weapon in the damp leaves as she struggled back to her feet. *I am no warrior*, she thought, as her heart hammered in her ears. The metal continued to flash in the sun. Dinah advanced slowly, making her way through the trees, her sword leading the way. Scrambling, Dinah clawed her way up a small embankment parallel to the flashing light to gain a better view.

The hill rose up next to a deep groove in the forest and Dinah perched on the edge, preparing to see a battalion of soldiers waiting for her. Instead she found herself looking down into a valley... *of heads?* There were dozens of them—Dinah quickly counted them as she carefully made her way down the hill. Dirt rose when her boots hit the ground with a thud. The forest floor had changed— all around this particular valley, the foliage was thick and dense, with ankle-high ferns and roots tangling the ground. Here there were only bright-green grasses that danced in the wind, their seeded tops brushing the carved heads. They were massive in size, most larger than Dinah's ridiculously large bed back at the palace. Some of the heads were propped upright, which made it appear as if the rest of the body was buried underground and they were simply popping up for a look around. Some of the heads lay on their sides, their lips brushed with the burnt yellow grass. One head lay completely upside down, the blunt cut of its square neck facing the sun. That head was wearing a crown, which allowed it to be propped that way, the sharp tips of the crown anchoring the head into the soil. There was something familiar about it.... Dinah ventured closer, making her way through the heads. She bent to look at the face and crown, her black hair brushing the dirt.

A wave of dizziness rushed over her as she realized what she was looking at: her father, the King of Hearts. She could tell by the crown, the same crown that encircled her father's head now, and by his heavy cheeks. Standing so close to the head made Dinah uncomfortable. Though he was made entirely of shiny bronze metal, it looked so much like her father—the same unbending will etched across his brow, the same bloodlust running through his eyes, the same hint of an ironic smile that never quite blossomed. The upside-down head stared at Dinah, its hard eyes piercing her chest. Her heart thudding, she turned away to take in the others. They were all kings and queens of some sort. She recognized several members of the royal family—her grandfathers and grandmothers, dating all the way back to those who had been present at the building of the palace.

There was Queen Millay, famous for her gracious hospitality and striking beauty. Her head lay on its side, the pearl crown on top of it covered with a creeping, soft, green moss. Next to her lay her king, another King of Hearts, King Royce. He was famous for not being faithful to his diligent queen, and for making his mistress the Queen of Hearts after Millay had died. Dinah did not see the mistress's head anywhere. Twenty or so heads of what Dinah guessed to be Yurkei chiefs were here as well—strong, solid heads of handsome warriors carved from stone, crowned not with a piece of gold or silver, but with feathers or elaborate fabric swirls that dangled down and framed their bright, glowing eyes made of blue gemstones. Dinah found these the most haunting—the eyes of the Yurkei heads made her feel as if they were watching her as she walked along, as she touched each face and marveled at its size and beauty.

Sunlight reflected through the low clouds and sent a rippling shadow over the heads, making them look for a minute as if they

were engaged in conversation—a never-ending dialogue of politics, land, and legend. Dinah was fascinated. *Who made these, and why? And when? How had they transported such massive sculptures into the forest without removing the trees that surrounded them?* Dinah let her fingers run over the face of the current Yurkei chief, Mundoo, her father's enemy. The metal was warm, perpetually kissed by the sun, and it felt soothing against her cut palm. Had she been Queen, would her head have one day graced this clearing? She hoped so. The valley was strangely beautiful, utterly unnerving, a good place for kings and queens to take their royal rest.

I will take Wardley here one day, she thought, *if I can find it again.* She wasn't convinced that she could—she and Morte had twisted and wound their way through these woods, not unlike the black snakes with silver eyes that she had seen in several trees so far. Together they had spiraled themselves into the deepest parts of the Twisted Wood, hoping to make their trail confusing and untraceable. How could she find her way back here, to this valley of her ancestors, to those who ruled when she would not? Her head should be here, not Vittiore's. She felt the blind fury rising up inside of her, that black hunger that clawed up her stomach and wrapped its arms around her heart when she was least expecting it. *How dare they take her crown away?* With a cry, Dinah flung her sword blade across the nearest tree, hacking and jabbing until the trunk was battered and flaking. She felt the tremors vibrate up the blade and into her arm, a jarring sensation that was more cathartic than painful. Until she stopped. Both of her hands throbbed with pain, but she didn't care.

"You killed my brother!" she sobbed, tears running down her face as she brought the blade of the sword down again and again against the rough trunk. "You killed him! That was my crown! It was mine!" In wide arcs, she slammed her blade against the tree, the

metal cutting into the wood deeper and deeper with each swipe. This wasn't swordplay, this was hacking, this was something else, something she had never known before. It felt glorious and dangerous at the same time, intoxicating.

Dinah continued until her arms shook with exhaustion. She angrily flung the sword away to wipe the tears off her face. Taking deep breaths, she leaned her head against the tree, her salty tears soaking into the now-exposed virgin white wood. From its towering height, the top of the tree let out a deep groan, and Dinah watched as the bark rippled up the tree like water. Several trunks twisted accusingly in her direction.

"I'm sorry, I'm sorry, forgive me." She rested her now-bleeding hand against the raw wood, feeling the deep scars and notches she had left. "I'm sorry. They killed him. They took everything." Sniffling, Dinah found herself looking again at the head of her father, the way his crown was dug into the ground, the way his neck bore the blunt cut of a sword. There was an aggressiveness to this statue that the others did not share. While the other heads were resting, his position was a punishment.

An unwelcome whisper was beginning to creep up her spine, a familiar, surreal feeling. It was the same feeling that she had awakened to that night in the palace, when a stranger in black was standing over her bed. *She was being watched.* Was it the heads? Dinah stared at the statues, her eyes jumping from face to face, but she saw no movement. They were not living things, only stone and metal. Dinah slowly picked up her sword from the base of the tree and held it in front of her, both sore hands clutched firmly around the hilt.

"Come out!" she screamed. "I see you!" There was only silence in return as the heads stared back at her, unmoving as the long grass waved in concentric circles around their necks. Dinah was

backing up slowly, past one head, then another. There was something here, she could feel it. *Had her father found her?* Dinah spun around and her eye caught a glimpse of white moving swiftly through the high green grass. She took a deep breath as she drew her sword. She would never make it to Morte in time. It was time to fight, time to die. She would not end up in the Black Towers. Her eyes darted from head to head.

She didn't see the bear at first, not until he was charging at her, letting out a roar that echoed off the metal heads and out into the wood. Dinah stood paralyzed with fear as the bear raced toward her. She felt like she was watching herself in a dream, unmoving, watching death race toward her. It was like she was underwater. *I need to move*, she told herself. *Move*! Finally, her feet obeyed and Dinah sprinted toward the nearest head—an upright Yurkei chief, whose fabric crown circled lazily around his head and then looped down low onto the ground. Without thinking, Dinah sheathed her sword and started her ascent, placing one foot onto his lips and pushing off the ground, grabbing hold of the chief's long nose. The eyes didn't provide anywhere to grasp, so Dinah moved sideways and pulled herself onto the man's ear by holding the tip of the large feathers that rested against his temples. A spasm of pain ripped through her hands as she pulled herself up and over the heavy swath of fabric and beads that circled his head. She leapt off the tip of his fabric crown and tumbled onto the man's head.

A roar came from below, so loud and terrifying that Dinah feared her head would rip apart. The bear had reached the head now. Dinah peeked cautiously over the edge. The bear was gigantic. He began pacing around the head, irately sniffing the ground where she had stood and pawing jagged trenches in the earth, feet deep. Rising up on his hind legs, the bear's head was level to the chief's eyes, just below Dinah's face. He opened his wide jaws, lined with protruding fangs, and let out a bloodcurdling roar. Dinah felt a rush of hot, rancid air blow over her face and she gagged as she smelled his potent breath—a mix of decaying meat and death. It reminded her of the Black Towers.

The bear raked his huge paws down the statue's face and the terrible screech of bone meeting metal filled the air. He was a daunting creature, tall enough that his head would brush the ceiling in her bathroom. His coat was two distinct shades of white—most of his fur was the shade of dirty cream, but the stripes that ran up from his stomach area to his visible spine were a bright, unspoiled white, a pure white, whiter than any garment or paint she had ever seen. His jaws snapped shut loudly as his milky eyes took in her face. Besides his massive mouth full of teeth, he also had two large fangs that rose up from the underside of his jaw. The head gave a tremor as the bear began rocking his weight against the statue. *He means to knock it over,* she thought with terror. The statue gave another tremble as the bear slammed his paws against the base and began digging in the mud around the chief's neck.

Dinah had read about the white bears of the Twisted Wood. They were sometimes passed off as myth, and many theorized that they had gone extinct decades ago. They were hard to kill, which was a shame since their pelts were worth a small fortune. Her entire body trembled as she stared down at him. The bear slammed his huge body up against the head again, and it gave a violent lurch. The bear huffed, frustrated, and continued digging around the base before rocking the head again and again, alternating one activity for the other. She was trapped. Sprays of dirt flew into the air. Dinah frantically looked around for some form of escape. The trees weren't within reach; besides, she was certain the bear could climb anything that wasn't stone. She could jump and run for it, but she was entirely sure the bear was faster. She would be dead in a matter of seconds. *Perhaps if she could entice the bear higher, she could stab its face with the end of her sword, or perhaps blind it.* That would give her the best chance.

Dinah could feel her chest compressing with fear as the bear's roars shook the statue. She leaned over the edge of the statue, her face low, the sword raised above her head. "I'm here!" she screamed. "Come and get me!" The bear gave her a confused look, its milky eyes focusing on her. Its jaws opened and it let out a loud roar before charging the bottom of the statue. It hadn't taken the bait, and Dinah braced herself for another impact. The statue gave another violent lurch when the bear's bulky body rammed against it. There was a moment when she thought the statue would stay upright, when it teetered on the edge of falling and staying, but then Dinah was flying through the air and the sword dropped from her hand. She landed hard on her side and rolled into the deep grasses. She barely had time to look up before the bear was charging again. There was nothing she could do. She closed her eyes and waited for the attack.

It didn't come.

Dinah opened her eyes. The bear was only about ten feet away from her, but it was crouched and still, the fur on its back raised up into a straight line. A thud echoed behind her, and Dinah turned her head. There stood Morte, his huge spiked hooves pawing the ground lustily. The bear began to pace back and forth as he eyed Morte's ten thousand pounds of delicious horse meat, but he was also eyeing the bony spikes that protruded from his hooves. Even a white bear had to think twice before attacking Morte. Dinah began slowly crawling backward, until Morte stood between her and the bear, which did not seem to notice her anymore.

The air stopped moving and for a second the valley of heads lay perfectly still, its grasses bent lazily over their stems. The forest held its breath. Dinah saw the sunlight glinting off her sword handle. It lay next to the bear, who was swiping the ground in front of it with a fluid sideways motion, creating a small cloud of dirt. Morte let a long hiss of steam radiate out from his nostrils.

With a roar, the bear charged, and Morte as well. They met in the middle with a terrible clash of claws and bone. They swiped and danced, both bleeding quickly—the bear from its face, and Morte from his side. Together they were tangled, chest to chest. The bear reared up on its hind legs and brought its claws down on Morte's side. The Hornhoov let out a high-pitched scream as the bear sunk his teeth into the horse's exposed chest, tearing off a large chunk of skin. Morte kicked the bear square in the chest before giving a great shake. Both the horse and the bear separated and charged again, tumbling to the ground in a flurry of thunder and blood. Morte landed on top this time and quickly reared himself up onto his back legs before bringing his massive hooves down onto the bear's torso. Dinah heard a sickening crunch as the weight of the hooves and the bone spikes crushed the bear's ribs and chest. Morte was stomping him to death.

The bear's massive paw swiped at Morte, tearing jagged stripes across his muzzle. Morte stepped backward, shaking his head. The bear rolled over with a roar and righted himself. His walk was unsteady, and blood flowed freely from his gut. Morte was circling the bear now, letting out angry snorts as flecks of blood flew from his mouth. The bear lumbered sideways and then raced toward his opponent again. The Hornhoov spun around, but the bear latched onto Morte's hindquarters. As the bear's teeth sank deep into Morte's flank and his claws tore red gashes down Morte's thighs, the massive steed let out a scream.

Unable to shake the bear by turning, Morte pushed up on his front legs. The bear lost his hold. With a strong kick of his back legs, Morte caught the bear square in the neck and sent the blood-covered beast sprawling backward.

In the sunlight, Morte's muscles pulsed and rippled with pleasure—it was obvious to Dinah that though he was injured, he was enjoying the fight. He whinnied happily as he paced the ground, even when his flank and chest were now exposed and bleeding. His crazed lust for fighting filled the air, a palpable stench. He turned to reposition himself. In that moment, Dinah saw instantly why the white bear would lose—the bear was acting out of instinct, out of hunger. His need was natural. Morte saw this as a battle—his brain was strategizing as they fought, and even though the bear outweighed him, Morte was *adapting*.

The bear charged again, but this time Morte was ready. Just as the bear reached him, Morte reared up and brought the bone spikes that surrounded his hooves straight up into the bear's neck and face. The bear let out a terrible whine as Morte forced him down to the ground and delicately detached his hooves. Morte tilted his head and looked at the bear before he reared up once more and brought his hooves crashing down on the beast's chest.

Dinah looked away. The creature was now utterly unrecognizable as a tangled heap of white and red. Morte stepped back and let out a bellow. It was a deep, terrible sound, a war cry, and it chilled Dinah to the bone. Morte began galloping wildly around his kill. The bear's body shifted, and Dinah watched its exposed ribs give a final shudder before the bear gave up his life.

Dinah stood quietly in the grass, her eyes trained on Morte, more afraid of him than she ever had been. Morte didn't even seem to notice her as he buried his head deep into the bear's belly and began eating. Dinah felt a wave of revulsion wash over her. She had forgotten that Hornhooves sometimes ate their kills. They were as satisfied with flesh and bone as they were with grass and grain.

With her hand pressed over her mouth, she turned away and walked back toward the overturned head of the Yurkei chief. Giant slashes lingered where the bear had ripped its claws across the stone. Dinah let out a long breath, suddenly aware of how close she had come to being maimed and eaten herself. This was the second time that Morte had saved her life.

After a while, Morte had eaten his fill of the bear and lay down in the grasses, nuzzling his wounded flank. Now hesitant to leave his side, Dinah raced to fetch her bag and returned quickly to the Valley of Heads. Inside, she found her old bloody nightgown. The birds in the trees began singing their shrill cries once again as she ripped it into several long pieces. Head bowed, she gingerly approached the Hornhoov. He gave a soft nicker as she grew near, and Dinah took this as a good sign. Using her waterskin, she poured her remaining water over the deep cuts in Morte's flank and chest. His giant head jerked in pain, but he did not move as she cleaned the wounds using the water and her hands. As gently as she could, Dinah laid the pieces of cloth over the bloody scrapes and used her hands to press them down until the blood dried against the cloth, until they would stay.

She stood and walked toward the dead bear, its chest and head nothing more than ground meat. This would take a strong stomach, she told herself, but it must be done. It was imperative to her survival that Morte trust her, understanding that she knew what he was. He wasn't a pet. He wasn't hers. Brandishing the dagger she had pulled from her bag, Dinah leaned over the bear, took a deep breath, and began cutting the bear's pelt away from its body. It was grueling work—by the time Dinah was done, the sun was setting low in the east and she could see that the night would be lit by a single visible star.

Blood was smeared to her elbows, her hair matted and sweaty, both of her hands trembling with pain. Her two broken fingers throbbed, and the cut in her hand seemed to have opened again, its blood mingling with the bear's. But finally she had it, she had the pelt. It was thick and soft, the size of a small blanket, shaped into a jagged square. In a nearby creek, Dinah rinsed out the blood.

Cradling the wet pelt in her arms, Dinah brought it before Morte. The Hornhoov sniffed at the pelt and raised his onyx head to look at Dinah. She held her breath as she laid it across his wide back, the trophy from his kill. Hand trembling, she reached forward and placed it just for a minute on his side. She let it linger there until Morte nipped at her arm. Her body weary in a way that Dinah hadn't previously known existed, she cleaned off the dagger, forced herself to swallow a piece of bird meat, packed up her bag, and took a long look back at the Valley of Heads. The setting sun lay heavy over the misty grasses, and the whole area simmered in a warm glow. The insect that resembled toast strutted proudly past Dinah, no doubt on its way back to the milky tree that gave it life. Dinah bit her lip and began walking east as the forest descended into darkness. She took only a few paces before she heard Morte's thudding hooves behind her, cracking branches as he walked. Soon, he was barely an arm's length away. The stench of death was all around him, but to Dinah, he was still a welcome smell.

CHAPTER TWO

The days stretched into a week, or so Dinah guessed by watching the rising and setting of the Wonderland sun, west to east, west to east. She would rise in the morning and take stock of her supplies in the bag—mentally repeating them to herself in an effort to maintain her sanity. *Five loaves of bread, ten pieces of bird meat. Three loaves of bread, seven pieces of bird meat. One loaf of bread, three pieces of bird meat.* Then it was time to find water, which, thank the Wonderland gods, had not been difficult. The Twisted Wood was full of tiny creeks crookedly spreading their fingers into little pools of water, perfect for filling her waterskin or providing Morte with a well-deserved drink. He often almost drained the pools, leaving behind a black puddle full of weeds and muck. Taking their time, they both rested and ate, slowly making their way deeper into the wood.

Since they had fled the stables, Morte was actually gaining weight on Wonderland's bountiful grasses and plant life. His inky coat glistened in the sun, his muscles hard and ready. He looked healthy and strong, even with his healing wounds. Dinah was not faring as well. As she ripped into her bird meat and bread every morning, she was painfully aware that she was starving, and that each meal meant that her provisions were dwindling. What would she do when the food ran out? She had been diligent about plucking any available fruit from the trees—a Julla Tree, with its sharp and fuzzy black melons, a pink peach tree, a handful of berries. Dinah would shovel them into her mouth, her lips dark with their ripe juices. Stepping over plants and overturned logs, she walked through countless trees stretching on forever. At night, when she settled into a thick nest of leaves or particularly soft dirt, she would set out to eat only a half loaf of her bread, and always ended up eating the entire thing.

This raw hunger was something she had never experienced—a constant jab of emptiness, an endless imagining of all the plates of food that had been available to her in the palace. She thought again and again of all the tarts she had thrown out, all the food left on her plate when she was done eating, of the banquets and balls where trays of food had been piled high above her head. Lavish displays of exotic bird breasts, creatively carved pies, bubbling wine glasses, and rich fruits. *All that food, wasted; all the food she had taken for granted.* This was what she thought about when she walked, when the hunger pains became so intense that she gasped out loud and Morte jerked his head up, alarmed. She thought about food, and what she would do when the food ran out. All the time, she walked. Her brown boots, once a deep, regal red but now covered to the tip with brown mud, crunched over dead tree branches, thick foliage, and exotic orchids.

Since the bear attack, Dinah had been more aware of how much noise she made. Hammering the tree with her sword in a moment of frenzy had no doubt attracted him. Her breathing was silent, and she tried to step softly, even when her legs felt as if they were made of iron. She tried to heighten her senses—what did she hear, what could she smell? She should have seen the bear—he was bright white, for gods' sake—and yet, her eyes had betrayed her. She had come within an inch of her life because she hadn't been paying attention. *It wouldn't happen again.*

Still, it was hard not to be distracted by the beauty around her. The deeper they descended into the Twisted Wood, the more breathtaking the forest became. The soft colors of the plains gave way to deep mossy greens, their fuzzy fingers reaching ever upward on towering majesties of trunks and branches. In the early mornings, the calm and quiet lull would be broken when white light radiated through the trees and heavenly streams of dawn covered the forest floor. One day, as she absently watched a red-striped otter flit in and out of a stream, she came very close to walking off a cliff. Behind her, Morte gave a loud snort and Dinah stopped, the tip of her boots sending a scatter of pebbles off the cliff and down into a clear river far below. Even that fascinated her; she had never seen such translucent water, or the minerals that graced the river floor. Silver layers of rock converged upon each other, giving the entire river a rippling effect, though the water's flow was quite mild.

They made their way down to the silver stream. The water was shallow—almost waferlike—and if she squinted, she could see tiny, waving underwater plants, their long fingers trailing downstream. Shimmery orange fish leapt and played between the thin silver layers. They swam backward, their shiny spotted tails weaving as they fought the current. With great bursts, they would shoot out of the water to wriggle backward in the air and burst hidden wings out of their backs. They would fly a few feet and splash back into the water to do it again.

Morte had allowed her to ride him a few times in the last few days, but only when she had grown so exhausted from walking that she found herself leaning against each passing tree to keep her balance. With an annoyed snort, he would saunter beside her and lift his leg. Dinah would climb up with a grateful sigh and feel the wave of relief that came with settling onto the already-warmed bear pelt, her legs draped over Morte's neck. Sometimes Morte would trot, but most of the time they would just walk, for hours, until Morte stopped and Dinah climbed down, grateful for the much-needed break for her perpetually sore muscles.

One day, lulled to sleep by his easy rhythm, she was jerked awake by the feeling of a cool shadow passing over her. Dinah looked up before letting out a small gasp. The trees had converged in a thick canopy of flowering branches, interweaving with each other to create a solid tunnel of flowers. The ground beneath, deprived of sunlight, had a soft and somewhat muddy texture and was covered by a thick maroon moss. The flowers looped down through the tunnel—pinks, purples, greens, and glossy whites, swallowing the sky. Strange white insects buzzed within the tunnel—completely rotund, they fluttered by on petite wings that barely seemed to hold them, nesting on the dewy orchid petals, waiting for their mate. Once the mate arrived, the two little creatures somehow hooked themselves together and created a warm light that glowed from both of them. Together they would float drunkenly through the tunnel.

Dinah was watching them in wonder when Morte gave a violent lurch under her—she was almost sent sprawling past his hindquarters, and would have been if she hadn't had her hand wrapped in his mane. Without warning, he was running—that pure, furious gallop she had only experienced when she was fleeing for her life. His body flowed like violent water beneath her, his speed unmatched by anything Dinah had ever seen. This time, she was able to enjoy it—the world flying past, the greens and purples of the tunnel blending together as they raced through dripping orchards and past velvety trunks. His hooves barely graced the ground. Dinah felt her black hair flying behind her, her gray cloak flapping in the wind. His muscles rippled and tensed with pleasure and release; Dinah could feel his excitement. She could sense his utter freedom and desperation in the run, and she let it course through her legs, up through her torso. For the first time since she had been awakened that night by the stranger's hand, Dinah allowed herself to smile, a smile that stretched into a laugh as Morte plunged farther and faster through the tunnel. *I'm flying!* she thought. Daring to reach one hand above her head, she let her fingers trail the heads of thousands of fuchsia orchids, their swollen tongues dripping down around her. The glowing lovebugs guided their way with subtle iridescent light, bouncing off of branches and flowers, occasionally whapping Dinah across her cheeks and brow. She didn't mind. She closed her eyes and enjoyed the swift wind on her face as Morte's speed intensified. The tunnel ended abruptly, with two tree trunks lying squarely in the middle of their path. Morte easily leapt over them—which was terrifying—and then began to canter at a normal speed. From there, the canopy dispersed, as it wasn't long before they were back in the forest. The air was frigid on her face, which Dinah was surprised to find soaked with tears.

Morte let her ride a bit longer that day. The more Dinah observed him, the more she understood why he had not heeded the King that day as her father bellowed out Morte's name in a blind rage. Morte wasn't anything like a normal steed. He didn't come when called, and he wasn't to be coddled and loved, as he wouldn't give it back. Sure, Dinah gave him any apples that she ran across, but only from a distance—tossed in the air. He was not Speckle. The bloody spikes around his feet and the dark look in his eyes reminded her of that every time she looked his direction. Morte was his own warrior. When her father rode him into battle, he had made the mistake of thinking Morte was fighting for him—he never understood that Morte wanted to fight for himself, that he had no loyalty to the man. The love of the fight and the blood—that's what Morte lived for, not to be the King's steed, not to be a vehicle for her father's glory. He didn't know or care that his owner was the King—he just wanted to fight. Morte came to each battle of his own will.

If her father had understood this, he would never have locked Morte up in that iron pen in the stables, in the dark. The animal had grown resentful in the pen, which explained why he hadn't killed Dinah and Wardley that day when Wardley tossed her on his back. This would never happen now, Dinah was sure of it. Morte had been waiting for a chance to run free, and he sensed that something important was happening. The sprint from the palace that had lasted almost a day would probably never happen again—that had been a combination of adrenaline and his need for freedom. She was fairly certain that Morte would not kill her, but she wasn't going to press her luck. Every night she slept a bit closer to his warm side, but she never touched him, nor allowed herself to sleep close to his bone spikes or huge mouth. When she closed her eyes, she could still see him burying his face in the bear's belly, his maw wet with black blood. It was a sight she would not—nor should she—ever forget.

Morte slept the nights away without a care, and Dinah watched him enviously as he slipped into the depths of slumber. Sleep did not come easily for Dinah anymore. At night, her thoughts wandered into dark places or even darker memories. Charles's body, lying broken on a stone slab. His beloved servants, Lucy and Quintrell, their throats open and bloody. The sound of the trumpets blaring from the castle and the Cards who had swarmed out of it, so ready to kill their Princess. The stranger, his black figure silhouetted in front of her balcony, the way his hand had wrapped around her mouth, truly the most terrifying moment of her life. She thought about Wardley and his brown curls. Wardley, who had saved her, Wardley who was probably in the Black Towers, black roots twisting into his body, into his brain, hollowing him from the inside out.

When she finally did fall asleep, she drifted from one bizarre nightmare to another. She would be in the Black Towers one minute and her father's chamber the next. The night before, Dinah dreamt that she had awakened to the sound of someone crying softly just beyond the trees. Curiosity propelled her forward, and she came to a large clearing in the trees, where one of the Heart Cards she killed sat on a log, softly playing a lute, a cat lounging lazily on his shoulder. Dinah had sat at his feet and listened to his weeping song as blood flowed down his chest, a crimson river creeping closer and closer to her white nightgown. She woke up screaming, covered in a cold sweat, and was unable to fall asleep until dawn began its slow rise.

Another week passed. Out here in the untamable wood, she thought a lot about her mother. Dinah had always tried her best not to think on Davianna. Her father had forbidden her to speak Davianna's name in his presence, so Dinah, young as she was, thought it was best if she just pretended her mother never existed. In a way she was grateful to him for the excuse—it was easier than facing the raw grief, the gray wave of nothingness that would roll over her if she turned her back for just a moment. But here, she was at the mercy of her memories during endless hours of walking. There was no one to talk to except Morte, and Dinah didn't want to upset the delicate balance they had formed by suddenly becoming very chatty. The good thing about Morte was that he didn't care if Dinah wept as she walked, or if she spent an hour staring off into the hazy woods. Allowing herself to remember Davianna was a gift that Dinah gave herself—she needed to feel close to someone out here in the wilderness. And so she delved deep into her mind, into Davianna.

Her first memory of her mother was the tips of her fingers, trailing over Dinah's face, tracing her cheekbones and lips with absolute devotion. Her mother had loved to be touched and to touch others—she was constantly resting her hands on the shoulders of those below her—Cards, lords, ladies, merchants, or even commoners from Wonderland proper, the town that surrounds the Wonderland Palace. They were originally struck by her beauty, but the touch of her hands left them overwhelmed by her grace. Davianna had been born the child of the Duke and Duchess of Ierladia, the largest and richest township on the Western Slope. Ierladia lay just south of the Todren and was the Wonderland stronghold in the North.

Like Dinah, Davianna was never allowed outside of her palace, though she was afforded every possible luxury. Negotiations between Dinah's grandfather, the King of Hearts at the time, and Davianna's father ensured her place at the throne, and from the time she was born, Davianna was groomed to be wife of the King of Wonderland—the Queen of Hearts. This accounted for the way she could float through a room full of the court's highest born with nary a thought, or how she commanded loyalty wherever she went. She was bred and raised on the idea of being a queen, much like Dinah. But unlike Dinah, Davianna loved her studies and dance lessons, whereas Dinah had mostly been thinking of ways to sneak out of them.

As a child, Dinah got the distinct impression that her mother loved being Queen. She wielded the crown with ease. As a mother she was gentle and loving, patient with her precocious daughter who was always yanking on her crown and smudging her dresses with chocolate-covered hands. Their relationship had changed when Charles was born, but Dinah never felt neglected; rather, she saw the large amount of care that Charles took and longed to be included. And so she was. Instead of croquet or watching ostrich riding, Dinah and her mother would feed and bathe Charles, or spend the day trying to teach him to walk, or taking him outside on the balcony so he could watch the ever-changing stars. Dinah didn't see her father from age three to five, when he was off fighting the Yurkei wars, and in that time she grew fiercely attached to her mother and Harris, her advisor and teacher.

Unfortunately, as Dinah grew older, she spent more and more time with Harris and less and less time with Charles and her mother. There were so many things to learn before one became Queen, and Dinah was terrible at each and every one of them. How to dress, how to wave, how to address each and every Card, how to take tea and how to send tea, how to eat tarts, how to ride Speckle. Her lessons took all day, but every night Harris and Emily looked the other way when Dinah slipped out of her bedroom door and ran past the Heart Cards all the way to the Royal Apartments to tell her mother about her day.

Davianna would always be preparing for bed, brushing her thick black hair with her pink shell comb and staring at herself in the mirror, her tear-filled blue-black eyes staring back at her, fringed with impossibly long lashes. Dinah knew she had a secret. She could see it in her eyes, in the way she held her body. Every night when Dinah came in, her mother looked as though she was preparing for the visit of a lover, although she was just getting ready for bed. She was always beautiful, always prepared. Together they would climb across Davianna's heart-shaped bed and her mother would pull her close and listen as Dinah whispered to her all the tiny details of her day—what Harris wore, what Emily said, the things she had learned, how she had cried after she broke a one-hundred-year-old teapot. Every night would end with her asking her mother why her father didn't love her, and her mother would just shake her head.

"Someday, you'll understand."

Like conspirators, they laughed and shared, mother and daughter, so happy to be close and unencumbered by anyone else. When Dinah was on the verge of falling asleep, her mother would always gently shake her awake to go back to her chambers. Exhausted, Dinah would slump back to her room, an annoyed Heart Card always following behind to ensure her safety.

Dinah's father had returned from war a changed man. He was angrier and increasingly cruel toward them both. She saw less and less of her mother, and when she did, Dinah was alarmed at her shrinking figure and the dark circles under her eyes. Her mother looked exhausted and sad. The care of Charles was taken from her and given to Lucy and Quintrell. Dinah would still occasionally visit her mother's chambers at the end of the day, but Davianna would often be sleeping, unable to take her visits, and Dinah would be sent back to her room like a child without supper.

On the eve of her ninth birthday, Dinah stumbled across a scene that she would never forget. Her daily lessons in the library had been cut short due to the sneezing of Monsignor Wol-Vor, the language tutor, and the Princess found herself with a few free hours—something she never had. Running happily down the hall, her pink dress in tatters behind her, Dinah made her way to her mother's apartment. The Heart Cards who normally stood guard at the Queen's door were oddly absent, and the door was cracked open a few inches. As she laid her fingers on the cool knob, Dinah could hear her father's voice—he was angry. She paused at the door, waiting.

"How dare you? You are nothing more than a common whore, low-born trash that washed up from the sea on the beaches of Ierladia! I am the King of Wonderland, and I will not be made a mockery of. Is this how you repay me? Who is he? Tell me! I should take your head for this!"

Dinah heard the sound of something crashing—dishes, perhaps. Something hit the door with a loud thud and Dinah leapt back, afraid. She could hear her mother murmuring, attempting to calm her father.

Then, "Don't tell me it's NOTHING!" roared the man who wore the crown. Dinah heard the sharp snap of skin against skin— a slap. She desperately wanted to help her mother, but she was afraid of her violent father, who told her terrible war stories that left Dinah feeling nauseated by his cruelty. Her hand lingered on the door as she heard her mother weeping behind it… and then Dinah walked back to her chambers, a coward.

She never told anyone about that day—not even Wardley. It was strange to think of it now, as she stepped over log after log, the muscles in her thighs clenching with the effort as she wove her way through the wood. A tiny stream crossed in front of them, and Dinah stopped to fill her waterskin. Morte lapped at the water and Dinah sat down on the muddy bank to rinse off her sore feet. The tinkling of the stream had a lulling power, and Dinah raised her face to take in the warm sun, resting for just a minute, just one more… one more memory….

Her mother had died on a winter afternoon, when huge mounds of pink snow were piled high against the iron gates outside the palace, and inside everyone was trying to stay warm. Her illness had been violent and sudden. One day, Dinah's mother had been there—her face thin and worried, but alive—and the next she was lying in her bed, drenched with sweat so hot that it steamed in the cool air. Her lips, once the color of a ripe fig, were blue and withered, and her eyes were somehow gone already—they looked past Dinah, as if the Queen were seeing someone else. The White Fever had raged through Wonderland Proper that year—a quick illness that turned a person's nails white before it swiftly delivered them to the grave, although it was curious that no one in the palace had gotten it, aside from her mother.

Dinah hadn't been allowed to touch her mother, or even to go near her bedside. She stood sobbing in the doorway, Harris's arms wrapped firmly around her, holding her back as she watched her mother's body convulse and twist in pain. Charles was not allowed in the room, and the King was nowhere to be seen as Davianna took her last breath, her eyes trained on Dinah as she whispered her goodbyes, her body shaking with the effort.

"Dinah, oh my wild girl. You so are smart, just like him. Be gentle my dear, take heart. Be a good queen. Take care of your brother."

Dinah wept, her fat tears dripping off of her chin. "I will Momma, I will. I love you. I love you."

The hint of a smile brushed across Davianna's face. "I love you too...."

The conversation had exhausted the Queen, and it wasn't long after that she fell into a heavy sleep, never to wake again. The rising of her chest slowed until it ceased. The Queen was declared dead. Her father, her servants, Harris, everyone who had known her mother, wailed. Cheshire's dark eyes filled with clever crocodile tears. The Cards came and went; a priest, wearing long red robes covered with hearts, rang a tiny silver bell outside her window. Another bell from somewhere down below rang in return.

Suddenly, the entire kingdom was ringing their bells, and the sound of it rose up through the courtyard and in through the open window as a swirl of pink snow rested on her mother's lips.

Dinah screamed and flailed in Harris's arms as the thin ruby crown was removed from her mother's head. The priest held it over open flames until the crown glowed a dim red, as if lit from within. She realized with a start that it was a precautionary measure, to cleanse it from the fever. He walked over to Dinah as he blew on the crown to cool it.

"The Queen is dead. Long live the future Queen of Wonderland." He placed the crown on her head, the heat of it scorching the tips of her ears. Harris turned and carried her out of the room, and as he turned, Dinah was given one last glance at her mother's face, her beauty siphoned away by death. As they covered her with a gray sheet, Dinah's wails bounced off the stone walls. Taking a cue from her father, Dinah had built a wall around that memory, thick as stone and impregnable to wandering thoughts. But here, in the depths of the Twisted Wood, it had been so easy to remember. She could smell the putrid air of the bedchamber, could see the fear in Harris's eyes as the hot crown was laid on her head.

Dinah wiped her eyes as she pushed her blistered feet into the cool stream. The relief was instant and it occurred to Dinah that she could possibly stay here forever, in this tiny lovely part of the wood, where all the trees were white and the huge dark-blue and deep-green veiny leaves stretched out over the ground. . But she couldn't. Not yet. After a few moments, Dinah pulled her feet out of the stream, delicately wrapped them with the remaining strips of linen and pushed them back into her boots, now instruments of torture. She watched silently as a fiery red hawk danced and dipped over the horizon, such a thing of beauty. She looked hopefully over at Morte, wishing he would lift his leg and have mercy on her. He did not, but rather stared off into the distance, his massive black head tilted with interest.

"I guess we'll be walking then," groaned Dinah. It was nice to hear a voice—any voice, even if it was her own. They continued walking northeast. Her march to starvation, as Dinah had begun to think of it, dragged on.

The tracking hawk continued to circle lazily overhead.

CHAPTER THREE

All day Dinah had felt strange. She had just eaten her last loaf of bread and there were only a few pieces of bird meat left. A creeping feeling made its way from her spine to her forehead. She convinced herself that it was just the sinking feeling of having no more food. Her time was up—she would either need to learn how to hunt or begin eating only fruit that she could find along their way, but that wouldn't sustain her for long.

Dinah was losing weight rapidly—already she had tightened her belt loop two notches, and when she had splashed her face in the stream that morning, she was shocked at how thin her face looked, how tired. Her hair was a raggedy tangle that would probably take years to work itself out, and her skin was marked with dozens of small cuts from thorny branches. The cut on her hand was healing well, but her two broken fingers still ached whenever she put pressure on them. The shocking thought that she might not survive this ordeal washed over her like a cold wave. *I cannot die from something as simple as a lack of food*, she told herself. *I survived the Black Towers, a father who wanted me dead, and a bear attack. I will not lie down and die just because I have run out of food. I will fight and I will learn.*

That day she kept a very sharp eye out for things that looked edible. She found a Julla Tree, but most of its spiky fruit had gone rotten. Dinah managed to grab three fruits that were edible and stashed them in her bag for the following day. She found a strange plant in the ground that sprouted something similar to the cabbage they ate at the palace. Tentatively, she rested a leaf on her tongue only to spit it out immediately. It was bitter and numbed her tongue, and she quickly rinsed her mouth out with water. *I'll die from poisoning much faster than starvation*, she told herself. *I can't just start eating things that I don't know.* And what she knew was so little. The Twisted Wood was filled with such fascinating and terrifying plants: huge rubbery vines that gave a shiver when she passed, and when she touched them, they released a puff of sparkling yellow powder; tubal roses that grew long instead of wide, whose petals collapsed inward when the sun set; carnivorous plants that feasted on small rodents—and once attempted to bite Dinah's ankle and would have broken the skin if she hadn't been wearing boots. There were thousands of ever-changing plants and flowers woven amongst the trees—those trees, always knowing—and none of it to eat.

Grumbling to herself while ignoring the sharp pain in her stomach, Dinah walked on, watching the blazing sun creep from west to east as dusk settled in like a thick blanket. Without warning, she found herself in a small clearing, marked by a unique tree that had small, perfectly round holes drilled into its impossibly wide trunk. Dinah walked up quietly to inspect the tree, noting that it was at least twice the width of her bedchambers. She padded slowly around the smooth trunk, letting her hand linger on its surprisingly glossy surface. It had the texture of marble, and yet it was thoroughly wood. It shimmered in the setting sun, the light playing across it like a warm ember. Dinah watched with amazement as rays of sunlight shot through the tree, and suddenly it pulsed with life, as if lit from inside. The tree was transparent and filled with a frozen golden sap. She could see everything inside it—every fiber, every bubble of air. This was an amber tree, something she had only seen in her picture books, rare because they were so valuable. Once found, they were immediately hacked down and turned into jewelry, furniture, and hand railings for the wealthy. The base of her tea table was made of this rare amber wood.

Dinah ran her hands over the trunk. It was so beautiful it took her breath away—why would anyone ever chop it down? There was so much more beauty in a living tree than a pendant wrapped around some noblewoman's neck. The tree pulsed with warmth that Dinah suspected didn't come from the sun, but rather from inside the tree. Her fingers trembled with the knowledge that its texture was changing underneath her skin. Whereas before it had felt like cool marble, it now was soft, like the jams she spread on toast. When she pulled away, her hands were covered with a dark, drippy syrup the color of molasses. Without thinking, she licked it. After weeks of stale bread and dried bird meat, the syrup was heavenly—rich and sweet, the best thing she had ever tasted. She licked her hands dry, covering her face in syrup, and went back for more until she felt sluggish with the sugar, drunk on this rush of goodness. She stumbled away from the tree past Morte, who had also been licking the trunk.

Dinah was wiping her hands on the damp grass when she looked up in surprise, her eyes catching a strange form in the trees. There was a house in front of her. Dinah leapt back in shock, her hand on her sword hilt. *How had I not noticed it?* The house sat snugly between two trees, their roots twisting up through the roof. This made Dinah shudder. Morte continued to drink with abandon. It reminded her of the Black Towers, of that root twisting itself into her mouth, up her nostril.... Dinah heaved up the syrup onto the ground, the thick sludge puddling at her feet, over and over again. Afterward, to her relief, she felt much better without its weight sitting in her stomach. Dinah gaped at the house as she crouched behind the liquid tree. There was no visible light coming from the house, no candles flickering in open windows, no guards against the approaching night. Morte flattened his ears back against his head and gave a loud huff. Dinah felt that familiar dread that had plagued her all day. Was this dangerous? Should she flee from the house? While longing to plunge back into the safety of the woods, Dinah found herself drawn to the man-made structure. It had been so long since she had seen anything related to humans and she longed to run her hands over the walls, to feel timber and bolts, blankets and cups. Also, she reasoned, there might be food in the house, something she could not ignore.

Scrambling on her knees, Dinah found a small rock and threw it at the door. It bounced off with a loud thud, and landed beside an empty bucket. Dinah waited a few minutes, but nothing happened, other than the wind tossing the branches of the trees overhead in a lulling whoosh. She drew her sword and approached cautiously, on silent cat feet. Dinah crouched low beneath the window and raised her head to peer through the beveled glass. She could see nothing through the thick glass, but she could sense that everything was silent and still. With a deep breath, she turned the door handle. The door swung open and rocked on its hinge. Dinah stepped inside, praying to find a fully stocked kitchen. The house was one large circular room with a beautiful high-vaulted ceiling and a dirt floor. On the right, an unmade bed had been overturned and books were scattered about, their pages flapping in the wind. At the front of the room sat a cold fireplace, cozied up to a sitting area that featured a well-worn rocking chair resting against the wall.

The blanket that had once been draped on the chair had been ripped to shreds and was tossed about the room.

To the left was indeed a kitchen that had been recently ransacked. Milk dripped from an overturned jug onto the floor, where a basket of food had been tossed aside. Hunger making her impulsive, Dinah raced toward it. She pushed past the overturned table, stepping over the blue-and-white spotted tea kettle smashed on the floor. She didn't care—all she saw were two loaves of bread, some onions, carrots, and what looked to be a burnt husk of thick meat—deer, perhaps. Ravenous, Dinah threw these things into her bag as the sun dipped behind the cottage, filling the room with a shadowy light. She gnashed at the bread. *Who had been here? Yurkei? Had an animal gotten in—a wolf? Something worse?* Dinah looked around. No. The chaos seemed a little neat for an animal, a little too intentional. What animal would leave food but rip pictures off the wall and flip a bed over?

Morte gave a nervous whinny from outside and pounded the ground with his heavy, spiked hooves. The dishes inside rattled. Dinah took one last glimpse around the kitchen before ducking out of the round house. She said a silent thanks to whoever baked this bread and grew these onions as she made her way behind the house, back into the woods. Morte shortly followed behind her before they both stopped short. There was a long field that stretched hundreds of feet behind the garden, and the body was there, lying face down in the dirt. He had been quite large but obviously strong—huge muscles, still as stone, that looked as though they had been carved out of his back. He wore a floppy hat and a lavender linen tunic, his feet bare and dirty. *A farmer*, Dinah thought, pressing her fingers across her trembling lips. Broken jars of the amber tree syrup littered the ground around him. Dinah felt all the air rush out of her lungs as she comprehended what she was seeing.

Out of the man's back arched a long arrow. It nestled between his great shoulder blades, a small blotch of blood surrounding the entry point. He had bled out from the front, the ground stained a deep red all around him. The blood was still wet, but it was cooling quickly and becoming one with the sticky syrup, a sickening swirling mixture of red and amber.

The fact that this hadn't happened long ago alarmed Dinah, but not as much as the blown red glass heart that topped the end of the arrow. She had seen these arrows before, adorning the backs of many Heart Cards that guarded the outer gates of the palace. She stood, the world spinning around her. It wasn't the Yurkei that had been here. The Cards had found her. Dinah swung the bag around her back and ran straight toward Morte. "Up!" she barked. Her panic was evident and for this he didn't hesitate, lifting his leg as she neared him. Dinah stepped without fear onto his spikes and vaulted herself onto his back, her legs curling around his massive neck.

From what she could tell, the tracks of the Cards (huge, impossible not to notice once she was looking) were heading north, and so she turned Morte east, not veering away from their previous path. From there, Morte ran. Her heart thudded in her ears as Morte raced through the ever-blackening woods. Farther and farther in they dashed, making an incredible noise, yet what chance did they have not to? Dinah could barely see, but Morte seemed to have perfect night vision—he easily navigated branches and deep holes in the earth without trouble. Every few seconds, she would glance back, praying that she wouldn't see a white Hornhoov emerging from the darkness. They had made it a few miles from the house when she heard the first faint shouts and clinking of armor. Fear surrounded her and made it hard to think. The sounds seemed to be coming over a dark ridge in the distance.

Tears welled up in her eyes and her hands shook as she clutched Morte's mane, turning him around, racing away. *I've come so far, so very far—it couldn't happen here. Not now... .* As they raced away, the sun disappeared over the Yurkei Mountains and all was black. The Twisted Wood became nothing more than shadows, an inky shade of trees and branches. Dinah could barely see Morte's head in front of her as he dove through the trees, straining to outpace the growing sounds of horses and men. The cacophony was coming from all sides now, so foreign and abrasive to her ears after so much silence. Their arrival raped the quiet wood, violating the peace of the trees. It was a violent commotion. They were so loud and they seemed to be everywhere, all around her, pouring down from every side. She couldn't see where they were, but they were getting closer—and there was nowhere to run where they wouldn't hear Morte crashing through the brush.

Dinah drew her sword and the thin swoosh of metal echoed through the trees. She wouldn't be able to fight through many of them—any of them, maybe—but she would not be taken to the Black Towers. She would force them to kill her, and she would try her best to kill her father. That was her only purpose on this black night; if this was going to be the way it ended, so be it. She would avenge her brother, his keepers, and her mother, killed by her father's neglect and cruelty. Dinah stood still and held her breath for a moment. Then her father's voice carried out through the darkness, commanding his troops, the sound of him sending a dagger of fear straight through her.

"She's here! Bring her to me, dead or alive. A lifetime's worth of wages and a position in the court will be given to the Card who can bring me either. Listen to me, men, do your duty and avenge your innocent prince! His blood will not be in vain!"

The voice stopped Dinah cold; Morte as well. They stood perfectly still as the roar of soldiers echoed all around them in the darkness. They were surrounded. A leaf crackled directly behind Dinah and she heard deep breathing.

"Hide," hissed a voice in the darkness. "If you want to live, hide; don't fight. Hide."

Dinah didn't need to be told twice, or have time to consider the source of her advice. She quietly dismounted Morte and bid him to follow her into a densely leafy area of the trees, stumbling many times over things she could not see. Something slithered over her boot and she forced herself not to scream. It was a consuming darkness. *The stars must be on the other side of the sky tonight,* she thought, *hiding from this terrible noise.* She could see almost nothing, save the tips of the trees as they reached for the gray night sky. The sounds of the Cards were all around her; the violent breaking of tree branches, the clanking of a cup against a thigh, horses pawing the ground, and a singular sound that chilled her blood—the thundering sound of another Hornhoov crashing through the brush.

She stood still, considering how best to hide. And how did one hide Morte? She looked over at him in the darkness but was surprised that she could see almost nothing—the black of his coat blended effortlessly with the trees and night. I have to disappear, she thought. Disappear into the night. *The dress.* Moving as quickly as she dared, Dinah untied the flaps on her bag and rummaged through it, her hands feeling for the thick, heavy fabric. When it seemed she had touched everything in her bag except for what she needed, Dinah's hand felt it—the heavy black dress. She pulled it out, unfurling it against the starless night. Dinah could barely see her hand in front of her face, let alone the pitch-black fabric of the dress. Dropping her sword to the ground, she pulled the dress over her head. It slipped over her easily, the ends of the dress brushing the ground. Reaching back, she felt that the dress collar was lined with a hood; Dinah pulled the thin black linen over her dark hair and face. It was long enough to cover everything, and the fabric dusted her chin. She pulled her hands into the sleeves so that they would not show and inched up next to a particularly wide tree, leaning into the trunk.

The voices were almost on top of her now—they would be on her in seconds, with their swords and horses and torches. She looked over at Morte, who stood as still as she was, white steam hissing out of his nostrils. It was taking every inch of his control not to leap into the fight. Dinah reached out and felt for his nostrils. She gently and carefully laid her hand over his muzzle. Her voice shaking, she murmured, "Still…, still…." The steam stopped and Morte knelt on the ground, becoming one with the thick foliage around him. Perhaps the animal knew he could not win this fight, not tonight, not while he was still partially wounded from the bear. Either way, Dinah could no longer see him; she pressed her face and body up against the tree and waited for them to come. Quivers of fear crawled up from her legs and infested her chest. Her knees felt weak. She clutched at her heart.

"Don't move," hissed the same voice from before. Was it above her? "Don't move, don't breathe and the Cards shouldn't see you." Dinah froze, a black statue in the woods. *Don't breathe. Don't think.* She closed her eyes as the Cards swarmed around them. Several of them trampled right past her—one almost tripping over Morte before he suddenly changed direction and veered to the right. *He should be thankful to be alive,* she thought, *as that would have ended in his very gruesome death.* Two brushed past the tree she was leaning against and Dinah clenched her hands inside the sleeves to keep from fainting. Unable to raise her head for fear of being seen, Dinah kept her eyes glued to the ground. She could see nothing except the occasional flash of a torch as it was waved in the darkness, the woods swallowing the light in their vast space. She could hear them scrambling, hear the swords being drawn and the arrows being cocked, the sounds of weathered breathing and water canteens and flags flapping in the wind, as loud as a trumpet's blast.

The voices of the Cards rose up from the trees. "She was here!" "I heard her, Your Majesty!" "She's over there!" The cacophony of sounds bouncing through the woods made it very hard to tell where each man was—and she could see that the Cards were disoriented and scattered. They were unaccustomed to the trees, to the starless night. To Dinah's horror, she felt the Earth shake beneath her feet and heard the singular plodding with which she had grown so familiar. She dared to raise her face a few inches. The white Hornhoov carrying her father had entered the trees, with Cheshire following behind him. Her father sat proud and furious atop a female half the height of Morte, but still gigantic. He carried a torch, so clearly visible in the darkness that surrounded the rest of the Cards. He wore his red armor, a black heart slashed boldly across the chest. The gold of his crown glinted in the firelight, his eyes lit up like flames. He held the reins on the Hornhoov in one hand and his Heartsword in the other, ready to kill. He seemed to stare right at Dinah, right through her. Beside him, Cheshire sat with his dagger clutched loosely as he scanned the wood, his black, catlike eyes searching each tree, his purple cloak draped over the flank of his steed.

The Hornhoov pulled her head in their direction and the King began thundering toward them. Dinah clutched the tree, pressing her face against it, fearing that her heart would actually explode.

"Stay still," ordered the voice. Dinah froze as her father's Hornhoov walked closer and closer to them, his torch only lighting the few feet in front of him. Carefully, she raised her head and saw her father staring right at her, squinting in the darkness, his face a mask of righteous fury. Dinah didn't move. He looked confused, as though he were unsure of what he was seeing. He tilted his head, his bloodshot eyes filled with rage and still squinting in the black night, looking right at Dinah but not seeing her. He was close enough that she could make out the sweat on his brow and smell the stink of drink clinging to his skin. She was sure he could hear her heart, which thudded with enough power to shake the tree.

Her father climbed off of the Hornhoov and began making his way toward the clump of trees where Dinah was standing. Hatred flooded over her fear, and she felt an intoxicating rush of fury circle up from inside her gut. *He killed Charles*, she thought. *And I will kill him now, a shadow in the darkness. Yes, my King, come ever closer.* Moving as slowly as she could, Dinah reached for her sword, her eyes trained on his neck, the only open spot in his armor. Suddenly there was a loud crash from the woods behind them.

"There!" yelled a soldier from a distance, "I heard something over there! I think it's her!" The King's face distorted with pleasure and he vaulted back onto the Hornhoov, turning her in the direction of the sound. Cheshire followed, giving a backward glance at the seemingly empty valley before raising his dagger menacingly and following behind the King. The King's Hornhoov kept trying to turn back—it could obviously smell Morte—but Dinah's father simply yanked the reins and dug his spiked heels in.

"Go, you blasted creature! Find her!" Together they galloped off into the darkness, the light from his torch dimming to a dull candle in the darkness.

"Go…," hissed the voice, and then Dinah heard the sound of a body dropping down from the tree above. "Who are—"

"No time!" snapped the voice, distinctly male, somehow familiar. "Yeh go! I'll lead them south. Quickly, for they will surely come back here." He was as invisible as she was, a hulking dark shape in the trees. Dinah flung the bag around her body and climbed onto Morte's back, strapping the sword across her shoulders. She leaned forward and pressed herself against his black skin, becoming invisible once more. Black on black, a shadow at midnight.

"Quietly now," she whispered to her giant steed. Morte seemed to understand as they silently headed east, his hooves gently kissing the earth. They moved far away from the tiny cottage and the roaming Cards, deeper and deeper into the black night, until the sounds of her father's army were no more. They walked quietly for hours, and Dinah noted that the flat floor of the forest was now increasingly sloping upward, harder and rockier. Hornhoov and rider moved silently through the trees, until Dinah spotted a small rock outcropping perched upon a narrow ridge overlooking the forest. Strategically, it would be a great place to watch for the approaching Cards, and besides, the trembles in her legs reminded her that they should go no farther. Without a word, she slipped off of Morte and collapsed against the rocks, exhausted from her ride and from the all-encompassing fear. Morte knelt behind the rocks next to her and fell quickly into slumber, leaving her alone with the starless night sky.

Comforted by the fact that she didn't think her father's army could sneak up on them in the dark—or find them in the dark, for that matter—Dinah let her eyelids flicker closed once, twice, and then she surrendered to her voracious exhaustion. She dreamed of a deck of cards on a glass table, being played by a black glove. The hand was detached from an arm, and tiny flecks of crimson dripped across the faces on the cards as they were revealed. Hearts. Spades. Diamonds. The King. The King. The King. Again and again.

Her eyes wrenched open again in the early dawn and she woke drenched in a feverish sweat, unsure of what had awakened her so suddenly. Then she heard the click of a boot in front of her and felt a cold steel blade pressed firmly against her neck. Trembling, she raised her eyes, her black braid brushing the tip of her sword. A Spade stood before her, his massive frame blocking the sun.

"Morning, Princess."

CHAPTER FOUR

Dinah curled backwards, knocking her spine against an overhanging rock. Picking up a handful of loose dirt, she flung it at the Spade's face and felt the ground for her sword. The Spade gave an annoyed cough.

"You won't be finding that now, yer Majesty." The Spade raised his other hand, which held Wardley's sword. He had two swords and she had none. "Yeh know, it's not very princess-like to throw dirt."

Dinah paused a second before she began slowly inching herself toward the Spade, hoping to scramble over the rock to where Morte lay snoring on the ridge above. *Why is he still sleeping? Curse that lazy beast!* The blade slid harmlessly over her throat as the Spade pushed against it.

"Don't be calling that monster of yours. I just want to talk to yeh, that's all." Her heart galloped wildly in her chest and Dinah glanced frantically around for the rest of the King's cavalry.

"Where are the others?"

"Ah, them. I left them behind." The Spade stepped forward into the light and Dinah gave a loud gasp.

"YOU!" She recognized the Spade instantly—his dark gold eyes, his grizzly gray hair, the tiny black heart tattooed under his right eye—but mostly because of the shallow two-inch scar that ran down his left cheek. "I know you."

The Spade smiled and drew his sword lightly across the mark. "Yes, yeh know me. You gave me this, you may remember, one day in the palace when I dared to steal a silly wooden toy from yeh."

"It wasn't my toy. It was for my brother."

The Spade grimaced. "He won't be needing that much now, will he? Wings might have helped more."

Dinah let out an angry scream before she feigned left, twisting past the sword, and managed to grab the Spade's black breastplate. He roughly shoved her backward with one hand. She tumbled in the dirt. He was so *strong*. She flung a rock at him, which bounced off of his armored chest.

"Do not speak of my brother, you filth! Where is the King? If I'm going to die, don't waste my time with silly banter. Kill me now and deny my father the pleasure." She paused. "Please, I beg of you. Please. It can't be him."

The Spade peered at Dinah with fascination. "Just as spirited as I remember yeh. Now sit down and shut yer yappy mouth and listen to what I say. My arm is weary from holding this sword and I want to put it down, but I'll need yeh to promise that you won't try to run, otherwise I might have to give you a matching scar."

Dinah sat back, her legs collapsing underneath her. She closed her eyes. *This is it, isn't it? This man will deliver me straight to my father, straight to my father's Heartsword or the Black Towers.* Dinah was sure that the rest of the Cards were nestled at the bottom of the valley, just waiting for them. The Spade wiped his face with his sleeve and tossed Wardley's sword into a nearby bush. He then dropped his sword down to waist level, his keen eyes never leaving Dinah's face.

"Well, Princess, shall I begin?" He stroked his goatee, peppered black and gray. "Yer father's Cards won't be coming along, not if we're careful. We can't wander about like fools, which is what you've been doing all this time. I'm not here for him, for the King of Hearts. I'm here for my own interests, and yours."

Dinah narrowed her eyes. "What?"

"I'm here to aid yeh. You can't make it very much longer, not without my help. Yer father will find yeh, maybe not today, maybe not tomorrow, but he will. And when he does...." The Spade pursed his thin lips together and drew his finger across his neck. "Well, yeh know what happens. Your father is a king entirely without honor." His eyes focused sadly upon the wood behind her.

Dinah stared at him, not understanding what he was saying. *He wants to help me?* She followed his eyes to the side, giving the impression that she was considering his speech before bolting off to the right. She almost made it past the edge of the boulder and opened her mouth to yell for Morte but the Spade caught her around the waist and flung her roughly to the ground. Dinah's healing fingers vibrated with pain, and the Spade reached forward and boxed her on her right temple, which left Dinah's head spinning. Blood seeped into her ear.

"I told yeh, just LISTEN. Oh, fer gods' sakes...." The Spade picked her up and easily propped her back underneath the rock overhang. "We'll try again. My name is Sir Gorrann, or Sir Gorr if you must. I've been a Spade in the Cards service for thirty or so years, and I am here to help yeh, if you will just settle down and start behaving more like a princess and less like a wild bear, damn yeh." Dinah was having trouble breathing and the world spun around as her hearing slowly returned. She was unsure of what was happening. Once more she tried to run, but Sir Gorrann delivered a swift punch to her stomach that left her moaning and gasping for breath on the ground. He gave a loud sigh.

"It makes me unhappy to treat yeh so, but until you stop trying to run and listen, it'll just be beatin' after beatin'." He settled down next to Dinah on a tree stump and pulled off his black gloves, flexing his hands. She laid her forehead against the ground, her hands and body curled protectively over her stomach.

"I can't... I can't... breathe."

"Aye, you've never been hit before, have yeh? More reason that you need protection, help to survive. I can teach you many things, Princess. How to survive, how to cover a track, how to fight."

"I know how to fight," wheezed Dinah before she spat her blood onto the ground.

"No, yeh don't. That handsome stable boy might have taught yeh a few things, but fighting wasn't one of them. Neither was being quiet. Yeh've been leading the King right to yeh, tromping around the woods on that devil of yers...."

"Wardley?" At his mention, everything in the world seemed to stop. "What do you know about Wardley? Is he alive?"

"Ah, now yeh want to talk." The Spade dusted off his black tunic, adorned with a glossy black Spade symbol. "Tell you what, Princess—I'll make yeh a deal. Yeh stop trying to run, stop trying to fight me, and make sure that horse of yers doesn't impale me on one of his bone spikes and I'll tell yeh everything yeh want to know about Wonderland and what's happened since yer... departure."

Dinah blinked in the rising sun, her eyes trained on the Spade's face. "I remember you. You left the gate open. You could have shut it, but you waited. I saw you. You paused...."

The Spade gave a quick nod. "That I did. Now, yeh charge me again and I'll knock yeh senseless and yeh'll get no answers about yer stable boy, yer guardian, or yer sister."

Dinah grimaced, pushed up with her elbows, the taste of mud in her mouth. "You mistake me, sir. I have no sister. I would rejoice to hear of Vittiore's death."

The Spade let out a gruff laugh, like a stone scraping over the ground. "That's the angry princess I remember! Now, be a good girl and call yer, uh, *horse* around. We best be on the move. If we stay here, the King's Cards will be on us in less than an hour."

"How do you…?"

The Spade gave a low whistle and a reddish brown mare approached on gently trotting feet. Dinah frowned. Morte would definitely not come if she whistled.

"Answer me this, traitor; why are you not with the King?"

The Spade gave a snicker as he mounted the mare. "Let's just say that I have my own interest in helping yeh. But that's not for yeh to worry about yet. Now, before I'll answer any questions, I need yeh to straddle that black thundercloud and ride, unless yeh feel like yer head would be best used as a decoration for the King's privy."

Dinah unsteadily climbed to her feet. "How long?"

"How long fer what?"

"How long until you answer my questions?"

The Spade gave a laugh. "I'll make yeh a deal. I'll answer one question each time the sun sets. Now, we really must go, otherwise the Cards will be flocking this area soon. Trust me 'bout that." He had her just where he wanted her, she was sure of it, but what else could she do? She could no more stop breathing than turn away from knowing Wardley's fate.

"How is it that you know what they are doing if you aren't with them?"

The Spade had already begun riding into the trees, which were looking ever more whimsical on this side of the Twisted Wood. "I know because I'm the King's best tracker, or at least I used to be. Yeh've led us right to yeh, and I'm not the only one he's using. They are tracking yeh even now, and after yer close call last night, I'm sure yeh know what that means. They will rush in like water, surrounding yeh from all sides. The darkness won't hide yeh again, not with the trees thinning out the farther east we go."

Dinah wiped her face on the heavy black dress. "That was you. You told us to hide."

"Aye. And if I hadn't, yeh would be headless right now, since yeh were determined to fight an entire army for one single moment of revenge against yer father. I hope I can teach yeh to think about the consequences of yer actions, to control that fury."

"My father murdered my brother."

"Not the first, I imagine, to be wronged at the hands of the King, vengeful bastard that he is, but that's a discussion for another time. We must move, otherwise I will be forced to knock yeh unconscious and throw yeh on the back on my horse and leave yer black steed here. I won't enjoy it, but it will surely be the easiest thing I do today. And, just for assurance that yeh won't take off with that very fast creature of yours, I'll be keeping both yer bag and yer sword, at least until I see fit to return them to yeh."

Dinah felt rage rise within her. "Who are you to order me around? No one, a dirty Spade! I've survived alone without you just fine."

The Spade turned his horse around and narrowed his eyes at Dinah. "Survived? Survived? What do yeh plan on doing once yer food runs out? Or when yeh need to venture away from the stream? Yeh weren't hard to find because yeh followed the water, and the Cards caught up with yeh without much trial. I wasn't fooled by that false trail to the Ninth Sea, but they were, so I let them dawdle around there for a few days. That steed of yers is fast, but they will catch yeh eventually, chasing until he is worn down or abandons yeh. Make no mistake, the Cards will run yeh off yer feet." He stroked his beard. "Maybe the King will mount yer heads together. Yeh were a blade's width away from being killed last night. Tell me, Princess, what is yer plan?"

He caught Dinah off-guard and she lowered her eyes as a warm shame rushed up her face. The Spade made a soft click with his tongue and the horse trotted up next to her. Her face bruised and dusted with dirt and clutching her stomach, Dinah tried her best to stand up straight to face the Spade. Her black eyes held his gold ones, sunken in his once-handsome face.

"My plan, my plan is that I'm waiting...," she started.

"Waiting for who?" He peered at her. "Who are yeh waiting for? The stable boy? The King?"

Dinah shook her head. "I don't know, I think so...." She realized then how foolish she had been. Thick clouds of doubt swirled over her. *I don't have a plan. Oh gods, where am I even going?* "I—" she clamped her mouth shut. There was nothing left to say. She had failed. She had no direction and no future, not without Wardley, and he wasn't here. Sir Gorrann was, however, and she could either follow him (and she would have to, otherwise she would not have food or clothing) or stay here and die. It was simple. From the depths of the Twisted Wood below, she thought she heard the faint blast of a trumpet. They were still looking for her and if she stayed, they would find her. The Spade was right. There was no choice. She pushed her hair back from her face and glowered at the Spade. "Fine. Let me get Morte."

"Oh, is that his name? He's a ripe ferocious animal that one. I've seen him in battle. Killed a dozen Yurkei right in front of me."

"You should ride him. He loves new riders."

The Spade chortled. "I don't think I'll be doing that today, Princess. It's time to head out. I'm sure yeh'll catch up."

"Don't call me Princess anymore," she snapped quietly. "My name is Dinah." He tipped his head in her direction as his brown steed disappeared under a clump of mossy green trees. Dinah stood still for just a second, letting the breeze rush over her. There was a new chill in the air, and she realized with a start that from the top of the rock outcropping, she could see the faintest outline of the Yurkei Mountains, once far on the horizon. The trees in the valley below groaned hungrily in the breeze and she saw several of them reach out to welcome the clean, frigid air. In the azure sky above, a red feathered hawk dove again and again into the wood, searching for food, spiraling with deadly efficiency as it sailed above the trees. Its feathers rippled like fish scales, and she watched as the flaming colors danced over its small form.

Something silver winked from the bird's neck in the morning light. She squinted. *A collar.* Dinah felt her breath catch in her throat. That was a tracking hawk. It was not hunting rodents, it was hunting *her.* She had seen this hawk before. The Spade was right. *It is time to go.* Dinah threw the filthy wool cloak over her shoulders and began to climb out of the rocky nest. Morte slumbered above, his spiked hooves pressed out in front of him. Dinah cleared her throat. He did not stir. She coughed again, loudly this time. One of his black marble eyes popped opened and he watched Dinah as she began to weave her way up the forest path, following the path of the Spade. She walked for several minutes before she spotted Sir Gorrann up ahead, his horse meandering through the woods as the Spade hummed a soft tune under his breath. He gave Dinah a smile as she came up the path behind him.

"Aye, yeh decided to come. That's the first good decision yeh made since leaving the palace."

"Shut up," replied Dinah. "I have no choice. You have my bag and my sword."

"That I do, Princess."

"I think I saw a tracking hawk."

"Indeed you did. His name is Bew and he belongs to one of the King's trackers, Sir Fourwells."

"Will he find us?"

"Not now that yer with me." The Spade raised his eyes, taking in the trees and the increasingly rocky landscape. "We won't have to flee long. I doubt the King will lead them out of the Twisted Wood. If they don't find yeh there, they'll probably head up to Ierladia, to pay a very unpleasant visit to yer mother's family."

"Why wouldn't they follow us?"

The Spade leveled her with an exasperated gaze.

"Because we're getting close to Yurkei territory, and the King does not want to be caught outnumbered."

The Spade blinked in the sun before reaching down and yanking a tall piece of wheat grass out of the ground to put into his mouth. "Yer just as smart as they say." The ground gave a slight tremor as Morte appeared at the end of the trail, his colossal body reflecting the bright sun as he climbed toward them with alarming speed. Sir Gorrann's mare took a step backward, almost tripping over an overturned branch. Even she knew better than to trifle with a Hornhoov. Sir Gorrann's face paled.

"Gah, massive, he is! Can yeh control him?"

Dinah gave a shrug and picked up a stick to fling into the trees. "Not really. I wouldn't touch him if I were you."

Before she could release the stick, the Spade's hand, nails black as soot, clamped onto her wrist. "What are yeh doing? No throwing sticks. No touching anything that yeh don't have to. Don't throw, don't kick, don't shuffle yer feet or run yer hands along the trees. It's going to be hard enough covering his tracks—" he motioned at Morte, who was munching on some tiny yellow flowers that popped open like bubbles when he crunched them, "without yeh leaving yer scent and marks everywhere. Yeh might as well have left a royal red carpet following us!"

They walked until the sun was high in the sky, breaking for a quick lunch beside the stream. The Spade pulled some dried meat and a small wrapped cheese out of his pack. Dinah's mouth watered at the sight of the cheese, but she forced herself to look away and appear happy with her stale bread. She didn't want anything from this man.

"Give me yer boots," he ordered gruffly, and Dinah obeyed. He rinsed them out in the stream, taking care to scrub the soles with diligence. He handed them back to her. "Step lightly. Think of yerself as air. Everything yeh do leaves a trace. Try not to tramp around the woods making as much noise as possible like yeh've been doing." Dinah watched in fascination as the Spade fastened two low-hanging pine branches to his belt so they dragged behind him. He pointed to the stream. "You and the horse need to walk in the stream for the next few miles. This is where I plan on losing them fer good."

It was easier said than done. Getting Morte to follow her into the ankle-deep stream was incredibly difficult. Eventually he was lured in by the large piece of meat Dinah had grabbed in the farmer's house. Morte didn't like the water on his spikes, although it was clear they needed it—swirls of dried blood colored the water when he finally stepped in. They followed the stream as it flowed uphill. Everything flowed uphill now—the land, the flowers, the plants. Dinah quickly sweated through the heavy black dress.

Walking in the stream was difficult. Several times she stumbled; her ankle caught on seaweed, rocks, and much to her horror, a silver-and-rose-striped snake. After a few miles, the Spade ordered her to leave the stream and walk in only her socks. He shuffled behind her, erasing their footprints. Every once in a while the Spade would lick his finger and hold it in the air or stop and tilt his head, listening for something inaudible to her own ears. Then he would correct their tracks, step by step. At one point, he made Dinah climb a tree only to climb back down on the other side. She protested loudly, until the Spade drew his sword. She grumbled all the way up and all the way back down as Morte watched her with amusement.

Several times Dinah would begin to talk only to be shushed by him, and once, without warning, the Spade pushed her down into a bush, laying his body on top of hers, followed by several branches and brush. Dinah let out a shriek and pushed against him with all her might, fearing he wanted to defile her in a way she had only read about, but his hands had only cupped her mouth. Dinah struggled until she saw the red shimmer of the tracking hawk above, dancing in and out of the tree branches overhead. She fell silent, though she was certain that the hawk could hear the loud poundings of her heart. After a while they hiked again through the bleached trees, until dusk fell and the woods turned dark. Dinah felt as though she were wandering through a gathering of ghosts, each one covered with dripping white linen. The Spade stopped abruptly and pushed his ear against the ground. After listening for a few seconds, he hopped to his feet.

"We'll camp here for the night. This is a good spot." He bound his mare, Cyndy, to a tree and looked at Dinah to see if she would do the same.

She laughed at the idea. "Try to tie him there. You won't live long, but, all the more reason to try." Morte collapsed in a moss pile a few feet away and began eating all the wild grasses within his reach. The Spade began gathering sticks into a pile. Dinah realized too late what he was doing. She dashed dirt toward the pile with her foot. "Stop! What are you doing? Don't build a fire, they'll see it!"

The Spade laughed as he produced a tiny muslin bag. "Ever see nightpowder?" Dinah shook her head. The Spade lit the fire with a flint, but as soon as he saw the first hint of a flicker, he dropped a pinch of the powder onto the growing flame. "Aye, the trick is to get it on when it's just a tiny thing. It won't work on a raging fire, or even a burning log."

Dinah watched in amazement as the flame grew, only instead of glowing with an orange heat, it was black, and emitted a clear smoke that disappeared into the sky. The flames still burned hot, and Dinah enjoyed the first feel of heat she'd felt on her face in a long time. The Spade roasted two rabbits he had speared that day and generously gave Dinah a whole one. She dove into it, relishing the drip of grease on her face. She threw the rest of her rabbit over to Morte, who cracked the bones between his teeth.

The Spade watched with disgust. "Unnatural, that is."

Dinah shrugged. When the Spade finished eating, he dropped the smallest portion of nightpowder into his pipe and leaned back against a rock. His ease infuriated her, and Dinah could contain herself no longer. "Wardley. What has become of him? And Harris? Tell me now, or I'll run with Morte, I swear."

The Spade inhaled a deep mouthful of his pipe and cleared his throat.

"So yeh want to know of the kingdom yeh left behind?"

"Yes."

He let a black puff of smoke drift out of his mouth and waft over Dinah's face. "So be it. What is yer one question?"

CHAPTER FIVE

Dinah thought long and hard before asking. "I would like to know any and all information that pertains to Wardley Ghane and the reasons behind any harms or dangers he might have encountered."

The Spade's drawn face scowled. "That seems like more than one question."

Dinah grinned wickedly. "I don't think so, I think it seems like a valid question. After all, I'm just asking about Wardley."

"Yer asking a bit more, and I believe yeh know that."

"I believe that is what you believe." Dinah continued smiling. She watched his features change through the flickering onyx flame. Dinah didn't know much about the Spades—of all the Cards, they were the ones most shrouded in secrecy—but she did know that Spades loved to tell a good tale with their comrades, bloody tales of wars fought, of limbs lost, and of battle fever, tales that would make any other Wonderlander squirm. Dinah was baiting him— she could tell by the way his mouth twitched and the grinding of his filthy teeth. Sir Gorrann longed to tell her everything. Dinah began her push.

"That's my question. I didn't try to flee today, though I think we both know that I could outrun your horse quite easily."

"Yeh wouldn't have made it to yer horse," replied Sir Gorrann with absolute certainty. "I can throw a knife into yer back faster than yeh can mount him. I'm not as skilled with a dagger as the Diamonds, but I can throw one. I can see easily that yer greatest weakness, Princess, is that yer impulsive, just like yer father. I can teach yeh to be better. Yer will training will begin tomorrow."

Dinah hated the way he so casually insulted her, and how he assumed that he knew her the way Wardley or Harris did. Once upon a time, she could have sent him to the Black Towers for such insolence. She instantly regretted her thought; thinking of the Black Towers made her stomach churn uneasily around the rabbit she had eaten. She would never send anyone there, not after seeing Faina Baker, not after feeling the black roots twist into her nostril. She trembled.

"Something bothering yeh, Princess?"

Dinah gave a haughty toss of her head, assuming a confidence she did not feel. "No. Answer my question, Spade."

The Spade stood up in the clear night, the black flames of the fire kissing the tip of his boots. A thin trail of smoke curled out of the side of his mouth and he began. "Well, if yeh must know, Wardley Ghane is alive." Dinah felt a sweet wave of relief wash over her, sweeter than anything she had ever tasted. The tremendous weight of worry broke from her shoulders and poured down her body and she wished that this feeling of clarity and respite would remain forever unblemished. A sob escaped her throat.

Sir Gorrann watched her closely. "I'll tell yeh what I know, what I saw that day. On the day that you fled—Wonderlanders now call it 'The Morning of Sorrows'—all of the Cards were woken by their commanders in the early morning with the surprising news that the Princess had murdered her own brother in cold blood, his servants, and two Heart Cards."

Two lies and a single truth, Dinah thought. *I did kill two Heart Cards. I lanced one through the heart from behind, like a coward, and hit the other in the head. Wardley killed another in the stable. That was three Cards.* The blood on her hands was growing thicker. The Spade continued, ignorant to her whirling guilt. "As the sun rose outside, we were instructed to put on our armor and march out to meet the Princess in front of the gates and to capture her, eh you, dead or alive." He gave a cough. "Our Commander, the great Spade Starey Belft, made it clear to us that dead was completely acceptable, due to the nature of yer crimes." The Spade cleared his throat. "I knew it to be a lie. The scar on my cheek said otherwise. The passion which yeh had defended that silly wooden toy for yer brother had shown me that yeh could never do such a thing. I asked myself in those seconds, as I pulled on my armor, what did yeh have to gain from the unspeakable crime of fratricide? Yer brother was never a threat to yer crown—it was yers for the taking, or so I thought. No, the only person who stood to gain from yer brother's murder was yer father. This all raced through my head yeh see, as I strapped on my armor and headed out to secure the gates. None of the other men seemed to question it—they were hungry for conflict, for battle, for something. The Spades have been dormant too long.

"We marched outside to take position by the gates, while most of our battalion followed the Heart Cards into the castle. We waited. The army of Cards returned and began to sniff around the stables. Then I saw yeh, a terrifying vision if there ever was one."

Dinah tilted her face, confused. The nightfire reflected off of the Spade's face, making his eyes glimmer like coins in the darkness. "What?"

"Aye! A terrifying vision. I saw yeh, Yer Highness, straddled across that massive black steed of yours, tearing out of the stable labyrinth like the devil himself was chasing yeh. I saw the wood exploding out from yer steed's body, a sword in yer hand, yer other hand clutching his mane, the cloak trailing behind yeh. I watched in awe as yeh plowed over helpless men without blinking, bent on revenge. I couldn't begin to fathom what yeh were doing, but yeh were terrifying. As yeh were sprinting to the gate, the other two Hornhooves came out behind you, killing and maiming any man they came across. Do you know they killed at least ten men?"

More blood, thought Dinah, *more death because of me.* The Spade gave a light laugh. It bounced off the rocky land around them.

"Wonderlanders are still talking about it—they are calling you the 'Red Queen.'"

"But I'm not the Red Queen. That's not me," blurted Dinah. "I was terrified. I was fleeing for my life. I didn't even fully understand what was happening. Wardley put me on Morte and sent him running for the gates."

"Yes, but the townspeople don't know that. They only know what the King tells them and that's very little. Because of The Morning of Sorrows, they *hate* yeh, but more importantly, they *fear* yeh. To everyone in the kingdom, it seemed like an attack, a last vengeance on Wonderland after killing your brother—a wild act, filled with fury. They believe yeh wanted to kill as many Heart Cards as you could before deserting the castle and leaving yer father to mourn his only son."

"That isn't true. I would never...." *But you would*, said a voice inside of her. *You did kill innocent Cards. You can and you have.* The Spade threw another bunch of branches onto the black flames of the fire, which leapt even higher, their invisible smoke choking Dinah's eyes. He continued.

"Yeh looked like a blood-thirsty warrior that day, Princess. I saw that wild fear in yer eyes when yeh passed through the iron gates, the look of a child, desperate to survive. I've seen it many times in battle. But that's not what the kingdom saw. Trust me, it will be to yer advantage in the future."

The future? Dinah pushed herself off the rotted log she was perched on. "I don't understand what this has to do with Wardley. Tell me about Wardley." She was getting annoyed.

"Ah sorry, I'm getting there, Yer Highness. Because everything that happened to your stable boy—"

"WARDLEY," snapped Dinah. "His name is Wardley."

"Everything was a result of your actions that day, you tearing out of the castle like a mad bear let loose. I stayed there long enough to see yer father and his small cavalry pass through the gates in pursuit of yeh, and I'm not sure I've ever seen a man so bent on the destruction of another. He longs for his vengeance and he will never stop thirsting for it."

In the past this statement would have sent Dinah into a flurry of tears, but now it just roused the boiling rage within her. She did not mourn the loss of her father anymore. He had taken everything from her. *I should have killed him in the forest last night,* she thought. *I had my chance for revenge and walked away from it.*

"When the King of Hearts returned from his pursuit, he was blinded with anger. He had lost the chase, and everyone in Wonderland knew it, especially the Cards. He slew three fruit sellers just because they didn't get out of his way fast enough, and there were a handful of townspeople that he beat so savagely yeh can hardly recognize them. He also finished off one of the white Hornhooves, only because she wasn't able to catch up with yeh."

The Spade ran his fingers across his knife belt as he stood and Dinah suddenly felt a bit unsafe as the anger in his tone rose.

"Wardley," she whispered.

"Er, right. I know a Heart Card who stands guard at the palace infirmary. He says that after the King killed the Hornhoov, he barged into the wing where they were treating yer stable boy and demanded his blood as well. He was crazed, knocking over carts and beds, hitting the midwives and sick-workers with his armored fists. The doctor on duty argued that Wardley's blood had already been paid and that he had a very real stab wound to prove his innocence. The King pushed past him, his sword in hand...." Dinah felt like she might faint under the bright stars shining that night, spiraled above in a glowing, circular pattern. "By some miracle, the King refrained once he saw that the blood flowing over the table and onto the floor all belonged to Wardley. He was unconscious, his wound raw and deep." Dinah winced, remembering the feeling of her sword separating his muscle, ringing against the bone, the pained face of the boy she loved.

"He had been found slumped over in the stables. Wardley's story was that he had slipped away from the Heart Cards when they were entering the castle to try and stop yeh—he figured yeh'd go for yer lame horse in the stable and he wanted to ferret yeh out, to take his own revenge on you for killing yer brother, a boy that he had grown so fond of. He heard a sound in the dark and when he woke up, there was a gaping bloody hole in his arm and a huge lump on his head."

Dinah said a silent prayer of thanks that Wardley was so smart, so crafty. Even in the Black Towers he had been astute and quick on his feet.

"The King wanted his head nonetheless, but was convinced otherwise by his council, Cheshire most likely, crafty snake that he is. The murder of such a handsome young Card, one who was so well liked and full of potential to become the Knave of Hearts would surely be frowned upon by the court and the kingdom. In the end, it was a political move." The Spade shook his head with a cavernous laugh. "Of course, his reputation for being one of the most skilled fighters in the Cards has since disappeared, and now he is known for being bested by the Princess in a stable. Yer father has blamed him for yer escape and he has become a laughing stock. He is called 'Wardley the Weak,' though always behind his back, as a wise man would not say it when he holds a sword in his hand. He still bears the Card clasp, but he mostly works on rebuilding the stables yeh so recklessly tore down."

Dinah tried to manage her breathing but the sob she had been holding in broke forth from her lips and she buried her face in her hands. Wardley, once the brightest star in Wonderland, the future Knave of Hearts, would be mocked for the rest of his life, all because he had saved hers. Her body shook with sobs before the Spade, who looked alarmed at her sudden rush of emotion.

Dinah was embarrassed. "I'm sorry. It was my fault... Wardley... he saved me. He put me on Morte and unlocked the stable gates. He gave me his sword and told me to stab him. I would have lain down and waited for the King if it wasn't for him." She wiped her nose on the corner of her sleeve.

The Spade's lip turned up in a half smile. "So I figured. Yeh don't strike me as a warrior. Yeh strike me as a terrified princess, denied of her kingdom, neglected by her father, a shell of a girl— one who has seen her brother murdered and her half sister crowned Queen."

Dinah jerked her head up. "Vittiore?"

"You must have fathomed that she would take yer place."

Yes, Dinah had imagined it, but it was always a waking nightmare, her worst fear come true, something that she reasoned with herself would never happen. Vittiore, walking up the aisle of the Great Hall as her court bowed before her. Vittiore, her long golden curls pressed down as the beautiful twisting crown that Charles had made was lowered onto her head. *My father has taken everything.* In her mind, she saw Vittiore, sitting in the heart throne next to her father, ruling Wonderland when she was nothing better than a piece of rotten fruit from the mountain villages. Dinah let out a blunt, angry cry and kicked the rotting log below her into the fire.

"That whore will never truly be the Queen. She is a pawn in my father's game, a tool that he used to push me out. She knew that my brother would be murdered and did nothing."

Dinah saw the flicker of a smile pass over the Spade's dark features. "Indeed. But she is beloved by the people. They are grateful that she survived the Rebel Queen's murderous rampage. The talk amongst the common people is that you tried to murder sweet Vittiore but couldn't get into her room."

"That is a LIE," whispered Dinah intensely. "I was never anywhere near her room that night. I only went to Charles's room, where I saw my brother...." Her voice broke, a mix of anger and grief. "I saw his broken body lying on a slab of stone. The stars were as dark as his blood that night and his eyes looked at nothing."

The Spade was silent, and for a few minutes there was nothing but the crackle of nightfire and the sounds of steam hissing out of Morte's nostrils.

Finally, the Spade cleared his throat. "There's nothing to be done now. Vittiore is Queen and sits beside your father. There is unrest in Wonderland because the King raised taxes to justify increasing the number of Cards and weapons. Many people in the kingdom are starving as he reinforces the Cards. When we left, turrets were being built around the perimeter of the iron walls."

Dinah wiped her tears away and worked at keeping her voice steady. "The Iron Gates? Did we break them?" She vaguely remembered the sides of the gates clipping Morte's shoulder before they were thrust open. The Spade laughed.

"Well, the King doesn't feel that the Iron Gates were enough to keep his traitorous daughter in, so he is strengthening them to make sure he keeps her and everyone else out."

Dinah gave a wry laugh. "To keep me out? What an idea. I have no intention of ever going back there. I'll be killed the moment I appear in Wonderland proper! I will never see the palace again." *Or Wardley*, she thought with sadness. *Or Harris. Or Emily. Or the beautiful stained-glass heart that sits outside my mother's room, the one that shades the world in red.*

The Spade took a last inhale of his pipe before dumping its contents into the fire. "Perhaps. But I think the King fears more than just the return of the Princess."

"The Yurkei?"

"This is the end of your answers for tonight."

"There is nothing more to tell me of Wardley?"

"No. His shoulder still healing. He spends his days in the stables, wiping the dung off of his face that is thrown at him by orphans."

But he is alive, thought Dinah, *he is alive.* She absently rubbed her hands together. *More blood on my hands,* she thought, *more consequences because of my actions. And Harris, and Emily—what had happened to them? Had her father chopped them down as easily as he had Lucy and Quintrell?*

She began to raise her voice when the Spade turned slightly, his ears pointed at the sky. *"BE SILENT!"* he whispered. Dinah froze in place. Without making a sound, the Spade ran over to his pack and withdrew a bow and arrow. Her heart thudded in her ears. What was he doing? Maybe he worked for her father. Perhaps he was an assassin sent her to kill her silently and bury her deep in the woods, where her body would simply disintegrate into the dusty ground. She looked around, taking in the moss-covered rocks and the thin white trees that ringed their nightfire. *There are worse places to be laid to rest*, she thought. *At least I'm here under the bright stars, though… if he wanted to kill me*, she reasoned, *he would have killed me while I slept. He could have pulled that knife across my throat before I had even understood what was going on.*

The Spade lifted the bow, his muscled arms quivering as he tracked something that Dinah couldn't see across the dark sky. Finally, he exhaled and released the arrow. Dinah heard a *thwap*, followed by the sound of something falling through dried leaves. The Spade darted into the woods. Dinah stood. *Now*, she thought, *now would be the time to run with Morte*, her legs shaking. *Go!* she told herself, but her legs didn't move. She stayed. There was something about this Spade, she reasoned, something different. Besides, the food was almost gone. And he was right—she didn't have a plan. Defeated, she admitted to herself that she had been wandering aimlessly through the forest, and it was a miracle that she had survived. Now she had help, or at least someone who wanted something from her, which in some cases was as good as help. He wasn't a friend, but she didn't sense danger radiating from him either. She paused, thinking of the rage on her father's face as she stood shadowed in the trees. *"But you can't trust that,"* she whispered to herself. *"You can't trust that feeling."* She never would have dreamed that her father would try to murder her, or throw her brother out of a window. Feelings meant nothing. *Whom could you trust when your own family turned against you?*

She quickly sat back on the rotted log, which gave a creak underneath her. *The day I find out what he wants,* she told herself, *is the day I will leave him behind in the dust.* There was a rustling from the trees and something landed with a sickening crack at her feet. It was the hawk, the tracking hawk, its beautiful deep red feathers mottled with black blood, an arrow through its neck. Dinah looked up at the Spade—and the admiration written across her face deceived her.

He gave a laugh at her surprise. "Chicken, Princess?"

For the first time in weeks, Dinah slept long and deep, without dreams of bloody Heart Cards or anything else that woke her in terror. It was late morning when she woke to a loud clanging. She shielded her eyes as she sat up. The Spade was clanging his swords together and watching how the blades ran over each other. Dinah was understandably unnerved by this.

"Morning, Princess." The Spade tossed a small loaf of bread in her direction and Dinah tore into it with ravenous bites. "Not very delicate, are yeh?"

She made a face in his direction.

"Now, get yerself up so I can begin yer training. Yeh need to learn how to fight, how to defend yerself. I've seen eight-year-old girls that can wield a sword better than yeh."

"I highly doubt that," replied Dinah, brushing the crumbs off of her cheeks. She handed a small piece of her bread to Morte, who almost bit her fingers off.

"On the contrary, I was raised in a village where every child could defend themselves."

Dinah was curious about this man. "Where was your village? And what makes you think your children could defend themselves?"

The Spade didn't answer and was silent before moving swiftly across the distance between them. Before Dinah could breathe, he had wrapped his thick hand around her arm and shook her roughly. "Don't speak of things yeh don't understand. If my daughter had survived, she would best yeh in a second."

"Let go of me!" she snapped, yanking her arm out of his grasp. "I thought Spades weren't allowed to have families. Your daughter is probably nothing more than your most fancy boy soldier—"

She didn't have a chance to finish. The Spade swept both of her feet out from under her, and Dinah landed hard on the small of her back. All the air rushed from her lungs. She barely had time to react before the tip of his sword drew a line across her cheek. He bowed before her. "Now we have matching scars."

Dinah leapt up and flung herself against him, and they both tumbled to the ground. The Spade easily flipped her face down into the dirt and then proceeded to keep her down with his boot, standing on top of her. Though his actions were quick and rough, his tone remained calm. "Yeh'll not say one word about my daughter, understand? Now, are yeh ready to learn?"

Dinah writhed under his foot before shouting at him. "Get off of me. I order you to stand down! Obey me! I command it!"

The Spade's gruff laugh echoed off the rock faces around them as he continued to balance on top of her. "Ah, Princess. Before yeh can learn to fight, yeh must let go of the idea that anyone in Wonderland gives a care about yer fate. Yer no longer a royal playing sticks with the stable boy. Yer no longer a princess, or anyone, for that matter. Yer a wretch, a wanderer in the forest.

Think about it. Are yeh her, are yeh that girl, the girl who would be Queen?"

Dinah considered for a moment, her face bleeding into the dirt. He was right. She was no longer the princess who loved to watch pink snowflakes swirling down from the cloudy sky, one who could command the bowed knee of every person in the room. She was here, in the middle of the wilderness. She was starving, she was broken and bleeding, and there was a Spade literally standing on her back. All this and yet, Dinah felt more in control of her fate than she had the past few months at the palace. There was a freedom in having nothing to lose.

"Let me stand. I said, let me stand!" She rolled over quickly, which caused him to lose his balance. Then she grabbed hold of the Spade's leg and dug her teeth into his calf. He let out a yell and hopped away. "Yeh bit me! Who bites someone?"

Dinah shuffled to her feet, unsteady, bleeding from the lip and covered with dirt. She spat on the ground. "C'mon you dirty Spade—teach me to fight."

He rubbed his beard. "Ah, there's the girl that slapped me for a toy, I knew yeh were there somewhere." He tossed Wardley's sword at her, and Dinah managed to catch it without slicing her hand open. This, however, was to be the highlight of her day. The rest of that morning was spent getting bruised, hit, and cut open by the blunt end of Sir Gorrann's sword. Every strike was deflected and every move of her body was dissected in an effort to find her weaknesses, which turned out to be *everything*.

As he flew around her, his voice never stopped lecturing. "Any move off balance and yeh belong to the enemy. A good swordsman can tell when his opponent is off balance and will use it to his advantage."

Dinah tried to maintain perfect balance while wielding the sword but it never worked—she was always tipped slightly to one side or the other. The Spade continued to knock her to the ground with ease, but after a few times she leapt up quickly, at the ready to fight again.

"That was good. Work on getting up. Getting back in the fight. Yeh aren't used to getting knocked down. Yeh must learn to expect it, to respond quickly when yer down. It can make the difference between victory and defeat. Every good fighter gets knocked down now and then. Now, give me back yer sword. We'll try again tomorrow to correct yer balance, but until then yeh do not deserve it."

Dinah clutched Wardley's blade close to her chest. *I have earned the right to this blade,* she thought, *I will not give it up so easily.* She felt bold. "Come and take it!" she declared.

He did, and left her lying on a rocky ledge, out of breath, with a bloody nose. Once the morning ended, Sir Gorrann erased all traces of them at the campsite and they continued to weave their way deeper and deeper into the Yurkei Mountains. The terrain was ever changing. The ground rose and fell in rocky slopes, like waves of rock that crested and broke upon the valleys, spilling their huge boulders upon gorgeous green valleys before rising again. It was a physically exhausting climb, and Dinah periodically looked longingly at Morte, only to have him ignore her completely. Only once, when Dinah slipped on a rock and tore her shin open from top to bottom did Morte pause and lift his leg. Dinah wearily climbed up onto his massive back while Sir Gorrann watched with fascination.

"Thank you," she breathed to him, letting her hand run over his smooth neck before he nipped at her. She loved the rhythm of Morte's muscles beneath her, the ocean of black that coated his whole body. He climbed easily through the jagged peaks with which Sir Gorrann's brown mare, Cyndy, seemed to increasingly struggle. The air became thinner and cleaner, and Dinah relished the sharp, cold breaths that cleared her mind.

They stopped to camp for the night, and Dinah was allowed her one question as the Spade stoked his nightfire. She asked about Harris, and learned that he had been imprisoned in the Black Towers. He was part of a group of prisoners being forced into slave labor, helping to reinforce the Iron Gates, and so Sir Gorrann said that Harris was outside for a few hours most days. He confessed that the old man looked broken, weary and sad. He was often covered with bruises and cuts inflicted by the Clubs. This news broke Dinah's heart, and there wasn't a day after that that she didn't think of Harris's kind face and soft hands. He had delivered her from her mother's womb, loved her the way her father should have, taught her everything she knew, and now he was in pain. It was unforgivable, and the white-hot rage she felt toward her father could have burned the Twisted Wood to the ground. To her devastation, she learned that Emily had been beheaded in a shabby public execution, based on the testimony of Nanda and Palma, Vittiore's ladies-in-waiting. The Spade didn't talk to her for the rest of that evening, and Dinah was grateful. She stared out at the Wonderland stars, bunched together in small clusters, and didn't bother to wipe the tears that dripped down her face.

Each day that followed in the next few weeks was the same. She woke sore but rested. Together, they gulped down a quick breakfast of bread and game before her training began. After days of working on balance, Dinah finally got her sword back, and with it her pride. She was covered in bruises, but each one had taught her a painful lesson, one that she would not soon forget. Pain cemented things in the brain the way reading did not. After sparring, they continued to make their way east, going painfully slowly as they navigated their way over pebbly ground and fields of strewn boulders. The Yurkei Mountains were upon them now, and the farther they got from the Twisted Wood, the less she feared her father finding them. The rocky outcroppings and grooves in the earth provided minimal protection once they reached the tree line, but there was no one around. The Spade had delivered them from the King's hands, as promised. In the evenings, Sir Gorrann would tell her of the politics and rumors swirling around Wonderland, some she knew and some she did not know. He told her dark stories of the Spades, stories that entertained while making her blood curdle. He never spoke of his own past, which made Dinah even more curious about where he had come from and why he was here. When she pressed him for answers, he simply walked away, leaving her in uncomfortable silence.

When the stars appeared, they watched with fascination as strange shades of light played over the mountain face, shifting swirls of every color, flickering like a flame as though they were reflecting an invisible sunset. It was beautiful, ethereal, and terrifying all at once. The light seemed to hover over one specific peak. She had never seen anything like it. Dinah did not relish turning her back to the lights, and slept facing them only to awaken facing the plain gray mountainside in the morning. Through it all the Spade remained, and with his training Dinah grew lean and strong. Another week passed. Thoughts of leaving his side slowly faded, and in the clear cold nights she was grateful to have a friend, if that's even what he was.

CHAPTER SIX

After their morning lesson—which consisted of repeatedly striking targets that Sir Gorrann had marked with charred wood—they started their hike early due to the abundance of ominous clouds in the west. The weather had turned in the last few days. Cheerful and glossy spring had changed into sopping warm rains and foggy nights. As she was almost constantly damp, drenched, or drying, Dinah had never known that being wet could be so miserable.

As they circled their way around boulders that resembled hulking granite giants, ones that even seemed to dwarf Morte, Dinah felt a question alight on her tongue. The Spade had shared so little about himself, and her curiosity grew more potent every day. Some days she felt as though she knew him better than anyone else; other days she was following nothing more than a shadow—listless, hard to pin down. Today had proved the most challenging climb so far, and both were exhausted from the rocky switchbacks that led up a nearly sheer cliff face. In a shocking twist, Morte had allowed Dinah to lead him with a leather rein that the Spade had given her. *It was a cruel joke*, thought Dinah. If Morte pitched off the side of the mountain, then she wouldn't be able to do anything to help him. She would plummet down with him, and both of their bodies would be broken on the rocks below. *Just like my brother.*

Still, a physical connection with Morte helped calm them both as they walked and tried not to look down.

Hoping that the discomfort and distraction of the climb would ease his fury, Dinah dared to speak the question: "Sir Gorrann, what happened to your family?"

The Spade flinched as he nicked his arm open on a sharp rock outcropping. "Damn! Look what yeh made me do. Been dying to ask, have yeh?"

Dinah shrugged, the motion giving Morte's leather reins a shake. "Perhaps. Yes. It's either that or tell me where we're going."

The Spade took a deep breath and stared aimlessly at the sky with his dark gold eyes. "Fine. I'll tell yeh. But not without some parameters. What I'm about to share cannot be repeated, understand? And once I tell it, yeh may not ask any questions about it. I'll not have you pestering me for feelings that I've long buried."

Dinah nodded. "I won't. Promise."

"Fine, then." He turned slightly back to look at her, his long gray hair blowing gently in the wind. "Cling to the wall, Princess, or this coming wind will rip yeh right off."

Dinah pressed herself against the stony slate at her back and continued to watch him silently. The Spade stared off into the distance, his eyes focused on something she couldn't see.

"I grew up in the Twisted Wood, farther north from where we've been. That's why I have a bit of an accent, yeh see? A small village called Dianquill. Yeh've probably never heard of it." Dinah shook her head, her eyes trained on the hundred foot drop before her. "I'm not surprised. It was a hundred people, maybe more. My mother died when I was just an infant. My father was a huntsman, and he supplied most of the food for the town, along with a few other men. It's how he made our living. Dianquill was also known for their berry harvest every spring. Most of my childhood was spent foraging in the forest for berries, looking for those rare fruits that would fetch a fortune from travelers stopping through.

"I was just fifteen years old when I met Amabel. I saw her out of the corner of my eye, this tiny red-haired girl, obviously hungry and dressed in filthy rags. She belonged to one of the strange families who lived deep in the woods. Their family couldn't afford to move to the village, so Amabel and her sisters came in to buy goods now and then before retreating back to their isolation. That day I gave her some Julla fruit that I had in my bag and she scampered off into the trees. A week later, she found me again while I was hunting. Her father had gone mad with a sickness and died, but before he passed he taught his daughter to be the best tracker in all of Wonderland. That's how she had found me, and that's how she found me every week from that day on. In return for food, she taught me how to track. Though I might seem skilled to yeh now, I am nothing compared to Amabel. She could track a deer for a hundred miles and at the same time follow the path of a man who had walked that land twenty years prior."

Sir Gorrann paused to take a long drink from his waterskin. "We married when I was nineteen, and I tell yeh, I have never loved another woman. Every morning when my eyes open, I can see her face—her long red hair, her bright eyes, wild as the sea. With my father's help, I built us a house on the edge of town. We were deep enough into the woods where we had some land and peace, but close enough to the village that I could continue to supply our family with income using my skills as a hunter. Hunting became almost too easy with Amabel's tracking skills. We had a bounty, and life was sweet and easy. We were so happy. And after our third year of marriage, we welcomed a daughter, Ioney. She looked like her mother. I thought I could never love anything more than Amabel, but I lost that battle the day I first laid eyes on Ioney. Our family was complete, and I wanted for nothing. I was a happy young man. Then they came. It was a damp spring day, not unlike this one...."

His voice sputtered out. The Spade had stopped moving, and Dinah held her position on the rock. Tears were gathering in his eyes, and she saw his weathered hands clenching with emotion. Though she was utterly fascinated, winding tendrils of guilt began to snake through her for asking him to recount these details. "You don't have to...."

"QUIET, GIRL!" he snapped. "Yeh asked, and yeh'll hear it. Be patient. It's been a spell since I've spoken of them." His mouth distorted with pain as he continued his story.

"As I was saying, it was spring and the warm rains had come and gone. I was out hunting a white bear, the same kind that almost took yer limbs, when I saw smoke rising from the village. I ran back, but it was too late. The entire village was smoldering; no building was left untouched. Several of my closest friends had been slaughtered defending their homes. The women and children had been left alive, but most of the men had been cut to pieces. My father was hanging from a burning log that had once been my childhood home. All of the villagers' food and livestock had been taken, their homes gone forever. An entire village, wiped out in less than an hour by a few cruel Cards."

Dinah's eyes narrowed. "Cards? From Wonderland Palace? Not the Yurkei?"

"I thought it was the Yurkei at first as well, but no. A friend who died in my arms told me that while some of the riders had been painted to look like Yurkei, they were undoubtedly Cards. The arrow buried in his stomach was topped with a red glass heart, so there was little doubt. Indeed, it had been Heart Cards, on their way to fight with Yurkei. Their provisions had run low, so they had taken what they wanted from my village. I closed his eyes and climbed upon my horse and galloped for my home, faster than I had ever ridden in my life."

Dinah longed to stop his story, to put her hands over his mouth to save her the horror of what was coming.

A tear made its way down his face. "I was too late, too late for my darling girls. The Cards had come across Amabel while she was tending our herb garden. She lay motionless on the ground, her red hair wet with the blood that flowed from her chest. Her hand clutched a bow and arrow, and I can only imagine that she intended to use it to defend our helpless child, my brave love, the love of my life. For this she had been shot clean through the heart. I longed to hold her there forever, her body still warm, but I had to find my daughter."

Dinah closed her eyes and pressed against the cool rock face, desperate to hear no more.

"Ioney was inside the house, although there wasn't a house anymore, just a charred pile of smoking wood and fallen timber. There was only bones left of my little girl, my Ioney."

Her eyes blurring with tears, Dinah looked away from Sir Gorrann, out into the open air before them, a vast view of honey-colored valleys and gray rock. Up until now, she had mistakenly believed that she was the only one who had suffered, the only one who had reason to grieve. Her childishness convicted her and she felt her face flush with shame.

The Spade continued. "Feeling sad that yeh asked, are yeh? 'Twas a dark night when I laid beside my love, and more than once I pressed a dagger to my throat, feeling that death would be such a sweet relief from the pain, hoping that I could join Amabel and Ioney, wherever they were. The only thing that kept me from burying it into my jugular was the thought of revenge. The next day, I buried Amabel and Ioney under their favorite berry bush in the woods, an unmarked grave. I planted Amabel's favorite orchids in a circle around their grave, sang them their favorite song and departed with my horse as evening fell. I took nothing with me aside from some food, a blanket, and every weapon I could find."

A wicked smile played over his face and Dinah feared she might be sick. "I rode my horse so hard he died after two days. I left him in the woods, barely stopping to put him out of his misery. From there, I tracked the Cards to the edge of the Yurkei Mountains, where they were attempting to find their way into Hu-Yuhar, the hidden Yurkei city, and failing miserably. It was a small group of only six men."

Sir Gorrann smiled and stroked his beard with disturbing fondness. Dinah was suddenly very afraid of him.

"I stalked and killed one each night, so that the rest might live in fear before their death's imminent arrival. They called me the Night Ghost and wrongly assumed that I was a Yurkei assassin. It took six days to kill them all, and I relished each one. When at last my vengeance was complete, I left their bodies in the Twisted Wood, just like they had left my Amabel to die. I lived for months in these hills, eventually finding the will to continue on living. I made my way to Wonderland proper. There was nothing left for me in my village, or in the Twisted Wood. I never wanted to see those places again, those places in my memory where I had first seen my wife, or where we had conceived our child."

Sir Gorrann cleared his throat and blinked before continuing along the uphill trail. His voice steadied. "I made my way to the palace, where I was blindsided by its size and wealth. Wonderland was not what I had expected and I was quickly eaten alive by city life. I wasted what little money I had brought with me on drink and women. I fell in with unsavory bedfellows, and soon was stealing to eat, then stealing to live. I was a good thief when I wasn't drinking, but unfortunately that was more often than not. I was caught breaking into a lady of the court's house while attempting to steal her jewels, so drunk I could barely stand. Her husband was a beast of a man and rightly beat me to a bloody pulp. I was thrown into the Black Towers." Dinah's mouth fell open and he managed to give her a rough smile.

"Yes, Princess, yeh aren't the only one who has seen the horrors of the Black Towers. Luckily for me I was in the Thieves' Tower, which only performs minimal torture. I was never strapped against its terrible roots." Dinah said a silent prayer that Harris was not being strapped to the tree. Seeing him devoured from the inside as Faina Baker had been would surely be enough to break her.

"I was imprisoned in the Black Towers for two years. It was a dark time, but I managed to befriend a young Club who told me everything he knew about Wonderland, the Black Towers, and the Cards. I was let out a year later and forced to join the Spades, for which I am ever thankful. Thanks to the Spades, I had food, a place to live, and a purpose. Eventually I became the lead tracker for the King, and that led me to being here with yeh now."

Dinah frowned as she sent a scattering of pebbles rolling down the steep mountainside. "I still don't understand why you sought to help me. You're a Spade, therefore you are loyal to the King and the Cards. You have betrayed your oaths in a grand way."

The Spade climbed up onto an overhead ledge to view their surroundings and then looked down on Dinah, who observed him with confused admiration. She scrambled up the path behind him, finally approaching the summit of the mountain.

The Spade stood before her, his stare intense. "Indeed, that's correct. I have broken my vows by helping yeh. I have abandoned the Cards. I have helped the most-wanted person in Wonderland. And for what? Surely yeh've assumed that there was something I left out of the story, and yeh would be correct. One person remains against whom I must take out my vengeance for the life of my family, a man who took everything precious from me. And even though it has taken me thirty years, I will have my vengeance, though not through typical means.

"The raid that killed my family was ordered by a young king, recently crowned by his father. He longed to impress his men, to show them his raw strength, so he rode out with a scouting party, devouring everything in his path. He was present at the raid that destroyed my village, but then was called back to Wonderland on royal business. This man I could not kill silently while creeping through the woods, for he is guarded night and day by fighters more skilled than I. To take his life is not enough. I must see him fall, to see everything that he loves stripped from him."

Dinah stared at the Spade as fat drops of rain drenched them both. Lightning snaked across the gray sky. "This is why I help yeh, and this is why we hike endlessly through these mountains. The man yeh called father is the man who ordered the raid on my village, and someday we will both have our vengeance for the loved ones that he has taken from us."

Dinah stared at the Spade, not sure what to say while her head reeled with potent thoughts and emotions. An empty hiss of air escaped her lips as she wiped a stray tear from her eye with the back of her hand, mingling with the rain that was now coming in sideways. Her pain was nothing compared to his loss, and yet she felt a sting of anger burning through her. His motivations had finally shown, and she was aware of just how close she was to a man who could have taken her life a dozen times before she woke.

Finally, she found the words she was looking for and began to speak. "Sir Gorrann, I am sorry for the loss of your family, but I have no intention of returning to Wonderland Palace. Not now, not ever. Now if you will please tell me where you are leading me, I'm certain we can—"

"QUIET, FOOL!" hissed the Spade, his head turning swiftly to the west. Morte's ears perked up. There was only silence, and then something. The crunch of a leaf, the sound of a step on the trail below them. "Hurry!" he yelled. "Someone's following us. We must make haste. Hurry yer steed. We must pass over this summit, and quickly. If he can't keep up, leave him behind. We must go now." Fear churned through Dinah as she gripped the leather reins, pulling Morte as quickly as she dared up and over the rocky slope.

CHAPTER SEVEN

Coming up and over the rocks, they ran into a sheer cliff face. An enormous slab of gray rock loomed before them, extending its jagged ends into the noon sun. Hundreds of boulders filled the small space, as if a giant had been playing with his toys and left them in a terrible pile.

"We're trapped!" Dinah hissed. "Where did you lead us?"

Sir Gorrann was scanning the face of the wall, up and down, searching for something Dinah couldn't see. There were several footsteps now, echoing off of the ledges below, the sound of more than a dozen men, inching ever closer. At first Dinah was confused as to why they had not been swarmed over already, but then she understood. Whoever tracked them wanted to push them over the cliff face. And Morte was with them. No man, Card, or Yurkei wanted to be the first one over the ledge. Sir Gorrann continued to search between boulders.

"What are you doing?" Dinah screamed. "We have to fight!" Finally, Sir Gorrann found what he was looking for. Two boulders, perfectly aligned, of equal shape and size. Upon first glance, there was nothing extraordinary about them, but on further inspection, their identical shape, marking, and color was unnerving. Dinah ran to Sir Gorrann, her sword drawn.

"Put that away," he mumbled. "You could not fight what threatens to push us off this ledge." As they crept around the boulders, the Spade took a bold step between them. What should have ended in a smacked head made him disappear completely. Dinah blinked several times before she was able to decipher this boggling—and genius—illusion. The two boulders were actually one, carved to look separate, like two stones. They looked as though they were pressed up against each other, but their carved lines hid a tall hole. On the outside, they appeared as two normal boulders. But from the perfect angle, the narrow doorway was easy to spot. Dinah knew she never would have been able to find it on her own.

"Through here!" shouted the Spade. Something churned in her stomach as she looked into the inky tunnel. It was a lurking, terrible feeling, a fear that distorted and confused. She recognized immediately—this was how she felt when the root had twisted into her mouth. The despair was unmistakable—there was evil in that tunnel.

"No. No, I can't go in there."

Sir Gorrann grabbed her arm and practically tossed her inside. "We have no choice, Princess. Move!"

She opened her mouth to object, but there were no other options. Head bowed, she followed Sir Gorrann's mare through the narrow opening. Morte gave a great huff and stomped the ground furiously, his hooves sending booming echoes through the quarry. The ground seemed to shudder. Finally, once Dinah took her hands off his reins, he ducked his head and entered the tunnel willingly. The sides of his flanks brushed against the wall. He was unfamiliar and uncomfortable in this rocky terrain. His ears were flattened against his head, and Dinah could see his muscles tensed and ready to run. She felt a sudden rush of panic.

Sir Gorrann, his mare, Dinah, and Morte were stacked end to end, moving as quickly as they dared. If Morte should panic and bolt, they would all be trampled under his crushing weight. Sir Gorrann glanced back at Morte, his face pale and drawn. He had obviously come to the same conclusion. They paused, their hearts humming loudly in their closely drawn quarters.

"This is a wicked place," breathed Sir Gorrann. "Let's hurry. Keep yer devil calm." The tunnel was maybe a half mile long, and from the moment they entered, an all-encompassing darkness draped them like a heavy blanket. Overhead, Dinah could hear the slight slithering of roots, a whispered hiss, and the sound of a thousand tiny legs. Something dripped onto her cheek, something warm and smelling of blood. Her hand brushed up against something wet and rubbery and she leapt toward the mare with a shriek. Morte was becoming more and more agitated, and Dinah forced herself to remain calm as a wet tendril caressed her cheek in the darkness. Something was crawling in her hair, something that made tiny clicking sounds with a sharp mouth. It scuttled across her forehead and leapt onto the wall. The walls around them were alive, raising their voices in a hissed chorus. *Evil, evil, evil.* Sir Gorrann pressed himself against the wall to let Cyndy pass, and Dinah felt his hand close around her wrist, grateful for the warmth of his calloused fingers. Something wet and long encircled their wrists and then slunk away into the tunnel.

"Do not run. Do not run." He repeated the mantra again and again, convincing himself rather than Dinah. Dinah did not need the reminder. As terrible as the tunnel was—and it was the foulest place she could ever dream, a place of nightmares—there would be nothing worse than being trampled alive and left to die in this place, to have your body consumed slowly by whatever demons thrived in this dark corridor. She would not run. If she ran, Morte would run, and they would all die. Her pace stayed steady, and her hand tightened around Sir Gorrann's in a show of strength. She would keep him calm. They stayed silent, afraid their voices would collapse the rock inward, or even worse, stir up the invisible creatures to aggression. A wild fear of the unknown pressed against Dinah's brain and she found herself remembering every dark thing that had ever happened to her. She saw death, bodies, the King. Charles, with worms crawling out of his eyes. Vittiore, wearing her silver crown. The dead farmer, the arrow in his back leaking blood.

She stumbled once, twice… again. Sir Gorrann was having a hard time as well, murmuring violent things to himself as he bumped off the wall, falling over his own feet. Some slithery heavy thing had settled on his shoulder, and he struggled to wrench it away. Dinah kept walking. She couldn't help him. Her hope was gone. The steam from Morte's nostrils was burning her elbow now, his muzzle pressed against her back. He was pushing, pushing, faster now. *We're going to die in here*, she thought. Another thought occurred to her—perhaps they were already dead. Perhaps this tunnel *was* death, in all its hideous finality.

She couldn't remember who she was. How did she get here again? Something was prying at her mouth. *Might as well open it*, she thought. *What could be the harm?* Then, there was light. A warm light appeared at the end of the tunnel, a hazy pinkish spot, warm and welcoming and safe. It throbbed through the darkness. Cyndy broke into a sprint toward it and Sir Gorrann followed, forgetting all previous instruction, so desperate to be free from this underground hell. Dinah did not run. She kept her pace steady, and Morte did not run. Slimy, terrible things detached themselves from her hair and wrists. Something slithered down her leg and back into the darkness. The light blazed through the dark. She burst through into its glorious pinkness, and fell to her knees beside

Sir Gorrann. He pushed her out of the way just before Morte's gigantic body collapsed in a heap right where she had been kneeling.

They lay on the ground, gasping, taking in heavy breaths of delicious, sweet air, so happy to be free of the tunnel. Minutes passed. There was nothing sweeter than being alive. Morte whinnied happily beside her, rolling on the soft carpet of flowers to erase the stench of the tunnel. When she finally felt balanced again, Dinah peered down at her hands on the ground. Purple flowers, the same color that Cheshire wore so often, opened and shut before her eyes, their blooms radiating individual rays of soft light. With each pulse of the petal, a tiny tendril of red lashed out, a pink light on the tip of the stamen. It was remarkable and strange all at once, and her eyes followed the ground until she saw that one flower led to a patch of flowers, and the patch of flowers led to a field. They were in an entire valley full of blinking purple and pink flowers, radiating light and— she held her hand over the tip of the flower. *Yes. Heat.*

The flowers radiated a warm heat when they popped open, which accounted for the heavenly air that flowed through this field. The grass was a bright green, and felt more like a soft pillow than a wooded forest floor. Dinah felt the overwhelming desire to slip off her boots and run laughing through the flowers. It could only be called a hysterical happiness. She was drunk with it.

"My gods," she heard Sir Gorrann mutter, and Dinah stood up. The Spade rested his hand on her arm and with a gentle touch tilted her head upward. They both looked in wonder... at the *mushrooms*. Thousands of enormous, swirly mushrooms filled the field. They were huge, as tall as trees in most places. Their stems were wider than Dinah, trunklike white stalks that led up into a thick, billowy explosion of color, the horizon like a bucket of upside-down parasols. They exploded from the ground, each unique in its varied colors and type, giving the overall effect of being in a hazy dream. Dinah turned in a circle. The valley was deep and long, a maze of color and fantastic curling shapes, each mushroom standing proudly against the sky.

Dinah blinked. She suddenly wasn't sure how long she had been staring at the mushrooms. Had she been here an hour or a minute? She looked over at Sir Gorrann. The Spade stood rooted in the same place he had been before, his mouth agape. Dinah shook herself out of the trance and began walking toward one of the mushrooms. Its cap was a brilliant yellow with swirls of glittering orange and red, like someone had taken a wet paintbrush to the top. Underneath the cap, a warm white light pulsed within its gills. They seemed to contract with each burst of light, as if they were breathing. The mushroom was utterly intoxicating, perhaps the most attractive thing she had ever seen. It seemed to be calling to her. Dinah reached out to touch the stem.

"Don't." The deep voice broke her trance and Dinah's hand jerked to a stop. The Spade walked up beside her. "Don't touch them. They might be poisonous, we don't know. On the other hand...."

"I want to eat them," whispered Dinah, her mouth watering at the thought.

Sir Gorrann scratched his beard, his hand trembling with want. "I do as well, which is exactly why I think we shouldn't. Let's continue on our way."

Dinah wanted to stay forever, but she simply nodded. Her eyes took in every stem, every inch of the mushrooms. Together they walked silently through the field, the fungi stretching out in all directions, seemingly never ending. Dinah watched with fascination as they passed a pink- and white-striped mushroom with a black stem and yellow gills, a bright blue mushroom the color and depth of the sky, and a deep purple mushroom with a stem covered in a thousand tiny mushrooms of the same color. The light in the valley faded into a soothing glow. It was something otherworldly, the most extraordinary thing Dinah had ever seen, the exact opposite of the dark tunnel from which they had emerged. Sir Gorrann didn't speak, but the Spade had drawn his sword for some reason that Dinah couldn't fully comprehend. Morte walked behind them, eating everything in his sight. There was no way Dinah could stop him in this valley of rich food, and she watched him with envy as he gulped down a pure white mushroom that appeared to be made of frosting. Her steps fell silently on the soft lawn. Twisty tendrils curled up from the ground, as thick as a man's arm, as they passed. The curls gave a tiny shake when her foot landed beside them, as if they were stirring from a dormant sleep.

I could stay here forever, thought Dinah. *I could lie underneath the mushrooms and simply watch their colors pulse with this... enthralling life.* Dinah let her eyes linger on a pink mushroom, its rich fuchsia the same color as the inside of a Julla fruit. Tiny glowing stars dotted its cap. "Oh," breathed Dinah, amazed at the beauty of it all. She reached for the mushroom. An odd cry echoed through the valley, such an odd sound in this peaceful haven of light and warmth. It sounded like a crane. The cry was followed by another, and then she heard a *whump.* She knew that sound. Her face distorted with terror as she spun around. The first arrow took the Spade off his feet. He flew backward onto the grass, a white quivered arrow protruding from his chest. Two more arrows landed on either side of him. The valley grew lighter as all the mushrooms suddenly radiated with blinding white light. A second arrow landed just past her feet, another in front of her. She blinked in confusion.

Wake up! She screamed at herself. *You are under attack!* Her thoughts finally connected and then she was running blindly, arrows falling around her like rain. Dinah plunged through the mushrooms, ducking and bobbing as arrows whizzed past her face.

"Morte!" she screamed. "Morte! Morte!" Suddenly, he was upon her, his black hide rippling with excitement. He barely even stopped moving long enough for her to step onto his leg and vault herself onto the nape of his neck. Then, they were flying, his muscles pounding like thunder beneath her. Through the mushrooms they plunged, the rainbow light a colored blur that flashed past. Dinah watched with horror as a line of feathered warriors appeared before them. Hundreds deep, each holding notched bows and arrows, each one trained on her, on Morte. *The Yurkei.* Morte wheeled to the left, but they were there as well, and to the right, emerging from between the mushrooms like ghosts in the darkness. *Had they been there the whole time?* Morte whinnied and backstepped. Something was wrong with him. He was stumbling, jumping, falling over his feet. The warriors slowly moved toward them. Dinah and Morte were surrounded on all sides.

Morte began to buck, and Dinah clutched his mane to keep from falling off. When he landed, she nudged him forward. If there was no passage leading away from the Yurkei, she would go through them. Morte would crush them under his mighty hooves, even if he was acting strangely. Dinah drew her sword.

"DINAH, STOP!" The voice plowed through the valley, strong and deep. The light from the mushrooms dimmed at the sound. She turned her head in surprise. It was the first time Sir Gorrann had ever said her name. He stood a thousand yards away, looking very much alive in the midst of a thousand Yurkei warriors that surrounded him, their arrows drawn, all pointing at her, pointing at him. Blood leaked steadily from his shoulder, but the wound didn't look terrible. There was no sign of a chest wound. *Armor,* she thought. *He still has his Spade armor on. Thank the gods.* The wild thudding of her heart shook her body as Morte wheeled and turned again.

Sir Gorrann raised his voice. "Dinah, do not fight! They will kill you with a hundred arrows before you cross their line. We are surrendering. Put down your sword." The Spade took his sword and laid it on the ground before raising his arms above his head. There was a murmuring in the crowd, and Dinah's eyes widened as the Yurkei parted like a sea. The mushrooms began to hum with light and sound. The warriors all extended their arms and pressed the base of their palms together, thumbs linked, fingers spread. Like wings. Dinah heard a familiar thudding, and her stomach clenched.

A tan Hornhoov emerged out of the dim light, and astride him, a fearsome-looking man. His hair was as white as snow, shaved back in a long strip that caressed his shoulder blades. Stripes of white paint covered his deeply tanned and muscular body, his radiant blue eyes visible even from a distance. On his head was a woven headdress of feathers, white and blue and gathered in a circle at the crown before cascading down his back. The rest of the Yurkei watched him with rapt attention, their hands still spread before themselves. He gave the slightest nod and their arms dropped back to their original position—aiming arrows at her and Morte. He was almost upon her now; Dinah was sure of his name. Mundoo, the Chief of the Yurkei.

A cold fear shot through her as she remembered all the terrible stories she had heard about this warrior chief. He raised his hand to her, his voice steady and calm. "Woman. You have trespassed into the sacred burial ground of the Yurkei tribe and will now be punished as such: give us your steed, your supplies, and all of your food and then you may go with your lives. Otherwise, you will be pierced through with the arrows of my strong warriors. They do not miss."

Dinah sat perfectly still, surprised at his perfect grasp of the Wonderland language. This seemed like a fair deal, but she did not want to part with Morte. Mundoo was eyeing him greedily—who knew what they would do to him.

Dinah coughed. "I have something of great worth to give you instead of my steed. Jewels and gold are worth much more than this horse. I can get you all of those and more."

Mundoo gave a nick of his tongue and his pale Hornhoov approached, eyeing Morte with aggression. The mare was almost the same size as Morte, the color of the purest sand, her white mane braided through with blue ribbons and paint.

Mundoo narrowed his glowing blue eyes as he neared them. "But that is not just a steed, My Lady, as you well know." As Mundoo grew closer, Dinah saw his bright-blue eyes widen just before he drew his own arrow, pointed straight at her throat, drawn in the time it took her to blink.

"Iy-Joyera! Iy-Joyera!" The tribe moved swiftly toward her, all arrows trained on Morte.

Mundoo stared past his quivering arrow. "This is no regular Hornhoov. I have seen this steed before. Iy-Joyera, the black devil. This is Morte, the King's horse. This beast has killed dozens of my best warriors and carried the murderous King of Wonderland upon his back as he burned and pillaged our villages." Mundoo was now very close to Dinah, their Hornhooves dangerously close to each other as they heaved and pawed the ground, desperate to fight each other. Morte stumbled again, and Dinah lurched down toward Mundoo. The tip of his arrow brushed her throat.

"Tell me! Tell me how a dirty peasant girl has the horse of a king and the speech of a noble. Tell me now or I will spill your blood here. I will let you watch as we kill your devil, one arrow at a time." Dinah raised her chin and stared deep into the Chief's eyes. She had no choice. They would no doubt kill her once they learned who she was, and it was better to die a quick death than a long one by torture. She would not go quietly, a meek, insecure princess. She would go out in a blaze of glory, a warrior who had come so far on her own, one who had made it through the Twisted Wood. She had seen death and pain, felt the blade of a sword on her neck and the thrill of the fear that preceded imminent death. She was a woman, not a girl, and she would not go without a fight.

Dinah raised her voice as she drew her sword quickly. "My name is Dinah, and I once was the future Queen of Wonderland until I escaped my father and made my way here. You will not touch my steed this day, nor spill my blood. I do not fear death from your arrows, but you should fear my sword and my rage." Morte rose up on his hind legs and she saw confusion and surprise register across Mundoo's face as she sliced her sword down toward his head. Mundoo's Hornhoov gave a skilled leap back, and Dinah swung into empty air before something hard and heavy hit the side of her head with a sickening crunch. The hazy light of the mushroom field went dim and Dinah gave thanks that her death had been quick and painless. She closed her eyes and waited to see Charles's happy face, just on the other side of the rabbit hole.

CHAPTER EIGHT

There it was again, the swirling darkness, the inky sky, the floating clocks. Dinah twisted and turned inside it, struggling to move. Something was wrapped around her arms—something like a vine? No matter how much she struggled, it wrapped tighter around her, strangling her, pressing her organs uncomfortably together. She opened her mouth to scream, but the vines were in her mouth as well. But now they were the roots, the roots of the Black Towers, twisting in and out, filling her with their visions. Blood on a sword, a white ghost emerging from the darkness, its claws outstretched.... Dinah's body jerked and she had the sensation of falling before something strong and hard encircled her waist and righted her. Awareness returned and she realized that she was bobbing up and down. She shook her head once and forced her eyes to open.

Morte. She was on Morte, but what was behind her? She managed to turn her head. The Spade was sitting behind her on Morte, one arm wrapped around her waist, the other one clutching the red leather reins with desperation. She could see why. Sir Gorrann had been blindfolded. Dinah's head dropped forward and she could see that she was bound with a heavy white rope, its texture not unlike the branches of trees. In her mouth was some sort of fabric gag, and she forced herself to breathe through her nose before she choked. The side of her head felt like a blunt object had been shoved through it, and there was dried blood crusted over her eye and nose. She tried to move her mouth and felt the Spade's hand feel its way up her face and gently remove the gag from her mouth. His lips brushed against her ear, an angry rush of words coming from his mouth.

"Do not say a word, not one godsdamn word, yeh stupid, silly Princess. Yer lucky to be alive right now, and because of yer impulsiveness, we almost both lost our lives. So like yer father, quick to rage and slow to think. Yer lucky that my hands found a rock, otherwise you would be strewn about the mushroom field in a thousand pieces." Dinah felt the waterskin brush her lips. "Drink some water now and yeh go back to sleep. I imagine we have more than a few miles to travel before reaching Hu-Yuhar."

Dinah could barely nod her head with the thundering pain in her temple, but she managed to swallow a few gulps of water. Sir Gorrann had thrown a rock at her? Her thoughts were confused, cloudy. There were the mushrooms and the Yurkei and their arrows and then... she couldn't remember. Why had the Spade taken her this way in the first place?

Morte's easy lilt rocked her back to unconsciousness, and when she awoke again the dusk was settling. She looked around. They were in a vast field of waving pale-green grass, as tall as most men, interspersed with curling lavender trees that whirled and leapt from their roots. The wind rippled the grass violently from side to side, and when she tucked her head to avoid a lashing from the grasses, the Yurkei didn't even seem to notice. A line of Yurkei warriors stretched out in front of them, and Dinah noticed that she was surrounded on all sides by Yurkei guards, eyeing her and Sir Gorrann with obvious loathing. She stared back unabashedly at the warriors, so different than anything she had ever seen before. Their skin was a dark toffee, the color of wet sand or burned bread. Stripes of thick white paint ran from under their eyes down their entire body, covering their arms and bare torsos. Each one had glowing bright-blue eyes that radiated from their dark faces. They each had white hair that came to a point in the middle of their forehead. Most had short hair, cropped to just below the neck, although Mundoo's was longer and braided down his back with stripes of blue. Each warrior wore pants (if one could call them that) made of white feathers that sat low and snug around their muscled pelvises.

They were strangely handsome and moved with a graceful ease that eluded every human Dinah had ever known. Their horses were all the same pale tan with white manes. The horses were smaller than the mares she had seen at the stable, but they seemed quicker and more connected to their riders. Together they moved, horse and rider, as though they were of one mind. All together, the Yurkei created an incredible mass of muscle and skill, each Yurkei in possession of a quiver hung across their backs, full of white arrows flecked with gray.

Mundoo rode at the front, the heavy footsteps of his Hornhoov echoing across the quiet landscape. He was taller than the rest, and Dinah could see from the rippling of muscles across his back that he was an impressive specimen. It was strange to look upon Mundoo, a name that struck fear into the heart of every Wonderland girl and boy and see that while he was no doubt a fierce man, he was still just a man. Stories of the Yurkei ran rampant in Wonderland—stories of the horrors they inflicted upon innocent towns, of how they beat their women, of how they sacrificed their children and gnawed on human bones. It was said that they mated with cranes, and that their offspring were the terrible white bears of the Twisted Wood. Dinah had always been skeptical of the Yurkei stories—mostly because she was skeptical of everything she learned—but she could see now with her own eyes that the stories were grossly exaggerated.

These men weren't so unlike the Cards. They dressed differently and spoke in a language that sounded like the flowing of water, but they were just men, not monsters. She had learned some basic Yurkei language in her studies, but the true lesson had been unspoken: they are the enemy. *Know the language of the enemy.*

Dinah struggled against her restraints as her arms fell asleep and her spine raged in protest from being bent forward for so many hours. "Yeh best quit moving," noted the Spade quietly. "Don't call attention to yourself."

"Mmm...." The Spade removed her gag for a short second. "Morte?" she gasped. Even with the blindfold, she could feel Sir Gorrann's disappointment boring into her as he put her gag back in place.

Finally, he gave a nod. "Amazing what yeh care about. Morte let me climb up—probably because I was carrying yeh. He's heavily drugged from the mushrooms—he probably isn't even aware what's happening right now. He's just walking. Otherwise, I think he would have killed a great many today." The Spade paused. "I want to warn yeh that Morte might not live long once we get to Hu-Yuhar. Yeh must understand that he has killed many, many Yurkei. *Iy-Joyera* means the black devil."

Dinah felt her eyes blur with tears and blood dripping from her head wound. She strained against her gag. "Whhhh...." Sir Gorrann pulled it out again. "Why... why did you lead me here?"

"Don't yeh worry about that quite yet. It will all play out." Dinah closed her eyes again, half-reassured, half-alarmed by the Spade's presence behind her. "Sleep. I'll wake yeh when we arrive.

Best get yer wits about yeh. And don't try to kill the Chief again, otherwise we'll both end up riddled with arrows."

I can't promise that, thought Dinah drowsily, on the edge of sleep as Sir Gorrann struggled to blindly put her gag back in. *Not if he tries to kill me first. I will fight for my pathetic existence, no matter how meaningless it is at this point.* Her head throbbed and she dropped swiftly into the soothing arms of sleep.

CHAPTER NINE

She awoke flat on her back, her eyes staring up at a circle of bright blue sky. She blinked a few times before her hands came up to wipe her watering eyes. Her arms were free. This was a good sign. She let her eyes play over her surroundings, hesitant to move. She was in a tent of some sort, but it wasn't triangular, or square. It was perfectly round and short, shaped like the tarts she had loved back at the palace. She knew if she stood that her fingers would brush the tip of the roof, and if she were just a bit taller she would be able to stick her hand through the open hole at the top. Dinah pushed herself up shakily. She was sitting on some sort of incredible mattress made of woven grass. Her back felt better than it had in weeks of sleeping on the hard ground. For the first time in a long time, Dinah's body felt truly rested. She stretched her arms out in front of her body—which led to a pulse of pain that radiated down from her head.

Tenderly, she probed the wound near her temple. Dried blood covered the area, and a lump the size of an apple protruded from just over her ear. Her head was pounding, and the pain pressing against her skull made her grind her teeth. She sat still for a few minutes until the pain decreased to where she could move around. Dinah took a breath. She was fine. She was alive. It was enough.

She looked longingly back at the mattress of grass and considered simply curling up and playing dead for the rest of the day, but she had a feeling that wasn't in her best interest. There were questions to be answered. Her eyes finally adjusted to the light of the tent and she saw that two Yurkei warriors stood silently near the door, their hands locked around their bows.

Dinah turned back to the mattress. A simple red tunic and a pair of white feather pants had been laid out for her. She dressed herself quickly, vaguely aware that the warriors' bright blue eyes watched her every move, even while their faces remained unreadable. She attempted to braid her hair, though the thick black curtain that she once so loathed was more a rat's nest than a hairstyle these days. Her boots were gone, and she hoped that they weren't gone forever if she was going to live through all this. She had grown quite fond of wearing boots.

When she approached the door of the pod-shaped room, the two guards parted. "Mundoo wish to see you," said one of them in heavily broken Wonderlander. Dinah nodded, hoping they couldn't see her growing fear. *They haven't killed me yet,* she told herself. *That's something.* The seething hatred in one guard's blue eyes was intense, while the other looked simply intrigued by her presence. Taking a breath, she pulled back the tent flap. White sunlight assaulted her eyes as Dinah struggled to comprehend what she was seeing. After a few moments, she let herself exhale, stunned into a respectful silence. She was in Hu-Yuhar, the hidden city of the Yurkei. She stood in a very narrow valley surrounded by rocky gray cliff faces on both sides that veered up and away. Past these towering walls of stone, the gorgeous Yurkei Mountains rose up around them, their tops always concealed behind a foggy mist that rolled and leapt like a child at play. The mountains were said to be topless, and the closer Dinah got to them the more she believed it.

The entire valley couldn't have been more than half a mile wide. The ground was covered by a lush, bluish-green grass. Horses were everywhere, roaming free—eating, running, sleeping. The valley floor seemed to belong to them, although she watched several hundred Yurkei going about their daily business on two narrow dirt pathways flanking the rock walls. Dinah looked up, shielding her eyes from the light that draped the whole valley in dewy sunshine. Hundreds of tents—shaped just like the one she had awakened in—protruded from the mountain side, hovering hundreds of feet above the ground like little clouds. Round and flat, they jutted out from holes in the rock or the edges of cliffs, or sometimes, just the vertical, flat rock face. Some sort of wooden structure secured each tent to the mountain with long wooden beams that twisted and wrapped under the pods, supporting them from below. *Biscuits*, thought Dinah, that's what the shape reminded her of. Round, flat biscuits.

Soaring through the space between the two mountain faces was a system of lofty bridges, made of the same wooden material that secured the tents to the cliff sides. Yurkei moved across the bridges with alarming speed: children chasing each other, women with baskets full of food or clothing, men carrying handfuls of arrows. The valley bustled with life, although most of it was taking place above Dinah's head. Something hit her shoulder, something blunt and hard. She winced and turned around. The Yurkei warrior who had looked at her with such loathing stood behind her, brandishing the butt of a long, curved spear at her. "You. Move. To Chief."

Dinah began walking forward, not sure of where she was going until several Yurkei children ran in front of her and proceeded to lead the way. Their long white hair flowing freely over their shoulders, clean of the white stripes that marked the men. Boy or girl, Dinah found it hard to tell. Altogether they were lovely, until one of them turned and spat in her face.

"C'hallgu Quon!" Then several others turned and followed suit. "C'hallgu Quon!" "C'hallgu Quon!" they chanted. *Bad Queen?* Dinah tried to translate in her mind as she wiped the spit off her lip. Small rocks appeared out of nowhere and suddenly Dinah was being pelted with all kinds of things: grass, rocks, spit, dirt…. She raised her hands to protect herself and the two Yurkei guards closed in on her, each taking one arm and barking orders at the children. Fervently, she looked around for Sir Gorrann, but his grizzled face was nowhere to be seen. She was alone.

On the sides of the valley, Yurkei women had lined up to watch her, this dirty and humiliated princess. She tripped over her feet as they stared, and she felt even more humbled by their wild beauty and piercing stares. The women wore only white feathered skirts that draped loosely around their legs and a white feathered band that hung loosely around their breasts. Each woman was muscled and lean, with smooth dark skin and shining blue eyes. Their hair was long and twisted back into several elaborate buns accented by sparse blue beads that winked in the sunlight. Dinah felt so out of place, a hideous monster with her pale white skin, black hair, and black eyes. Their eyes narrowed as she passed. The tunic was given to her with a purpose, she realized. She was wearing red, the color of Wonderland Palace, a color to remind those around her exactly who she was. Red, the color of blood, the color of the oppressor. *I should have gone naked*, she thought, stumbling again. *I might have attracted less notice.*

The crowds parted in front of her as she approached a massive white rope ladder that seemed to hang in midair. Dinah glanced up, her neck straining to take in its height. Far above, carved out of the two mighty rock walls that lined the valley, two cranes faced each other—their wings outstretched, their chests puffed out. Two long necks elongated into huge heads with terrible, open beaks. The carvings were so large that the beaks were almost touching, though they began on opposite sides of the valley.

"Meir hu-gofrey," murmured the Yurkei warrior who had looked at her with such curiosity. "Our protectors and gods." Dinah nodded. She knew that the Yurkei worshipped the birds, and that Wonderland's fascination with birds had grown out of their early meetings with the Yurkei. In between the two birds, a single large pod was suspended between the curves in their necks by the same wooden rope material she had seen in the valley. The Chief lived there, she guessed, suspended perpetually between two warring birds, each the size of a mountain.

Dinah stopped and stared at the ladder. It blew about in the wind, looking weak and worn. "I can't."

The angry Yurkei warrior pushed Dinah up to the ladder and placed her hand on the bottom rung.

"Climb," he demanded. "Climb."

Dinah looked up. The pod was suspended hundreds of feet above the earth. A fall from even the middle would surely either kill her or break every bone in her body. She took a deep breath and began making her way up the rope ladder that somehow blew in the breeze but still managed to be strong and unbendable beneath her white-knuckled grip. Hand over hand, she made her way up with the two Yurkei warriors lingering behind her, obviously annoyed by how slowly she was climbing. A strong gust of wind rocked the ladder, and Dinah pressed herself against it, wrapping her arms and legs around the rungs. She heard the roaring laughter of Yurkei children from below as they watched her desperately cling to the ladder for dear life as it lifted off the ground and blew out behind the warriors, lashing like an angry tail.

"Up, up!" shouted the guard behind her. Dinah clutched the ladder, afraid to move, afraid of the long fall that would break her body on the jagged rocks below. The ladder twisted and swayed, and Dinah let out a cry before murmuring nearly forgotten prayers from childhood as she clutched the rung before her. She was frozen, unable to move. The ladder began to twirl in the wind, faster and faster as it cracked and whistled. She could hear the peals of laughter below and the angry roar of the wind that ripped through the valley. *I'm so afraid,* she thought. *Have I ever been this afraid? I'm going to die here.* The rung underneath her hand was growing slippery with sweat, and Dinah's foot was tangled between two others. *I can't. I can't move,* she thought.

Before she could finish her thought, the kinder of the two guards began rapidly climbing up the ladder after her. He reached her in seconds. Once there, he moved slowly, circling around the ladder until he was on the opposite side, his face inches from Dinah's. He dangled from the rope with one hand as he untangled Dinah's footing with the other. He switched hands then and wrapped one palm around the wooden rope as it twisted in the breeze and the other tightly around her waist. "I will help," he murmured. "Step."

Dinah closed her eyes and reached for the next rung, secured by his hand supporting her waist. Her foot found the rung. Without thinking, she grabbed the next rung and the one after that, even when the wind wrenched the ladder sideways so roughly that Dinah almost lost her grip. The Yurkei warrior held onto her as she slipped and strained her way up. At times it seemed hopeless, but still she climbed. She climbed up past the breasts of the enormous cranes, past the crests of their giant necks and finally, straight up into the vast white pod strung between the two birds, like some saucer that the fowl had dropped from their mouths.

The Yurkei warrior was the first one through the pod, and he rapped his hand twice against a wooden bracket on the outside. A square of fabric was pulled from the bottom, and with a leap, he disappeared up into the hole, reaching back to help Dinah. Her feet dangled in the air lifelessly as he held her arms, and she looked up with fear into his glowing blue eyes, her life completely in his hands. He gave her a shy smile and yanked her up through the opening, setting her down roughly inside the tent. Dinah's legs and arms were shaking so terribly that she simply rolled over onto her back, her lungs heaving and contracting with each long breath. Her hands wouldn't stop shaking, a cold sweat pouring from her skin. It felt good to be on a hard surface, but she couldn't forget the fact that this fabric tent was suspended hundreds of feet in the air. It was unnatural to be this high, and she longed to feel dirt underneath her fingernails. She was a child of the earth, not the sky. Her heart gave a terrified thud when she realized that she would also have to climb back down the ladder, which would be less physically exhausting but infinitely more dangerous. She closed her eyes and focused on breathing. After a few minutes, a man's voice broke the silence.

"Did you enjoy your climb, Princess?" Warily, Dinah rolled over and pushed herself into a sitting position. She tried to force her heaving breaths down into her ribs, to appear more in control. Mundoo stood before her, looking resplendent in a full headdress made of blue feathers, wearing nothing more than a feathered loincloth and some sort of wooden sandal that laced up the ankle and calf. The white painted stripes she had seen on him before were gone, now replaced with elaborately illustrated white drawings and symbols that coated his skin. His muscles were lean and hard, his eyes brilliant and blue. He sat calmly on a huge throne of carved golden birds, which much to her surprise, was not unlike the Heart thrones in the Great Hall. In fact, the more she looked at it, the more she realized it was the twin of the thrones in Wonderland Palace. One was carved of hearts and the other of birds, but otherwise they were the same. Carved by the same maker at the same time, no doubt.

Stand up, Dinah told herself, *now! You look weak.* She forced herself shakily to her feet and raised her head. Mundoo stood and motioned to his guards. "Lu-feryir." The guards turned and walked toward several open flaps around the bean-shaped tent and out into the open air. Dinah gasped, thinking that Mundoo had ordered them to kill themselves—then realized her foolishness when she saw that the ropes suspending the pods high above the earth were also walkways that led into slim tunnels carved right into the breasts of the stone birds.

"Would you like some water? The ladder climb can be... strenuous for those who aren't used to it." Dinah waved his water away. She didn't want anything from him except for mercy, though her throat longed for liquid.

"The ladder climb was to make me look weak." She raised her chin. "Your Highness."

Mundoo gave a small laugh. "You know, you don't remind me of your father, not much. Your pride and your blatant lack of self-control, perhaps. But otherwise...." He peered into her dark eyes. "I do not see the man in you who has killed so many of my own."

Dinah lowered her eyes. "My father, the King, murdered my brother in cold blood so that he would not have to share the crown. He tried to kill me, his own daughter, but not until after he murdered *his own son* by throwing him from a window. He has pursued me through the Twisted Wood, so close I saw his breath and smelled the rage wafting off of his body. I have no love for my father and the fact that you see none of him in me is the greatest compliment I've been paid."

Mundoo smiled and lifted his hand to Dinah's cheek. She forced herself to stay steady as his tan, weathered hands caressed her jaw line. "And what of Wonderland Palace? Do you have loyalty to them? To the Cards?"

Dinah considered her answer carefully. *I am a mouse in an eagle's nest,* she thought, *and one wrong move will deliver me straight into his mouth.* "I have no loyalty to Wonderland while it remains under the rule of the man who murdered my brother."

Mundoo's bright blue eyes sparkled as a smile crept over his face. "Well answered. I see you are adept at the language of ruling and politics. I should not be surprised." Mundoo stepped back from her and began pacing around his throne. "You must know the history of my people and Wonderland. Our legends say that the Yurkei arrived here hundreds and hundreds of years ago, flown here on the backs of great birds. We lived in peace with the land, and made this place—Hu-Yuhar, the hidden city—our home. We had no need for war, for weapons, other than to hunt. And then one day, strangers came, born by a boat from a distant land, from the 'Other Worlds' as you call them. They had many weapons and many great and shiny jewels that impressed our foolish Chief at the time. These men established Wonderland Palace and proceeded to push us back into the mountains, though originally they had agreed to share all of the land. Your father's father's father declared war on us, and we have been battling the line of Hearts ever since.

"And for what? We long for nothing more than to live in our lands and have peace. It's true—when a Wonderland village comes too close to our lands, we will burn it to the ground, because we must fight for each inch of grass. You Wonderlanders take and take and give nothing back. This is a vast country, and yet the Palace feels it must own every inch, from the Western Sea to the edge of the Yurkei Mountains. As our ancestors said, *Yu-Fhullei-Ja-Drayden, Ja-Drayden*—what cannot be, cannot be. As you are probably well aware, I have spies in Wonderland Palace, and I hear whispers that your father is laying out the groundwork to start his great war. He longs to push us into the sea, the place from where his ancestors came, with their red hearts and taste for blood and tarts. He seeks to find and destroy Hu-Yuhar."

Mundoo gave a sigh and rested his hand upon the throne as he gazed at her. Dinah could see lines of worry etched across his strong face. "And so we come to you, you who rode so boldly into my territory astride the black devil. What do I do with an exiled princess? Most of the people down there would have you publicly executed. Look down." Dinah stood still as Mundoo raised a few flaps on the side of the tent. Then he wrapped his hand around her neck and pushed her face toward the light. "Look down Dinah. See them, see the widows out there who lust for your blood to be spilled for their warriors who never returned. You may have been exiled from Wonderland and the King himself may wish you dead, but that matters little to a fatherless child or a woman whose bed will never be warm again."

Dinah kept quiet as she looked down at the throngs of people below, Mundoo's warm hand against the back of her head. Nothing he said was untrue.

"Executing you, your Spade, and your steed would be the easiest course of action. But I think that we can find a better use for you. How much do you know of your kingdom as it currently stands?"

"I know that the city is restless because of raised taxes. I know that my father is growing ever more paranoid and that he is amassing the Cards in great numbers; for what purpose, I am unsure. I know that he has placed Vittiore, his puppet, on the throne next to him, and that he rules with an ever-harder iron fist. He is preparing for something, but it is of little concern to me. I am no longer a member of the royal family. I am now simply a girl who has no home."

Mundoo smiled. "If only I could believe that. I hear your sister is very beautiful, with hair like the sun."

"And a mind like mud," replied Dinah, sharper than she intended. "She does nothing that my father does not tell her to do. Vittiore could not rule over an anthill."

"Interesting. But your father, he is a clever man, no?"

Dinah thought of how her father had beheaded Faina Baker right in front of her just to teach her to not put her nose where it didn't belong. "He is intelligent, yes. He is a skilled fighter, but he is also brutal and unforgiving, and a drunk. It has made him slow in recent years. He is full of hatred, for reasons I do not understand. The cleverest man in the palace is Cheshire. Most of the decisions my father makes come from him." In her mind's eye, Dinah saw Charles's tiny body crumpled under a starry sky. Her voice rose. "I have nothing but hatred for the King. I would gladly take his life. I attempted to in the Twisted Wood until the Spade intervened."

"So I have heard." Mundoo stared at her, his unflinching blue eyes piercing her tingling bones. "I find you very interesting, Dinah, exiled Princess of Wonderland. Stories of your escape from the palace have echoed through this land, even here into Hu-Yuhar, our home. You are called many things: the Queen of Death, the Red Queen, the Rebel Queen, Rider of the Black Devil. Some even say you are a ghost, or an omen of the future...."

"I am no one," replied Dinah. "I am simply Dinah, an exile who stumbled into your mushroom fields by accident."

Mundoo raised his eyebrow. "By accident? Yes, that is *interesting*. No one stumbles into our sacred burial ground by accident. No. Your Spade led you there, though his reasons are yet clear."

"No, we were…," Dinah found the words dying on her tongue, and the twinge in her heart told her that Mundoo was right. The Spade had led her there. She had thought they were fleeing the King, perhaps over the mountains to the Other Worlds, but instead, he had taken them east… right into the Yurkei's hands. "I trusted him," she gasped, her throat dry and raspy.

Mundoo stood and handed her a small wooden bowl filled with water. "Drink. I insist. It pains me to hear your voice."

Dinah, feeling humbled, gulped the water noisily.

"You should know not to trust anyone when you possess so much power."

"I do not possess power," she answered, wiping her mouth. "I possess a sword, a bag full of filthy clothing, and a horse."

"Ah, your horse." Mundoo untied a piece of fabric that was lashed to his glorious throne and the roof of the tent pulled back, like an egg with its shell removed. The sky opened up above them, and the room was filled with the whirling cold wind that had so easily tossed the ladder. Dinah barely had time to duck before a giant white crane flapped into the tent, its huge wings sending bursts of air across her face. The crane landed on the throne and gave a loud squawk at Dinah. Mundoo continued, seemingly oblivious to the dangerous-looking bird. "Morte will be put to death in one week, when the moon is at its fullest. A price must be paid for all of the blood he has taken from this tribe. Believe that I will find no joy in killing a Hornhoov, rare and exquisite creatures that they are, and I have never seen one quite like him."

"He hasn't done anything," Dinah knew it was untrue as soon as the words passed over her tongue.

"No? With my own eyes, I saw him crush three of my best warriors without even a backward glance, at least, not until he came back to taste their flesh." Dinah remembered the bear, Morte's muzzle covered with the smear of blood and the way her stomach had turned. "The beast WILL die. And then we shall decide what to do with his rider. I have much to think about. My spies have given me reason to believe that your father is preparing to launch a large assault on my tribe, perhaps bringing the fight here, to Hu-Yuhar, within a few months' time."

"But your city seems impregnable. It is surrounded by mountains on every side."

Mundoo smiled as the crane rested its head on his knee. "So one would think, but I do not underestimate your father. We have our weaknesses, just like any city. But that is for me to consider. For now, you will stay here as our guest. You will attend our feasts and ceremonies, and I would encourage you to talk with our tribe, to learn. You may not leave the valley, and you may not enter any homes. You are to keep up your training with the Spade, and I will command my strongest warrior to help give you instruction and build your skills. You are not to go near Morte, lest we call for your blood instead of his. And if he suddenly disappears or is set free, you die, along with the Spade. I will make you watch as we take him piece by piece."

"Where is Sir Gorrann?"

"He will be waiting for you back at your tent. We spoke earlier this morning, and he handled the climb even worse than you did." Dinah's mouth curved into the smallest of smiles as Mundoo strolled up behind her. At least Sir Gorrann was alive. "We will speak again, Princess, but for now you must go. You have met your guards, Ki-ershan and Yur-Jee. They will follow you wherever you go. I would encourage you not to stray from their sight. Yur-Jee lost his eldest son to your father's Heartsword, so I would be careful not to anger him. Passion can lead a man to violent ways."

Dinah nodded and turned to go. The sunlight winked in front of her face, just for a second, and then there was an arm around her neck, a body pressed against her back. Mundoo had moved so fast. Dinah didn't understand what was happening. The pain came swiftly as something sharp and hard was shoved into her, through her. Her shoulder exploded, and everything went white. She grasped his outstretched hand, where she saw a thin wooden knife made of the same white wood that held the tent aloft. It was as slender as a knitting needle, and now covered with red. Mundoo took a breath and shoved it into her back again, just over her shoulder blade. *He was killing her.* She didn't feel it going in, but the pain when it was pulled out was worse than anything she had ever felt. Dinah let out a muffled scream as the blood rushed forth over her shoulder. The pain was deep, like a thousand scalding irons were being pushed inside of her. She stumbled backward before falling to her knees with a choking gasp. Mundoo knelt behind her and wrapped his thick arm around her neck again, his lips brushing her ear as he pulled her close. Dinah gurgled and choked. His hand was covered in blood.

"Don't be afraid, Princess. It's not a fatal wound I've given you, and it will heal quickly. You will not die, you have my word. That was for swinging your sword at my head. I am the noble Chief of the Yurkei and a man of honor, but I wouldn't want you to think that we were friends, or that you can escape from my watchful eye. Though you are exiled, you are still the seed of my enemy, and I won't forget it, not until I have justice for my people." His hot breath lingered over her face. Dinah's shoulder felt as if the muscles were detaching, strand by tiny strand. She let out a cry and he smiled. "I'm sorry to cause you such pain, but I must leave you with a reminder not to betray me. The Yurkei have been hunted, executed, and tortured under the red heart of Wonderland. Your blood is but a small drop in the bucket that must be filled before justice is served. We are a peaceful people, but like sleeping serpents, we will strike when someone steps too close, and the Kings and Queens of Wonderland Palace have stomped on us for decades. I am an honorable man, but not a safe one." He released her violently, and she fell face forward onto the wooden floor of the tent, writhing in pain. The Chief called for Ki-ershan and Yur-Jee, and they appeared through one of the open flaps of the tent door.

"Take her through the mountain," Mundoo instructed with a wave of his hand. "Make sure no one hurts her or the Spade until I have made a decision regarding their fates. Feed, clean, and clothe them. See that they are well cared for, but closely watched. Call for Ge-Jursi to use Iu-Hora's potions to heal her." Dinah's whole body curled up in blinding pain as she cried out. Yur-Jee raised his voice to argue with the Chief, but Mundoo silenced him with a raised hand. "Do as I command. Ach-julik."

Yur-Jee bowed with his hands spread out before him into the symbol of the crane. Dinah's guards clamped their hands around her arms and pulled her out through one of the tent's open doors. Her shoulder felt as though it had been set on fire. She gasped for air, unable to breathe through the pain. They pushed her out onto the rope walkway that led into the breast of the crane. Dinah stumbled repeatedly, which made walking on the thin, knotted-rope walkway even more terrifying. Blood dripped down from her shoulder until it coated her bare feet, and she struggled to stay conscious. She slipped. Ki-ershan pressed his bare hand over the wound to stop the bleeding. Dinah could see the ground hundreds and hundreds of feet below her as they struggled to stay on the thin rope bridge. The crowd watched her in silence as drops of blood fell from her body. They seemed satisfied.

"Walk," grunted Yur-Jee, roughly pushing her forward, so hard that Dinah would have gone flying off the edge if Ki-ershan hadn't yanked her back. "Ja-hohy!" he snapped at Yur-Jee. *Stop*, thought Dinah, half-delusional. *Yes, Ja-hohy means stop. Thank you, Harris*, she thought madly.

Something twitched in her shoulder and suddenly it felt as if the bone was separating from her muscle, somewhere deep inside the cut. She gave a scream and stumbled forward, her knees hitting the rock outcropping that led into the mountain. Overjoyed at the cool feel of the stone, she laughed hysterically to have solid ground beneath her, even if she was still in a giant stone bird, hundreds of feet above the ground. The urge to brush her lips on the mountain was overtaken by a throbbing, angry pain, and she struggled to stay conscious. She heard raised voices and shouting. Sir Gorrann's face appeared in a hazy blue sky over her, the thin lines of his face creased in worry.

"What did he do to yeh? Dinah, are yeh all right? Dinah! Dinah! Yer Highness, let me see." His hands cradled her face, her shoulder. The Spade turned her over gently, peeling Ki-ershan's hand back from the wound, and she heard a sharp intake of breath. "The Chief should not have done this. Why would he do this? Yur-Jee, please get me some bandages and a healer. NOW!"

Dinah closed her eyes. When she opened them again, there was a beautiful Yurkei woman leaning over her, her glowing blue eyes trained on Dinah's wound, her resplendent white hair soaked red at the tips where it had brushed in her blood. She listened silently as the woman sang a wailing song over her as she rocked back and forth and applied some sort of gray paste to Dinah's wound. The paste smelled like the mushroom fields—warm and potent, a decadent perfume. The pain suddenly receded into a dull, stabbing sensation, and Dinah breathed a sigh of relief, her hand reaching up to clutch the woman's shoulder. "Thank you, thank you, thank you...," she repeated it over and over, her tongue becoming numb.

The woman smiled, showing her small pearly teeth. "How do you say... in Wonderlander? Ahh... well... Su-heyg... hu-sang...." The woman clapped her hands. "Oh yes, hu-satey." Her blue eyes stared unflinchingly into Dinah's. "WELCOME. Welcome to Hu-Yuhar."

CHAPTER TEN

Dinah slept for two days after that, two glorious days on the bed of woven grass, two glorious days of rest. Occasionally, she would be awoken by the pain. She'd eat and relieve herself, before surrendering her consciousness. Sir Gorrann sat quietly beside her bed, always watchful. He must have slept, but Dinah didn't know when he did, and she didn't really care. The healing paste made her dreams bright and vivid and joyful. Charles, weaving feathers into a hat. Harris, adjusting his spectacles while they feasted on wine and grapes. Wardley, astride Corning, his brown hair glowing like warm chocolate in the sun, his arms reaching for her. Wardley... she thought of him often in the few minutes between waking and falling back asleep. Wardley, her love, whom she probably would never see again. Wardley the Weak, as he was called now. The shame she felt at tarnishing his name was at times unbearable, so it was easier just to sleep.

When two days had finally passed, Dinah begrudgingly decided that it was time to leave the confines of her warm, cozy tent, though she felt she could stay forever—eating, sleeping, and dreaming. Sir Gorrann roused her early and made sure that she ate a plate of eggs and strange amber fruit. As Dinah bit into the egg, a rush of yellow yolk ran down her chin. She stared at Sir Gorrann, who was devouring his eggs, still famished after the last bite.

"Did you lead me here?" she asked. The Spade wiped his face with a feathered napkin.

"Perhaps. Perhaps it is not yet time to ask."

Dinah flung her plate across the room with a fury that surprised even herself. Her wound screamed in protest and she let out a tiny whimper. "Why? WHY WOULD YOU DO THAT? Why would you take us here?"

The Spade stood and brushed off his lap. "I'll not answer that question for yeh now, not now and not while yeh are acting like a child. But I would say, ask yerself if yeh trust me. Ask if yeh would have survived without me. And when yeh are done, I will take yeh down to the river to bathe because I have never seen anyone look so disgusting, and your wound will need washing and redressing."

He left the tent without another word. Dinah stewed for a few minutes in the bright white light of the tent. He had led her here. But why? To provide the Yurkei with the revenge they so desired? To ransom her off to the King, who would then kill her? No matter how many situations she came up with, not a single one of them made any sense. The Spade had saved her, protected her, taught her to fight. One did not give one's enemy a sword and instruct the arm to wield it. The more she considered it, the less sense it made. But what choice did she have? She couldn't change the fact that she was a well-rested hostage of the Yurkei tribe who had been stabbed by the Chief. Mundoo had *stabbed* her. Dinah remembered the venom in his voice, the anger that had bubbled up beneath his wise speeches.

She sat and considered for a few minutes. Sleep had made her a new person, one who had the capacity to think instead of just surviving hour to hour. She could bathe, but not alone if she wanted to wash her wound, which felt sticky and burning hot. Finally, with a cry of pain and a stream of curses that would make the Spade proud, Dinah righted herself and pulled a tunic over her head. She ducked out of the tent to find Ki-ershan waiting for her. He nodded his head toward a dirt path that ran behind her tent. "Thank you," she whispered. He smiled back at her. Ki-ershan was definitely her favorite of the two guards. He followed behind as Dinah proceeded to walk slowly down the path until she arrived at a tiny freshwater stream that ran the length of the valley. Her wound still pulsed with pain, but it was nothing compared to the pain she remembered from the wooden knife. Sir Gorrann waited for her at a bend in the trail, and they walked together in silence toward the bank.

She stopped at the stream and stared into the water. It was small, barely ten feet across, but it gurgled and danced in the morning sun, its water so clear that it was almost like looking in a mirror. Dinah had thought she had no embarrassment left after being paraded through the valley in her bright red tunic and then forced to climb the ladder into the sky, but she had been wrong. In the shiny blue stream, there were hundreds of Yurkei bathing, playing, and washing clothing. The women all bathed naked, their perfect lean bodies glistening in the sun, their skin smooth like rich tea. Dinah saw Sir Gorrann glance away, a red flush rising in his cheeks. Dinah slowly undressed herself, trying to cover all that she could with her tunic before lowering herself quickly into the icy water with a wince as it converged on her wound. All eyes watched her as she came up, no doubt disgusted at this pale, bruised creature with black hair and the darkest eyes they had ever seen. The intense cold took her breath away and she immediately started shivering. A strange gray paste seeped from the wound. Sir Gorrann climbed in after her, struggling to cover himself as well, giving his own gasp at the cold water. He dunked his head and then emerged, shaking the water out of his gray hair. He then began to scrub her wound with fervor. The moment was anything but intimate, as they were both freezing and working as quickly as possible.

Sir Gorrann raised his voice to whisper in her ear. "Yer wound... it's almost healed. Amazing. I've never seen anything like it." Indeed, he was correct—her wound was healing nicely after two days of rest, and whatever healing paste had been put on it had sealed it shut. Her shoulder had a constant ache, and when she raised her arms there was a thin slice of pain, but Mundoo had kept his word—the wound would not kill her. He had left her a scar, a remembrance of him. Dinah watched as the clean water around her became cloudy with the dirt and muck scrubbed from her skin. There was something in the gentle way the Spade touched her shoulder, something that made Dinah realize that even though he had led them into the mouth of the Yurkei, she deeply trusted him. He would never hurt her, she knew it instinctively; the same way she knew the stars would change each night. Sir Gorrann cursed the Chief as he scrubbed at the bloody wound.

"He believed yeh deserved this, no doubt, but it didn't have to be so deep. He should have just left yeh alone. What with the coming battles...?"

"Why should it matter?" replied Dinah. "If anything, I'm going to be executed in a few days, just long enough to see Morte put to death. Mundoo no doubt wants me dead, he just wants to prolong the process. And why wouldn't he? It's no secret that the Yurkei are not fans of the royal family, nor should they be." She raised her eyes to Yur-Jee, who watched them with barely concealed hatred from the banks of the stream. "Mundoo might lose his chance," she muttered. "There are plenty of people here who would like to see my head on a stake, sooner rather than later."

"The Yurkei don't behead," said Sir Gorrann calmly as he dunked his head under the stream. "They drop their prisoners from the wings of the cranes onto the stones below." He stopped, suddenly aware of what that image would do to Dinah. "I'm sorry, Yer Highness. I forgot."

She spread her fingers in the water, seeing Charles on the stone slab. "Don't be sorry. It would be fitting to die like my brother. There would be a great balance to it." Dinah was suddenly aware that the noisy stream had grown very silent. The Yurkei women were climbing naked out of the water and gathering up their children with whispered words of compliance. The children struggled, unhappy to have their playtime cut short, but the women carried them away, everyone wet and nude and healthy. Within seconds, Dinah and Sir Gorrann were the only ones left in the stream. Dinah heard the crunch of branches behind her and turned, her arms wrapped tightly across her chest, her heart thudding beneath them.

Two huge feet stood before her on the bank—gnarled, gross feet—huge slabs of meat marked with callouses and scars. They led up to the tallest man Dinah had ever seen. It was strange seeing someone with a similar skin tone here in the depth of Yurkei country. His hair was a honeyed brown rather than white, though it was long and cut in the Yurkei manner. His hair came to a downward point on his forehead, his eyes a dull green. A jagged scar ran from his chin up past his cheek, mingling with the white stripes of paint that ran from under his eye to his shins. He wore only a feather loincloth and his massive muscles bulged underneath, taut with veins. Thighs and arms like tree trunks stretched out from his jaggedly rigid stomach. He was a giant, the most massive man Dinah had ever seen, one that would dwarf even her father. In one hand he clutched an elaborately curved bow and arrow. In the other was a Heartsword.

Dinah's stomach gave a lurch when she saw the sunlight flicker off the double-sided blade. Only her father and the highest-ranking Cards carried Heartswords. She stared in wonder, her arms pressed tightly over her round breasts. The man glowered at them before throwing his weapons on the bank. Without warning, he reached down and plucked Dinah straight out of the water by clasping both of her arms at her side and lifting, as easily as if he had picked up a rag doll. Something felt as if it was ripping inside her shoulder. She struggled, but it was no use. His grip was as strong as iron. Her feet dangled above the ground. Sir Gorrann struggled to climb out of the stream, his eyes on the man.

The man sneered as he looked into Dinah's surprised face. "This skinny dark-eyed girl is the great Princess of Wonderland? The one who bested her father, who stole his horse and left a bloody trail behind her? It can't be. You are barely the size of my thigh and weak as a newly hatched worm. Are you her, this legendary warrior, the Rebel Queen? Answer me, child."

Dinah strained her neck to look up at him, water streaming into her eyes. Her mouth seemed unable to form words.

"Speak up!" he bellowed, his breath blowing her hair back. Dinah bit her lip, the fury inside of her poking its head out of slumber. She twisted to free herself, but it was of no use. Instead she fixed her black eyes on his.

"I am Dinah, the former Princess of Wonderland, and this is my guard, Sir Gorrann, a Spade, and one of the most feared trackers in the Cards."

"So I have heard," he said. "A naked drowned rat and her old man guardian; this is who I am to train?" With a laugh, he set her down on the ground. "Pleased to meet you. You can call me Bah-kan. As you may have noticed, I do not look like most of my brothers here in Hu-Yuhar. You may be wondering who I am, that my Wonderlander speech is so perfect." Dinah was, indeed, wondering all of these things. She nodded.

"My given name is Stern Radley, and I was once the highest-ranking Club Card in the King's army."

Dinah let out a gasp. Stern Radley was *famous*—in fact, his giant statue guarded Charles's room. There were poems and stories about him, Stern Radley, the bravest Club to ever live.

"You're famous," she stuttered, her lips blue with cold. "And dead!"

The huge man let out a bellow that seemed to rustle the trees around them. "So Wonderland Palace would have you believe. My Yurkei name, the true name you will call me, is Bah-kan, which means the Tall Warrior. I am here to train you." His eyes traveled over Dinah's form. "You have my permission to dress." He set her down roughly.

Dinah staggered over to her red tunic and white feather pants, as light as a whisper when she pulled them over her stinging wet skin. Sir Gorrann climbed out as well, his hands covering his groin as he eyed Bah-kan.

"Stories of your mighty death resound in the halls of the Cards," he said forcefully. "How is it that you are now a Yurkei warrior, though you bear the highest honors of Wonderland Palace?" His tone was accusing. *Traitor.*

"Ah, that's a story for another time. For now, we must go. Mundoo insists that training begin today, for both of you." He gave Sir Gorrann a hard slap on the shoulder. "It's good to see another Card, even if it must be a Spade. It's a wonder you kept her alive. Spades aren't exactly known for their abilities."

Sir Gorrann lunged naked toward Bah-kan, who brought down his palm straight against the Spade's chest without flinching. Sir Gorrann flew back into the stream as if he was thrown there by the gods. He surfaced with a furious look on his face, water streaming from his gray hair. Dinah tried to control it, but laughter was churning its way up her throat and before long she was laughing so hysterically that she was doubled over. Tears reddened her eyes. The whole situation, everything, was so terrible, so strange and confusing, and yet, she could only laugh at Sir Gorrann simmering in the water, looking like a drowned cat. The giant Yurkei warrior standing guard laughed quietly to himself as she quickly pulled her hair into a low bun.

Bah-kan cleared his throat. "I'm glad to give you a laugh, Princess. Your training will commence in a few minutes. Follow this path by the river, turn right at the waterfall and then come to a rest in front of the livestock pen, just below the knee of the crane." He wiggled his eyebrows. "Perhaps you are just as mad as they say, just like your brother. Personally, I can't wait to find out." Bah-kan gathered up his weapons and stomped off. Normally this sort of insult would have sent Dinah into a rage, but instead it just made her laugh harder. Eventually, the Spade joined in, laughing while he floated on his back in the stream, his nudity out for the world to see as he spat water into the air. It was a good while before they trekked their way back to the valley floor, dripping wet and laughing the entire way.

Unfortunately, the laughter didn't last. Bah-kan was a brutal fighter and a merciless trainer. He had no stomach for weakness and made a game out of fighting them with one hand—and sometimes with no hands. Crowds of Yurkei gathered around them each morning to watch Bah-kan humiliate and exploit their weaknesses. The focus was on Dinah, but he also sparred with Sir

Gorrann several times a day. Those fights were incredible to watch, and Dinah felt that she learned more from watching those than when she herself was in the ring. Even Mundoo, who took mysterious journeys into the mountain tunnels during the day, made rare appearances to watch the fights. Bah-kan would arm himself with the Heartsword, Sir Gorrann with his sword and dagger. Bah-kan would begin with a charge—a sight that would stop lesser men dead in their tracks. Sir Gorrann would spin out of the way, light on his feet, the tip of his sword snapping out to catch Bah-kan as he passed. Bah-kan might be huge, but he was quick like a much lighter man. He spun around the opposite direction and swung his Heartsword arm up from the ground, hoping to catch the Spade's neck. Sir Gorrann bent backwards and removed his dagger from his boot before winging it at Bah-kan. Bah-kan deflected the blade with the Heartsword. Then they met in the middle.

Swords flew and clanged through the valley, the swift dance of warriors, one that attracted even the best Yurkei warriors to watch and dissect. Bah-kan would preempt the Spade's strokes and parry with his own, the Heartsword close to his breast to act as both shield and weapon. Sir Gorrann was the more cautious of the two, the more calculating. He saved his advances for those times when he had the best opportunities. Bah-kan had the advantage of strength, but he also was an intelligent fighter, one who weighed challenging maneuvers before charging in with fearless abandon. They were well matched. There were several times when Dinah feared Sir Gorrann would lose his life, when Bah-kan's blade came a little too close, but he always leapt out of the way at the ideal moment, or cried to yield. Bah-kan would bellow at the sky and beat his breast before helping the Spade to his feet. Bah-Kan was unstoppable, she realized, perhaps the best warrior she had ever seen in her life. He was the lethal combination of a highly disciplined Card mixed with the best traits of a Yurkei warrior—equal parts brutal and graceful, moving as if he was dancing on air. Dinah realized quickly that there were none in Wonderland or Yurkei country that could best him, aside from perhaps Xavier Juflee, the Knave of Hearts. But she wasn't sure that even he could beat Bah-kan.

After the fight, several Yurkei women would rush over to Sir Gorrann to tend his wounds as he recovered on the side of the dirt circle, spitting blood and the occasional tooth onto the ground. For some odd reason, the Yurkei women found him quite fascinating, and more than once Dinah caught him winking in their direction. Dinah and Bah-kan sparring was much less exciting, since it took only a few minutes before Dinah was face down on the ground, beaten and exhausted in every possible way. Still, she was proud that she could meet most of his blows with a somewhat broad counter strike of her own. She was no longer swinging into the air with large, heavy-handed strokes, but rather with quick strikes of her blade combined with rapid foot movement. She was no longer simply flinging her sword around out of fear of being hit; she was calculating her next move. She danced around Bah-kan, and once managed to land a hard blow just above his ribs that left him gasping. The Yurkei surrounding them had whooped and stomped their feet.

Bah-kan gave a tiny laugh and then plunged forward, rage playing across his white-striped face. Dinah jumped high to avoid a low stroke and brought the butt of her blade down hard on his knee. It was like striking a rock, and the vibrations that shot through her once-broken fingers made her wince in pain. Bah-kan was upon her then. He swung the Heartsword across her chest but stopped midswing, twisted around, and punched her in the back of the shoulder—right in the spot where Mundoo had sunk his thin blade. She screamed.

"Bah-kan!" shouted Sir Gorrann, angry.

Bah-kan shrugged. "An enemy will look for her obvious weakness. Why shouldn't I?"

Surprised by the white-hot pain blowing through her shoulder and distracted by rage, Dinah swung her sword at his arm. It was a mistake. He caught the blade with the end of his Heartsword and wrenched backwards. Dinah's sword went sailing into the crowd and she was left empty-handed.

"Your Highness!" Dinah looked up just in time to see Sir Gorrann toss his knife in her direction. She caught it and turned to meet Bah-kan again. The crowd was silent as Bah-kan shifted his weight from foot to foot, as if thinking of a million ways to kill her. Then he spoke.

"Your father, the King of Wonderland, is a whoremonger and a cheat." The Yurkei cheered at his words.

Dinah clasped her hand around the dagger. "I agree!" she yelled back.

"And your father was a whore as well, except that he slept with sheep." The crowd laughed and Bah-Kan let a smile draw across his face. "Your half-sister is a dozen times more beautiful than you, and the crown looks so lovely upon her head. I hear she is a good queen."

Dinah felt the fury rising up inside of her, the clawing black heat that she so often pushed back down. Still, she remained calm. "You are surely right. She is lovely, even though she is a false queen."

Bah-kan sidestepped and then charged, his Heartsword raised as if to carve her in half. Dinah rolled in front of him, clipping him at the shins and making him tumble. As she passed, she nicked the back of his calf with her dagger. Bah-kan roared as he landed, and Dinah scurried to her feet, the dagger poised to throw. For a second, she had the advantage. Bah-kan was distracted by his bleeding leg, and the Heartsword was down. Then he spoke again.

"Your mother was just as well-known for her whoring as she was for her mad son, who would have benefitted from an infant drowning. The Mad Hatter should have been left at the bottom of a lake."

Dinah screamed with rage as the fury overtook her and she flung the knife at Bah-Kan. The blade was thrown so sloppily that it bounced off the edge of his Heartsword even though he never moved it. With inhuman speed, he reached out, caught it in his hands and flung it back at Dinah. She watched as it buried itself deep in her chest armor. Without the armor that Mundoo insisted upon, she would have been dead, but that was the least of her cares. Seeing nothing but her all-encompassing rage, she launched herself upon Bah-Kan and ripped at his ear with her teeth.

"Your Highness! Dinah! Stop!" She felt Sir Gorrann grab her waist and tug her back.

Bah-kan shoved her off with one hand. "Control her! Gods, she's just as mad as people say!"

The crowd stared as Sir Gorrann carried her, squirming and screaming, back to her tent. That had been a dark day, but the training continued. Each and every morning her lesson was learned: when she let her fury get the best of her, she lost control of herself, her fight, and her focus. Bah-kan assaulted her with words and insults each fight after that, but Dinah never rose to the challenge. She remained calm and in control and told herself that revenge was best taken with a blade—not a violent tantrum. Bah-kan's strength and skill always bested her in the end, and would forever, but Dinah grew exponentially as a fighter each time his Heartsword met her blade. Between the training that Wardley had given her growing up, the time she had spent learning from Sir Gorrann in the woods, and the brutal, one-on-one fighting with Bah-kan now, Dinah felt increasingly more comfortable with the blade in her hand. The next day, she faced off sword-to-sword with a dozen different Yurkei warriors, and more often than not, she beat them.

When she boasted, Bah-kan laughingly reminded her that it wasn't the accomplishment she thought it was—the Yurkei's main weapon was not a blade, but a bow and arrow (a weapon with which Dinah was utterly useless). In a real battle, she wouldn't get within a hundred yards of them unless they didn't have their bows and arrows; even then, if they just had daggers, she would still lose. This didn't matter to Dinah. When her opponent was laid out on the ground in front of her, her silver blade held against his heaving throat, a rush of pride and fury flooded Dinah's system. She loved the feeling of winning a fight. It was no wonder her father had found battle so intoxicating—when you didn't know if you would live or die after this moment, the moment when you found that magical opening in which to slip your blade was otherworldly grace.

After their seventh day of training, Bah-kan released Dinah early, saying that he had to visit his wife and brood of children, who lived at the other end of the valley. Dinah smiled at the thought—Bah-kan and his large Yurkei wife, and their tent full of monstrous children, all taller than the rest of the Yurkei children, with dyed white hair and shining blue eyes.

Dinah was exhausted and wished to go to bed, but Sir Gorrann stiffly informed her that she must find other ways to occupy her time. When she put up a fight, he insisted that he had pressing matters in their tent; he wouldn't tell Dinah what they were, but gently shoved her out the door after checking her healed wound.

Dinah suspected his pressing appointment was with one of the Yurkei women who was fond of watching him bathe every day, but she kept her mouth shut and gathered a small meal of eggs before leaving. Sir Gorrann lowered the tent flap in her face after ordering her to find them some ripe fruit in the Yurkei orchard. Dinah sighed. It was late afternoon, and the falling sun was just beginning to cast a hazy golden glow on the valley. Free time? Without her guards? It was a foreign concept to her at this point.

After a few minutes of consideration, she decided to walk the length of the valley to the orchard. She still had an hour or so before the sun set in the east. She longed to see what rested behind the highest mountain ridge, the northernmost hill with a winding staircase carved deep into its steep side. Dinah took her time getting there, and found herself wandering along the outer mountain face of the valley as the Yurkei settled into their tents in the late afternoon. Dim lights from white torches flickered within the fabric tents, giving the valley an enchanted, mythical glow, like ethereal clouds had floated into its midst. As she walked, Dinah saw the lowered eyes of the tribe as she passed them, a sign of disrespect. The Yurkei's distrust and anger toward her remained, but she was no longer spit upon or had rocks thrown at her when she left her tent, and that was a vast improvement. Many of them crossed the valley to avoid walking next to her, and Dinah wondered if it was just that they didn't want to chance touching her, of if they were afraid of her. Her sessions with Bah-kan and Sir Gorrann were growing in popularity, and while she always lost, she was a strong fighter.

Time passed slowly here, and Dinah wandered aimlessly through the valley for a few hours; her only excitement was when she pressed herself against the mountain to avoid a group of tan ponies galloping through. The twilight hours of the Yurkei

Mountains were their playtime, and the thundering of hooves had become a comforting sound each night when Dinah fell asleep. The Yurkei life was so peaceful, so different than the life she had grown up with at the palace—a life of politics and games, of tarts and dresses and Cards. Here, one simply lived and toiled against the ground. It was about community and a natural life. Possessions didn't matter much to the Yurkei—only land and horses mattered to them, the wilds around them, the mountains and the birds, all the things they worshipped in one way or another. It was, of course, *land* that her father desired from them. And if she had been crowned Queen beside him, as she had desired her entire life, she probably would have consented to the Yurkei raids, and eventually to a war—after all, they seemed to come every thirty years or so. Wonderlanders feared the Yurkei while at the same time desiring their freedom and the connection they had with the wild nature of Wonderland itself. Her head spinning, Dinah watched a stunning pale mare run feverish loops across the valley. In the distance, dozens of white cranes folded their wings in a massive twig nest that nestled against a rocky outcrop. *I could stay here*, thought Dinah with surprise, *I could be happy here.* She could become a Yurkei warrior, live in a flat tent that was suspended from the mountainside and learn to love the heights of the ropes strewn between the two mountains.

Yes, she could be happy here, perhaps in time. There was no Wardley, so a truly perfect life was ruled out, but what could she do? He would never find her here, and she would never return to the palace, lest her head grace the white marble slab that took so many. This valley could hold a possible future for her, and yet, her heart kept its distance from the idea. The truth, if she thought about it, was that there was no blissful ending to her story. Her punishment had not been decided, but whenever Mundoo got around to planning it, Morte would be put to death. Her fate awaited his, and if his was any indication, then she should understand that this brief reprieve from death was just that. Mundoo would be right to let her fly off the wings of the crane, for if she was Queen, she certainly would have put the daughter of her most-feared enemy to death. Perhaps Mundoo was having Bah-kan train her so that later it would be a fair(er) fight to death when her time for execution came. A show for the crowds, a glorious bloody death for those who desired justice.

Her wandering thoughts were interrupted by a delicious smell entering her nostrils. It was a distinct smell, warm and fruity, so unlike the earthy aromas of the Yurkei food. There was a hint of cherry and rose, fresh baked bread and cream. How was that possible? Was she dreaming? She sniffed the air again. *No. The smell is real.* She carefully followed the aroma into a small orchard that sat at the far west end of the valley.

The trees were thick, the swath of fruit trees perhaps a quarter of a mile long. Petite lemon trees dripping with yellow fruit nuzzled up next to lush apple trees, their trunks pushed against floating mulberry trees. Even higher, some fruit trees hovered, connected to the ground by some sort of shiny blue vine that snaked along the path, its purple fruit the size of marbles.

The orchard in itself was marvelous—truly, a wonder—but nothing could compare with what Dinah was smelling: *home. Tarts. Tea.* In the back of her mind, she knew that she was being led, and yet, the smell was everything she missed: Harris and Wardley and warm baths and the palace. *Her palace.* Lights flickered ahead of her in the orchard and she slowed her walk. A nagging voice inside ordered her to draw her dagger, and she obeyed, shielding her eyes from heart-shaped lanterns that seemed to float among the trees. Finally, she emerged from the trees into a small clearing. A long table, magnificently set with towering tea cups in every shade and adorned with buckets of flowers, stood before her. The table was covered with all of her favorite Wonderland tarts: raspberry and cream, whipped limes and butter roses, deep cocoa mixed with powdered jam. They rested alongside haphazardly piled plates and cups, candles and steaming glasses of hot tea.

A bright pink checkered tablecloth brushed against the tall grass, and in the middle sat a cake. It was a plain white cake with a simple design frosted on the top: a heart, a single red heart. Dinah's own heart clenched, and she clutched her dagger as she began to back away from the table. A light stirred in the trees, and she watched as a tall figure dressed in an elaborate purple robe stepped forward and sat down at the table. His long fingers reached out and grasped a cup of tea before pulling it up to his thin lips. He blew on the steam and took a long sip.

"Mmm. Hello, Your Highness," he said silkily, before setting the cup back down. "Won't you have a cup of tea with me? Nothing would make me happier."

Dinah felt the air whoosh out of her chest and saw the orchard spin around her. The man leaned back in his seat and gestured to the table. "Please sit. You wouldn't want it to get cold." Cheshire's wicked grin seemed to stretch to the end of the valley. "Cat got your tongue?"

CHAPTER ELEVEN

Dinah was having trouble breathing. Her lungs pressed against her chest, her head against her shoulders—everything, everything was tucking itself into a wild panic and she couldn't quite understand what was happening. There was a table full of food, lights in the trees, and then there was the man—THAT man—responsible for so much pain, for turning her father against her, for helping her father murder her brother and crown Vittiore. Cheshire, the cleverest man in Wonderland. He was right there, his impossibly long body stretched out on a wooden chair, sipping tea like he hadn't a single care in the world. A peppered goatee had stretched across his rubbery face since she had last seen him, and his black hair and eyes glistened with malice in the flickering candlelight. A purple rope tied over a plum tunic cinched his waist, and as he took a lavish bite of one of the cocoa tarts, sugar dusted the tip of his brooch, which was adorned with jeweled symbols of the four cards. It symbolized that he controlled ALL of the Cards.

Dinah noticed the dagger that sat innocently in front of him—its handle turned inward—his weapon of choice, at the ready if she should attack him. Unmoved by her presence, he licked the tips of his fingers.

"Mmm... this one is delicious." His voice jarred Dinah back from the dark paralyzed place in her mind, and her hand brushed the tip of her dagger. His eyes followed her fingers. "I wouldn't throw that, Princess. I'm sure your skill has improved since arriving here, but if you do that you will get none of the answers you seek, and I believe you seek answers more than you seek revenge, at least at this moment. Trust me when I say I can give you *both*."

Dinah narrowed her eyes and pulled her dagger out of its sheath. Her voice finally clawed its way up her throat. "Tell me one reason why I shouldn't I kill you where you sit," she hissed. "Tell me why I shouldn't slit your throat open right here, and then dine on these tarts as your blood pools over the table. I'd do it happily."

Cheshire's eyes sparkled as he looked through her. "Because then you'll hardly enjoy them. Tarts and blood are not complementary on the palate. Also, it's bad manners, or so your mother should have taught you." *My mother. How dare he?* Dinah was on him in a second, holding his neck and pressing the blade of the dagger against his main artery. She yanked his head back by his greasy black hair. Tarts spilled from their elaborately orchestrated places as his legs slammed against the corner of the table. He twisted suddenly, and Dinah loosened her grip on the dagger, wary of cutting into his thin neck skin. She did want answers—but she also wanted him to feel the fear that could overcome a person in seconds, like diving into icy water. He twisted quickly and furiously, and she pulled back her blade, and then suddenly he was behind her, pressing his body against hers, his hand not on his dagger but wrapped around her mouth. She had made a fatal mistake.

His mouth brushed her ear. "Does this feel familiar, Princess?" he hissed. Then he lowered his voice significantly and Dinah felt chills rush up her spine. "Perhaps from the night I saved your life and sent you running with a bag strapped across your shoulders? The night when I told you to *GO NOW*, and yet, like an idiot, you visited Charles's chamber instead?" Dinah's body went weak. Cheshire—he was the stranger who had saved her life? She stopped struggling and stood stunned in the clearing.

Cheshire slowly removed his hand from her mouth and tucked a hair back behind her ear. "Now Dinah, be a good girl and sit down. I have much to tell you, and you look famished. Have some tea and tarts. I would be bereft if you broke my favorite teapot by flailing all over the place. It was not easy to get all of this out here."

Her body shaking, Dinah let him lead her to a chair at the other end of the table. She still clutched her dagger and Cheshire made no attempt to take his own—an elaborate show to make her feel more in control, no doubt. At the other end of the table, he settled into his chair and took another sip of tea as he straightened the tablecloth and tea cups.

"Now. Where to begin? I have so much to tell you, but I guess we'll start at the beginning, since most of the things I dabble in start with ME anyway."

Dinah stared at him, hatred simmering in her eyes.

"I was born in Verrader, a small fishing village by the Western Slope. I'm sure you've never heard of it." Dinah hadn't. "My parents were poor but well educated, due to the diligence of the priests in that town, who felt that every child deserved a decent education, misguided as they were. They raised me to be a fisherman, like them, though they also raised me to memorize the literature and languages of Wonderland. I hated fishing, and I grew up dreaming of the day when I would leave that sorry little town, with its brutal children who would rise up to be nothing more than fish mongers and innkeepers.

"As a child I was teased mercilessly, only because they could see I was fiercely intelligent. Even more damagingly to their pride, I had no interest in the life for which they were destined. My father found this disappointing as well, and when I turned twelve he began beating me to within an inch of my life with disturbing frequency.

"On the day I turned sixteen, I left home, but not before I plundered my father's hidden wealth. There was a large rock on the shore, one that he walked past each day. There was a nest of seaweed at the base, and as I understood it, most seaweed decays and disintegrates. Even as a young child, I had noticed this seaweed didn't. It stayed fresh, because he refreshed it every few days. My suspicions were correct—that was where my father had stored his money, buried deep in the Earth, under the seaweed. The money was plentiful. He had been hiding money there for years, storing it away for booze and women, though my mother and I went hungry most days. I took all of his money, and spilled to the local builder that my father had been bedding his wife.

"The next day, I took my father's horse and rode east for Wonderland Palace and the life that I had dreamed of. Upon arriving there, I immediately found work in the jewelry shop, counting numbers and keeping accounts. I'm good with numbers, books and things that can be, how shall we say, manipulated? The accountant that had been there before me suddenly took ill, and I took his place at the shop. I updated all of the accounts and made sure that everyone's debts were paid to the jeweler—something that the previous accountant had been too lenient about."

Cheshire shook his head. "The people of Wonderland dream of being appointed to the court, and so they spend their money on jewels to dazzle the royals who, as you know, never notice such things. The people wanted these jewels and yet didn't want to pay for them. Within a year, I quickly settled all of our debts, and by doing this I became well-known in Wonderland proper for being a man who got what he wanted. I caught the eye of a local banker, who hired me, and then the eye of another well-known banker, who put me in charge of everything when his main account man disappeared. Upon my arrival, I was presented with a problem from the man who owned the bank: there was a very large amount of credit lent out to a wealthy merchant who had avoided or beaten every collector sent to collect."

Cheshire sighed and tipped back his chair, his feet up on the table as he munched on molded mint. "I learned early in my life that each man has something they value above all others—and my job was to find out what that thing was. After watching him for a few weeks, I learned that this man had a bastard son that he held dear, a young one, barely three years of age. He was his pride and joy, though he hid him from the world. One day, while he was out with his whore mother, I took the babe from her and held him prisoner at the bank. A squirmy young thing he was, but to my credit, I did not have him bound and gagged; no, he was a child, and so we simply locked him in a room, and left him alone with food and water. The man came right away with all the money to pay his debts. We gave the child back, but burned the seal of the bank onto his heel, lest his father forget to pay the debts he owed. He left Wonderland shortly thereafter.

"Somehow, Wonderland Palace had heard word of this transaction and hired me on at the King's bank. Two years after I started as the accountant, I was one of three Diamond Cards managing the King's treasury. I had a way with numbers, a way of getting what I wanted from those who owed the King, be it peasants or visiting lords. I was the third highest-ranking Diamond in the Cards, and I lived a life of counting and calculating."

Cheshire paused to take a sip of his tea and motioned Dinah to do the same. She shook her head and dumped her tea onto the grass. Cheshire looked exasperated.

"It's not poison, Your Highness, but I won't fault you for being cautious. You're smart, like me. I mean, gods know people have tried to poison me over the years." He took a breath and gave a deceptive smile, his unnaturally white teeth glowing in the darkness.

"I apologize if this next part is hard for you to hear, but it's something you must know. One night, I was invited to attend the Royal Croquet Ball, something I believe you are familiar with. I too share your distaste for such things, but I see them as necessary for social climbing. That night, a radiant young woman was visiting the court. She was from Ierladia, and rumor had it that she was the King's bride to be, the future Queen. Her name was Davianna."

"NO." cringed Dinah. "No, no."

Cheshire leaned forward, his face sincere. "When I saw your mother, my world changed. Understand this—all my life I had gathered things for other people—money, goods, revenge. It was my skill. And yet, for the first time, I saw something I wanted for *myself.* She was the most beautiful woman I had ever seen, the most beautiful woman *most* men have ever seen. Her hair was thick and black, like yours, and one could rest a lemon on the curve of her hips. Roses envied the red of her lips, and figs the dark purple of her iris. *She took my breath away.* Davianna danced with many men that night—mostly the King—in the way of a traditional ball.

"I waited my turn and took her arm. I couldn't breathe or think. When she danced with me, both of our worlds seemed to stop. There was an intense connection, a feeling that we had been waiting for each other our entire lives. We fell in love instantly, a thing of fairy tales, but a truth nonetheless. She did not love your father, who was already a brutish man, a drinker, but she married him, because she longed to be Queen and we both agreed that Wonderland needed a steady hand to rule. I loved your mother for eleven years, with both my soul and body."

He paused and put his cup down, his black eyes staring at her through the shimmering tree lights. "Together we conceived a child and named her Dinah. You, my beautiful and strong daughter."

Everything seemed to stop for Dinah and she gripped the teacup so hard it shattered in her hands. Her mind was having trouble keeping calm, and she heard a cacophony of voices raise up inside of her, all revolting, all of them in a state of shock. A drop of blood dripped from her palm onto the table.

"*Lies*," she whispered.

Cheshire gave her a sympathetic smile and continued. "I'm sure that's difficult to hear, but let's not forget that the man you thought was your father tried to kill you, and murdered your brother. You should relish the realization that you do not share his blood. Davianna and I loved each other for a little over a decade. Eventually, the King of Hearts began to suspect your mother of having an affair. Every waking hour I could, I spent with her, and there were many times when the King came so close to catching us that I barely escaped in time. In your tenth year of life, Davianna fell ill, very suddenly. I suspected poison, and I still do, though I have never been able to prove who did it or why." He took a labored breath and Dinah noticed a slight tremble of his lip. "I never got to say a proper goodbye to her, except when they gathered the highest ranking Cards to pay their last respects as the life slowly drained out of her. Imagine, seeing the love of your life dying in front of you and being only able to exchange formal, pleasant words of comfort in front of the King, your heart feeling like it will burst inside of your chest.

"I dared not say anything, because who would watch over you if I was executed? And what would happen to you? The King already suspected that you were not his because of your dark hair and dark eyes—so unlike mad Charles, with his blond hair, surely your father's child. Your mother, the breath of my life, died that evening. The King was left alone to grieve, but I arranged to have an urgent account matter to discuss with him that very evening. In his drunken grief, he confessed to me that he thought his late wife was unfaithful. I volunteered to root out the culprit, and a month later, with the proof to show, I gave him the head of the Diamond Cards, a handsome young man named Kenrik Ruhalt. Poor Kenrik—he denied it, all the way up until your father beheaded him in a secret execution in the dawn hours. I was given his job, and eventually worked my way up until I was the King's Chief Advisor, the Head of the Cards.

"Was it cruel? Yes, but I had to get myself into the best position to control the King—to make sure that he acted as a steadfast ruler, as it was not his natural inclination—and most importantly, to keep an eye on you, my daughter."

Cheshire smiled and looked down at the table. "You were ten then, and I had already interceded where I dared to make sure that you had a good childhood, even before Davianna's death. I arranged for the Ghanes to move into the palace so that you might have a friend in Wardley, since before his arrival you were a lonely, moody child. I convinced the King to hire gentle Harris as your guardian, instead of the cruel Governess Forsythe, who was the customary teacher for the royal children. I made sure that you were kept safe, as safe as you could be, from the King's rage. I encouraged him to go to war with the Yurkei when you were very young, so that you and your mother could have some peace.

"But, as you know, the man you have called father for so long is a rapacious and obsessive man. He was sure that you were not his child, and was convinced that you could never follow him to the throne because you would soon marry and either banish or execute him. He told me of an idea that he had been thinking of for a long time, the idea that he would create his own heir, the heir he had always wanted. He needed to find a child, a child about the same age as his daughter. A girl, for a boy would be prone to rebellion, and what he needed was someone who could be his puppet, someone who he could control without problems arising. As his advisor, I warned him against the idea, but I had long suspected that he would never put you on the throne. I did all I could to keep him away from you, but his rage and paranoid delusions were growing, though he kept them concealed behind a charming mask of contempt. I could never risk my position as advisor—who would watch over you then? So I agreed to help him find his little princess.

"The King told his council that he was going off on a hunt, but instead we rode hard for the outer villages on the lower Western Slope—isolated sea towns where we would go unnoticed. On our way there, we chanced upon a small hut with a fire burning outside, far outside of any town or village. A woman and a small girl were making necklaces out of seashells. The girl was breathtakingly beautiful, ethereal almost, and most importantly, she had yellow hair, the exact same color as the King's. That night the King burned a small heart onto her back to remind her who he was, and rode homeward with her strapped to Morte's back. A few Cards followed behind with her mother, Faina Baker, and threw her in the Black Towers upon their arrival to Wonderland proper. The girl was christened Vittiore—a noble name—and put in front of the court as his long-lost daughter. You were there that day, and I watched your face as your world fell apart.

"It was that day that I realized that your life was in danger, and that the closer you got to your coronation, the more your father would try to get rid of you—either that or try to persuade you to give up your rightful throne. That would never work—even as a child, you longed to be queen."

He grinned.

"Your thirst for power matches my own. I showed you the tunnels that afternoon, for it was all I could do at that moment to help you. Someday, I thought to myself, you would have need of them. I started trying to clue you in to your father's motivations, to the fact that a vast conspiracy to crown Vittiore was growing up around you, one that I was a part of, but I undermined it whenever I could. Your father made his stance during the Royal Croquet Game and I knew it wasn't long before he would try to have you murdered or exiled. I passed you a note at the dinner that evening, in a small bottle. It might seem coy, but I wanted you to figure it out on your own. After all, I knew my daughter to be intelligent and curious, just like me."

Dinah's throat was dry and stinging, her eyes filled with tears. *This couldn't be true. It couldn't be.*

"I shouldn't have worried. Using the tunnels, you made your way to the Black Towers and discovered the truth about Vittiore, even if you didn't put it together right away, for by then Faina Baker had gone mad. Your father was hungry for a shift in power, and once he learned of your excursion to the Black Towers, he decided to behead Faina. It was a message for you, but its true purpose was to remind Vittiore of what would happen if she ever rebelled against him. It was unthinkably cruel, but it was a well-instructed lesson that neither of you were to put your noses where they didn't belong.

"Time passed. The King's patience for you was running thin as your coronation day drew near. A sort of madness had overtaken him, and he began muttering dark, violent things. I worried for your safety. I pressed the King to reveal his plans to me, but he refused. Even his most trusted advisors remained in the dark."

Dinah's hands were gripping the tablecloth, her nails tearing through the thin fabric. Her world was collapsing, inside and outside. Her watery eyes made the stars look like they were falling. She stopped breathing. She stared at Cheshire as he continued, but all she saw was Charles.

"On the night of your brother's murder, I was out meeting with some colleagues of mine who lived in the court just outside of the palace—Lords Delmont and Sander, I'm sure you know them."

Dinah nodded impatiently.

"I returned late, much past the midnight hour. Your father burst into my chamber, unannounced and covered with blood. He was hysterical. I calmed him down, but could not hide my horror when he told me that he had just thrown Charles from a window, and murdered Lucy and Quintrell. He said that he was going to frame you, so that you might never ascend to the throne. Instead, it would be off with your head, or you would be thrown into the Black Towers for the remainder of your life. As he rocked himself by the window, muttering of justice and how your mother's bastard would be tried for her crimes, I knew that every moment of my life had boiled down to this one. How could I help save my daughter, without revealing the truth to the King?

"I told the King to change, bathe, and gather his Cards to help apprehend you. I ran—how I ran—first to the kitchens and then to the weapon room. I knew you would never survive without food in the wild—you were raised in a palace that gave you everything you ever needed. After I packed your bag, I ran to your room, where I knocked Harris and Emily unconscious. For a few seconds, I watched you sleeping, my daughter, the pride of my heart, with a face like her mother's, and a fierce intelligence not unlike my own. I had never seen you so close, so perfect, the blood of my veins sleeping before me. I vowed I would do whatever it took to help you survive. Then you awoke... and tried to kill me."

He gave a chuckle, and Dinah remembered the horror of waking up to the dark shrouded figure in her room.

"And though you did not follow my exact directions, you did escape, and in what GRAND fashion! You left behind a bloody mess, you stole your father's Hornhoov, and then outran him and his army in a chase that the peasants will be talking about a hundred years from now!" He clapped his hands. "I couldn't have planned it better myself. It was genius, a statement of your power. After you left, the King quickly declared you a traitor to the realm and placed the crown on Vittiore's head. The coronation was the biggest that Wonderland had ever seen, and I believe she was glad to receive it. The King left immediately after she was crowned to resume the hunt for you, and it was the opportunity I had been waiting for. A chance to find you, to make sure that you were surviving in the Twisted Wood.

"Whispered sources told me of a Spade tracker that had a long-standing grudge against the King and I sought him out. I made a deal with your Sir Gorrann. He would track you down—with the King in tow—but would find you beforehand and take you deep into the Yurkei Mountains, where you would be safe from the King. He tracked you a little too well, but as you can see, he kept you safe, fed, and began training you to fight."

Cheshire rubbed the front of his neck where Dinah had poked him with the dagger. A smile played across his face. "The Spade did well. I joined the King on this mission to hunt you down, and as soon as I knew that you were safely in Sir Gorrann's care, I quietly took my leave from the King's side and followed an alternate path up to Hu-Yuhar, but not before I convinced him to abandon his chase and return to Wonderland Palace." He absentmindedly fingered his sparkling brooch.

"I saw you in the darkness that night, standing so still in the black dress I had packed for you. I was so proud that you had used it so well, and so furious that you would put yourself at that much risk, all for a chance at revenge. Please forgive me for my delay." He gestured to the elaborate table. "One would not call me a light packer. But, finally, here we are, father and daughter, reunited at last, without secrets or lies between us. I have longed for this moment."

Dinah's voice caught in her throat. She longed to throw herself at him, to take his life, to beat him, to embrace him, to weep and laugh, all at once. She felt nauseated and dizzy, confused and elated. *It was too much.* She could barely strangle out a single bitter sentence. "Why? Why are you here?"

His fingers stopped moving against his cup and he cautiously stood and walked slowly over to Dinah. Kneeling before her, he bowed his jet-black head in the moonlight and then looked up at her, his white smile stretching wide over his thin face.

"Why? Because you are my daughter, the pride and purpose of my life, and I have come to aid you as you reclaim the throne in Wonderland. Why? Because you are the true heir of Queen Davianna, and your claim to the throne is stronger than Vittiore's, who is a pauper, related to no one. She sits pretty on her stolen throne. I will help you take your vengeance against the King, with a mighty army of the Yurkei behind you. Why? Because you were born to wear the crown, and I will not see Davianna's daughter slowly waste away in the Yurkei Mountains. Dinah, you must become a conqueror."

Without warning, he pressed his lips to her hand and Dinah felt a wave of revulsion wash over her. She yanked her hand back as if she had been burned.

Cheshire stood and walked to the end of the table, where he gently picked up a covered silver cake platter. He set it in front of Dinah's chair. "A gift for my daughter."

"I don't want to see it."

"You must."

Shaking, Dinah lifted the lid. Underneath it was her crown— the gold and ruby crown, a ring of hearts that blazed like fire, the crown she had left behind. Cheshire picked up the crown and lowered it onto her head. She had forgotten how solid it was, how its points dug into her skull, and the flush of happiness she felt when it rested heavy on her temples. This crown, her crown. The lanterns in the trees flickered, and she heard the rustling of a crane's wings overhead. She looked down at Cheshire, kneeling in front of her. His black eyes met hers, a mirror image, her enemy, her father?

His voice boomed through the trees. "Rise, Dinah, and become the Queen of Hearts. It is time to embrace your fate."

The night held its breath. Dinah looked down at him, his black eyes glittering in the starlight.

Embrace your fate.

She ran.

CHAPTER TWELVE

All she heard was the crashing and breathing, alternating with each step. Twigs and branches breaking and snapping as she plunged through the Yurkei orchard, far away from Cheshire, far away from everything he had said. Her breath, loud and jagged, full of pain and confusion. The crashing and the breathing, that was what was happening now, and it was the only thing she could do, the only thing she could think about.

Sharp branches ripped at her arms and legs, their thorns piercing her soft flesh as she rushed past. The dark branches arched their spindly arms overhead as Dinah escaped deeper into the orchard. There were strange blue lights flickering in the trees, but then again, what wasn't strange in Wonderland? Something large sailed over her head and Dinah heard a foreign cry as she raced through a bramble bush, her legs moving faster than she had ever known they could. It was just her, just the breath in her lungs, the ragged sound of her sobs wrenching out of her chest and the crunching of the leaves and twigs under her boots.

She ran. It didn't take long for her to come to the end of the forest, and when she emerged from the trees, she was surprised to see a sheer cliff face rising up before her, looking like bone in the white moonlight. Dinah buried her face in her hands as she gradually remembered where she was: the Yurkei valley, surrounded by mountains. There was nowhere else to go, nowhere but up— there was no escape. She looked around for a few minutes before spotting the winding path that Sir Gorrann had mentioned a few days ago. It was steep, looping over on itself as it snaked its way up the mountain, narrow but well-worn. Dinah found herself running up the path without consideration. She just needed to flee, to anywhere, to anything. It was all too much. The path climbed higher and higher into the sky, until Dinah was surrounded by a thick white mist that clouded her vision. She pressed her back against the wall and continued her crablike climb until the ghostly mist gave way to cool air.

Dinah was out of breath when she reached the top of the cliff face, gasping for air, for clarity. She swayed on her feet and was surprised to find herself toeing the line of consciousness. The healed wound on her shoulder ached and pulsed with each frayed inhale, and Dinah found herself heaving onto the pebbly ground. She rested her head on the cool stone for a few minutes, focusing on breathing normally again. Wiping her mouth, she pushed off of her knees and looked around.

She was truly alone in this wondrous place. The ground before her was flat and made of stone—a circular platform carved from the mountain and dropping into air on each side. Small etchings had been carved into the ground, tiny little marks that told an ancient story of sacrifice and redemption. They were the religious markings of the Yurkei tribe. She ran her fingers lightly over them. Harris would have loved to see this—he found the Yurkei religion fascinating. Dinah lifted her eyes and looked out past the edge of the stone circle. She could see the entire Yurkei valley if she stood on one side—the floating white tents attached to the side of the mountain, each of them emitting a dim glow from a flameless light.

The great stone birds stood erect and silent with Mundoo's tent suspended between them. The flowing creek behind the tents gurgled contentedly. It was a quiet night in Hu-Yuhar—the only noise coming from the herds of wild horses playing in large groups below, their happy whinnies soothing to her ears.

Dinah let her eyes wander to the northernmost part of the valley, and they rested upon the subtly lit forest, where Cheshire waited for her, his long hands clasping a tea cup. He was still there, no doubt biding his time before he could crush everything she knew into a fine powder, like the sugar that dusted his brooch. Cheshire—her father? Dinah pressed her hands against the unyielding stone. *Could this be true? And if it was?* Should she be grateful that her own father did not try to kill her, but rather saved her life? Or should she be furious that her entire life was a well-orchestrated lie? The truth had been kept from her, not only by Cheshire but by her own mother, the only person who truly loved her. Her mother, Davianna, who had loved Cheshire and betrayed the King, her mother with her soft hands and deep laugh, those hands that wrapped around Cheshire's waist as they danced in the Great Hall, the same hands that had always caressed Dinah's face so lovingly…. Dinah shook her head to clear the image. Was this just another of Cheshire's games? It was possible, but there was an unmistakable thrumming in her heart that told her it was not.

Part of her wished that she had slit his throat before he could speak. *Or did she?* Dinah didn't know what she wanted. Her emotions whirled, a churning storm inside of her. Was she to become a grateful, doting daughter? The warrior he had been training her to become? An exiled princess, a Yurkei prisoner? Was she full of rage like the man she believed to be her father, or full of grace like Charles, now her *half* brother? If she was not the daughter of the King of Hearts, but the daughter of Cheshire, now a traitor—what was she now? Who was she now?

"Who would you have me be?" she angrily called to the stars, tonight all circling around one singular bright star that lingered lazily over the mountains. Her voice rose to a strained yell, choked with emotion. "I SAID, who would you have me BE?"

"I think yeh know," answered a familiar voice.

Dinah didn't bother to turn around. "How did you find me?" she sniffed.

He gave a gruff laugh. "I'm a tracker, remember? It wasn't exactly hard—there was nowhere else for yeh to go but up. Yer in a damn valley." She lowered her eyes, refusing to look at him. "You best not go any farther though, lest Mundoo think you are trying to escape. I fancy breathing."

She spun around to face him. "You work for him, for Cheshire. You betrayed me. You lied to me."

Sir Gorrann walked up beside her and Dinah heard the crunch of his heavy boots echoing over the cavernous drop. "I never lied to yeh. Yeh never really asked about Cheshire. Did he hire me to find yeh? Indeed. And did I? Yes. I saved yer life, girl, and I would save it again. When Cheshire came to me, he dangled a promise: if I was to find yeh, I would get to see for myself that the King was brought to justice, hopefully by yer hand. Not only that, but I would see him stripped of all power and pride. That is what I long for—for him to suffer as I have suffered. That's what I long for—justice at last for the King of Hearts, justice for Amabel and Ioney—this is something I have longed for for many years. Only his wayward daughter could give it to me."

He paused and scratched at his beard as he stared at Dinah, framed by the bright stars. "Though it pains me to tell yeh... truth be told, after a while, things changed. Dinah, I've grown a bit fond of yeh, and I'll fight beside yeh, whatever yeh decide." He looked gently into her eyes, his face etched with the love of a doting father.

"Yeh remind me of her, my Ioney, if she had been given the chance to live. Yer fierce and strong, full of rash emotion. Hear me that my loyalty is to yeh, and yeh alone. If yeh ask me to kill him—" he gestured his head toward the forest below, to Cheshire, "I will. Though, keep in mind, he might get me first. Cheshire is already four steps ahead of wherever you think you are. He knows what you will be thinking a month from now. Listen to me, girl, don't ever underestimate that man. And don't blindly trust him. Ever."

Dinah pulled her knees into her chest and shivered as she stared at the white-washed valley that stretched out toward the east. "That man—you mean my father?" Sir Gorrann did not reply, but instead made quick work of building a small fire against the night chill from a dried bird's nest. His skill was remarkable, and soon warm flames crackled and hissed as they sat together in silence.

Finally, Dinah spoke, her voice breaking with emotional exhaustion. "What does he want me to do?"

Sir Gorrann shifted in his seat and withdrew a pipe. "Isn't it obvious? He wants yeh to take what's yers. The crown. Yer mother's throne at Wonderland Palace. He wants yeh to rule."

"And what do you want?"

Sir Gorrann blew a stream of smoke into the air, the tail end smelling of horses and sweet leaves. "I want yeh to do what yeh believe is right. I long for the King to be brought to justice, but I'll bring him justice one way or another, now or twenty years from now, either at yer side or by some other means. I'll not make yeh carry my burden."

Dinah frowned. "Justice." She laughed wildly. "Do I not long for that as well? The King killed my brother. Cheshire saved my life."

"That he did. And from the sounds of it, more than once. But yeh don't owe him anything. Yeh do not want to owe a man like that. Do yeh understand? Yeh don't." The Spade was getting upset. Dinah shushed him with a glance. He took a breath. "Do yeh believe him? About him being yer father?"

Dinah shut her eyes. *That was the question, wasn't it?* She didn't want to believe him. She wanted everything to go back to how it was long before—when she was a child in her mother's arms, when Charles was still alive, when the King of Hearts was still her father and she could look on him with pride, even when she trembled with fear at his fury. Back to a time when Wardley was near, an apple in one hand and reins in another. Dinah considered carefully before she spoke.

"I don't want to believe him, and yet, when he said these... *things,* I could feel that pieces of my life that were scattered about were clicking into place. Everything fits together now, in a way it didn't before." She shook her head. "It's gruesome, but there was a conclusion, a finality about it. It makes sense—why I don't look anything like my father—er, the King—or Charles. Why the King hated me my entire life, why he beat my mother, why he so frequently escaped to go to war. Why he never wanted me to share his throne." She let out a low scream before beating one clenched fist against her chest. "Gods, I am such a FOOL!"

No sooner had her voice echoed over the rocks than a loud clamor of high screams echoed back. Both Dinah and Sir Gorrann froze in place. The screams grew louder, until Dinah realized that what she was hearing was a growing cacophony of high-pitched bird calls. It was growing louder, a terrible sound. Crawling on her hands and knees, Dinah cautiously peeked her face over the edge of the stone circle and immediately felt her stomach drop. What she had guessed to be nothing but white-washed stone below was actually birds, hundreds of thousands of white cranes nesting fifty feet below the edge of the cliff. Their rising sound was deafening, and Dinah felt her pulse quicken. The birds could kill them both. With newfound understanding, she glanced back at the religious markings on the ground, the dark brown spots that stained the stone in certain places. She closed her eyes and saw a prisoner, tied down to the stone, left for the birds. *A sacrifice. Oh gods.*

Sir Gorrann looked over the edge with a grimace. "These cranes are holy to our hosts. The Yurkei worship them. They are at once gods and a food source, equal parts in the chain of life." His eyes too lingered on the brown stains on the rock face. "We shouldn't stay here long."

Dinah watched the cranes in silence, her black eyes wide with fascination and fear. The birds eventually calmed down, their wings tucking back, settling into their one massive nest. Dinah thought she spotted the carcass of a horse. It was still moving slightly. Their cries faded, and Dinah spoke quietly. "Cheshire wants me to reclaim my throne. He thinks I am a conqueror. A conqueror without an army."

"The Yurkei will fight for you."

"Fight for me," she laughed out loud. "They *hate* me. The Yurkei will fight for Mundoo. They have no interest in fighting for me. Have you seen their faces when I walk by?" She saw them then, their glowing blue eyes following her every move, their brows knotted in fury. "And there aren't very many of them, not compared to the Cards."

"Have you ever seen the Yurkei fight?" replied Sir Gorrann. "One Yurkei can best four Cards." He shook his head. "They move with an unnatural swiftness. It's unnerving."

"It's still not enough," she corrected him. "If it did happen, which I'm not saying it will, how could it... happen?"

Sir Gorrann took his time phrasing his careful reply, one eye trained on the simmering crane nest below. "Cheshire has been meeting with Mundoo for a few days now."

Dinah bit her lip. *So that's where Mundoo had been going.*

"They are still hammering out an acceptable treaty. From what I can gather, in return for fighting for yeh, they will get all their lands back inside the Twisted Wood, and a promise that we will never try to take them again, by any measure."

Dinah shook her head in amazement. "What are we talking about? Just a few hours ago, I was a prisoner of the Yurkei, and a few weeks before that, an outlaw, and before that a princess!"

Sir Gorrann shook his head. "Yeh never were just a prisoner."

"Maybe I just want to be a prisoner! Or a nobody! Maybe I just want to stay here and live a normal life. Have you considered that?"

Sir Gorrann's golden eyes studied her face. "Yeh don't want that. I know yeh."

Dinah felt a blush rise up her cheeks. "It doesn't matter. What you're telling me is that I'm to lead an army to Wonderland Palace that will surely be defeated? Am I correct? You're saying that I should lead this fray all in a doomed attempt to sit on a throne because my mother once sat there?" Her voice was growing ever louder, more and more agitated. She felt the fury rising in her chest, the black boiling. She leapt to her feet. "Look at me, and tell me—who am I, Sir Gorrann? Who do you see when you look at me? Do you see my father's daughter? Do you see Cheshire? Do you see a whimpering girl, or a Yurkei warrior? A spoiled princess? A conqueror? And who are you? A lonely man? Do you hope for a crown upon your head, Sir Gorrann?"

She was yelling now, and she could hear the agitated squawks from below as the birds began to stir once again. Thousands of wings began to flap in the night air, the stirrings of flight.

"Shut yer mouth, girl! Be quiet! Do yeh long to be pecked to death?" Sir Gorrann was growing agitated as well. His face was contorted with an anger that seemed to light up the valley. "Yer acting like a child, that's what yeh are! A spoiled brat who has been given everything! And now, a man brings an army to yer feet and yeh aren't sure what to do? That's not for me to tell yeh! I'm just a dirty Spade, a tracker, a broken man, I know yeh see that!"

They were furious with each other now, yelling in whispers, their sentences overlapping, spit flying from their mouths. Sir Gorrann's forehead pulsed with a purple vein. "Who am I, yeh ask? I am not who I once was, a man with a wife and a daughter. We become who we must to overcome pain and to make things right again! Everything I have done, I have done to get justice for my family! I have not brought yeh this far to have yeh ask someone else what yeh should do!"

Sir Gorrann pointed to one of the vertical rock faces that divided the west and east sides of the valley. His small fire had thrown its light, and their large shadows danced across it. "I know who I see! No matter what Cheshire said, yer still the same person that yeh were before yeh came upon that tea table. It's not his arrival that has changed anything; it's just yer understanding of the past. There's nothing I can tell yeh, but I would say to look with yer own damn eyes!" He began walking toward the sloping path that led down to the valley. "I'll say goodnight, for yer in a right mood. And if yeh don't be careful, those birds aren't going to stay dormant."

"Go away," she said quietly. "I don't want to see anyone right now." The black fury was stirring inside of her. She would not let his arguments push her over the edge of sanity.

With a huff, he began descending down the winding path, muttering to himself about "Cheshire's mad daughter." Dinah was suddenly alone, comforted only by the crackling fire that continued to project massive dancing shadows on the rock walls. She felt swept away by a surge of emotion, as if she was drowning in a tidal wave of her own confusion. A thousand different hands were reaching inside her head, each yanking at a string. Her once-father, the King of Hearts. Her now-father, Cheshire, with his slippery feline smile. Sir Gorrann. Mundoo. Bah-kan. Wardley, Charles, Harris, Faina Baker, Vittiore. Their faces ran together, each one a part of her, but none of them giving her the answer she needed. Images chased each other through her mind, a game of insane tag: Wardley, kissing her under the Julla Tree. Her mother, looking at her reflection in the mirror. Charles, a finely crafted hat in his hand. Lucy and Quintrell, bloody and piled in a closet. An empty table. She closed her eyes and felt the heat from the fire sear close to her face. Then she willed the thousand voices to be quiet.

Unconsciously, she raised her arms, the pain of her shoulder making her wince through the confusion. *Be silent,* she shouted to the voices in her head. *Be silent!* she commanded again. *Silence!* Finally, she pushed them down until it was only her own voice that she heard. She lowered her hands. *Be quiet, all.* There was a stillness within her, and Dinah allowed herself to reach inside to gather her thoughts. When she opened her eyes again, she looked up at the rocky cliff face and immediately saw what Sir Gorrann had been pointing at. Stunned, Dinah lifted her chin in a way that she hadn't done since she fled the palace. With the fire leaping behind her, the shadow of her figure loomed huge on the rock walls: a giant, almost larger than the mountain itself. And on her head, the shadow of the crown that Cheshire had placed upon her.

Dinah reached up and felt the brim of the crown with her shaking fingers, the gold warm from the growing flames. She had forgotten she was wearing it, she was so used to its weight and feel.

It was natural for her—she had been practically born wearing that particular crown. It stayed put even as she had torn through the trees and bramble. It felt *right* on her head, and the spikes that dug into her temple gave her a steadiness that she hadn't felt in a long time. She stared at her shadow, and the commanding figure with the crown shimmered in the flames. Her mind cleared. The answer was here. *This was who she was, who she had always been.* She was no one's daughter, no one's warrior, no one's scapegoat or prisoner. She wasn't a spoiled princess or the savior of a foreign people. Dinah raised her eyes to the circling stars, and her shadow straightened in accordance.

I am the Queen, she thought.

That's who I am. I am the Queen of Hearts, born to sit in one of two Heart Thrones. I am the Queen of Wonderland and I will have the crown that my brother made for me. I will take it with fury and swords and whatever help I can find. Pride blossomed in her chest, and every inch of her skin felt alive with promise and purpose. Suddenly aware of everything touching her, pressing against her skin, clinging to her neck, Dinah began taking off her clothing. She flung down her dagger and pulled the red tunic that represented Wonderland off over her head. Off came the feathery Yurkei pants and the boots that had been tucked into her bag, a million years ago. When she was finished, Dinah was without an inch of clothing on her body, without chains to bind or gifts to bribe or tools to shame her. She was naked, with only the crown on her head, a crown that was her right by birth, by the line of her mother. *I am the Queen.* Everyone in Wonderland would bow before her. She wasn't afraid, not anymore. *I am the Queen.*

Alive in every way, Dinah flung a large burning piece of wood over the edge of the cliff, where it landed with a fiery burst in the massive nest. The air instantly thrummed with the sound of a thousand wings, and Dinah watched without fear as the sky filled with the enormous white cranes. They rushed at her with beating wings and sharp beaks, but she stood firm, naked and flushed, with only a crown on her head. They circled her, their loud cries coming ever closer, their beaks brushing her skin. "Go!" she screamed. "GO!" All around her was a sea of white feathers, but Dinah dared not close her eyes. There was a moment where the seething flock hovered just above her and all around her, an angry hissing and squawking swarm, considering an attack on this strange creature wearing a crown and blazing with righteous anger. Dinah's black eyes stared at the birds, unflinching, daring them to touch her. The birds seemed to pause, violence on their minds, calculating the odds of taking on this latest sacrifice. Then, at the last moment, they rose into the air in an ever-widening spiral, blocking out the stars, the rock, everything. She had faced down the gods and won.

I am the Queen of Hearts, she thought, *and I will take my throne.*

The cloud of birds disappeared over the mountain and the air was silent again. She stood before the mountains, the painfully cold breeze whipping around her body. Something had changed here on this ledge, this piece of etched rock stained with an ancient religion. Dinah saw her path unfold before her, confident of what she needed to do and who she was. *I am the Queen of Hearts.* She was a queen, she would have her throne and when she had that, she would deliver Charles his justice. This was her fate and she was, for the first time, unafraid for her future. The path to war was suddenly the least scary option of all, because it was *right.* Once the birds had completely disappeared into the night sky, she breathed deeply until her heart stopped pounding. Dinah left the fire to burn itself out, but not before she glanced once more at her impassive shadow, so ferocious and secure, with the pointed tips of her crown brushing the top of the cliff face. A nagging voice told her that while she wasn't as mighty as *that* queen, she would have to try to be. No matter the fear that would inevitably get her in her way, she had to try.

Dinah begrudgingly pulled all of her clothing back on and gave one quick glance at the Hu-Yuhar valley below. A crowd of Yurkei was gathering, and their voices gave way to silent awe as she made her way down the steep path carved into the rock wall. A nervous group of men waited for her at the bottom of the narrow staircase: Cheshire, his purple robes billowing in the wind and his hands resting together as if in prayer; Sir Gorrann, his weathered face a mask of concern; Mundoo, fierce and proud, the leader of his people; and Bah-kan, who towered over all of them, terrifying and vicious, clutching his Heartsword. The men watched her as she made her way down, her emotionless face betraying nothing. Hundreds of fascinated Yurkei gathered at the bottom watching her with their piercing blue eyes, almost luminescent in the darkness. She drew ever closer to the small group of men who had played her like a pawn, those men who had deftly moved her toward her destiny. Cheshire's face broke into a wide smile when he saw the crown on her head. He quickly bent at the knee and bowed before her in grand fashion. Sir Gorrann followed. Mundoo and Bah-kan simply nodded in her direction. They would not bow before her.

Mundoo cleared his mighty throat. "Princess. We have much to speak about."

Dinah wouldn't realize until later that three simple words would forever change the face of Wonderland.

"It's Your Highness," she corrected him. "And I imagine we do."

CHAPTER THIRTEEN

Seasons changed the landscape with alarming ferocity as the next few months flew by. *Even the grass was different here in the Darklands*, thought Dinah, as she watched the pale-blue ferns ripple across the murky landscape. Everything was softer and wetter. Her steed pawed impatiently at the ground, thirsty and ready to plunge his head into the swirling currents of cool water that ran just beneath the moss. Her hair, damp and twisted with white ribbons, blew out before her and Dinah shuddered in the morning air as something round and glowing slithered just underneath the foamy brush. She had expected the South to be warm and humid. She had been right about the humidity, but with the still, moist air of the Darklands came a certain chill in the early morning, the wet air holding on to the bite of night.

It had been a hellish march south—they had lost several Yurkei along the way, between the hidden bogs and the strange poisonous creatures that seemed to lurk under every rock. Disturbingly, the Twisted Wood seemed downright tame compared to the Darklands. As she dug her hand into her steed's tangled mane, Dinah hummed a song softly under her breath, a song her mother taught her so very long ago. A song, she now knew, Davianna had learned from Cheshire. The landscape was brutal, but even with danger surrounding her on all sides, Dinah felt stronger than ever. Her crown rested on top of her head, its rightful place, and Dinah felt powerful in the high saddle. Her stomach grumbled loudly. She was hungry, as she had been ever since they started their march southward. Moving a small army required much food, and there was never enough, it seemed, to satisfy everyone. Everyone could eat at least five times more, even the future Queen, who slept in a battered tent, curled around her sword. Dinah was still humming when Sir Gorrann's trotted up next to her on Cyndy.

"Sir Gorrann, good morning."

He didn't waste time with pleasantries. "Yer Highness, there is a conflict between two of the warriors. Ju-Kule and Freyuk are about to come to blows. Yeh must come quickly—their quarrel will surely end in even more divided loyalty amongst the Yurkei."

Dinah nodded her head and with a click of her tongue sent her steed galloping toward the camp—a small city of circular white tents that held a thousand Yurkei warriors and, so far, about three hundred rogue Cards. *Wonderful,* she thought, *another problem, another small battle.* Planning a war, it turned out, was very complicated and took months to prepare. She bit her cheek nervously as she thought back on all the conflicts that had followed her down from the mountains.

The night she had accepted her fate as Queen, after she had descended from the Yurkei Mountain, she had, along with Sir Gorrann and Cheshire, climbed up into Mundoo's tent. The fear had returned when she stared up at the ladder, but this time she had something other than survival at hand—she had reasons to live: vengeance and the throne. As the ladder billowed out behind her, Dinah forced herself to climb without fear. *I am the Queen.* Almost immediately after they began their tense discussion, it was very clear that each member of the war council entered with their own agenda. Mundoo longed for his people's complete autonomy and independence from Wonderland Palace. In return for his people's support in battle, he demanded the release of all their former lands back to the Yurkei, all the way north from the Ninth Sea up through the Todren and to the East, from the Twisted Wood until the end of the Yurkei Mountains. He also decreed that a representative of the Yurkei people was to sit on the Queen's council, once established, and would have a vote in Wonderland's affairs that both did and did not concern the Yurkei. It was a steep price to pay for her army, one that she would surely feel later if she was indeed crowned Queen. Part of the Yurkei lands included Ierladia, her mother's hometown, the largest Wonderland stronghold in the North. The negotiations over Ierladia had taken three days, but in the end, a compromise had been reached. Mundoo agreed that the citizens and buildings of Ierladia would remain unharmed under Yurkei rule. While the Yurkei would ultimately own the city, Ierladia would still function as it always had—by doing trade and commerce with Wonderland Palace. The Yurkei would then reap a hefty portion of their taxes as the owners of the city. Tax was a strange concept to the Yurkei, but eventually they seceded to Cheshire's plan.

Dinah's newfound father came with his own set of demands: he would take his seat as the Queen's main advisor, and the head of her council, and he would remain in charge of all of the Cards, as well as the acting Diamond Card in charge of the treasury. His powers would increase to include a seat on the Yurkei council and he would have the power to hold or release prisoners at his will. Without expressly saying so, Cheshire made sure that he would be the most powerful person in the palace, aside from the Queen. Bah-kan wanted lands within Yurkei territory and a royal pardon for his desertion of the Cards, and he would have it, but only if he agreed to be Dinah's personal bodyguard until she was crowned. Sir Gorrann said that he would negotiate with Dinah alone, but so far he had remained silent and impassive, wanting nothing apparently.

After the negotiations were signed and sealed, four swift horses bearing Yurkei riders were sent to store the documents in the four corners of Wonderland, so that there might always be one treaty that remained safe, even if the rest were destroyed. After the documents were sent on their way, Dinah nervously prepared for the ancient Yurkei sealing ritual. Wearing little more than a few feathers, Dinah stood perfectly still for hours as the words of the treaty were painted on her body with white paint by silent Yurkei women. The words trailed down from her eyes in straight lines to the edge of her toes, and by the end, there wasn't an inch of her skin unmarked with white paint. The words of their treaty trailed from her cheeks, her belly, her fingertips. Mundoo had the same treaty inscribed down his immaculate body, and when they were done, both Dinah and Mundoo were led into a ringed circle of fire, a subdued crane tied to each of their wrists. The Yurkei rose in song, an unnerving wail that resonated through the narrow valley.

For hours they sang as Dinah and Mundoo stood perfectly still until their legs trembled beneath them. Finally, with a desperate shout, the two parties neared each other as the stars swirled above. When they were close enough to touch, the cranes leapt from their wrists and flapped toward each other. Mundoo and Dinah were yanked together as the strings holding their cranes twisted and tangled while the birds fluttered and fought. The warm words written on their bodies smeared together, the melting paint mixing with their sweat and tears as they struggled against one another. Finally, a Yurkei priestess gave a shout and they both released their birds into the sky. The words were now one, their sweat was one, and their heat was one. Dinah's black eyes met Mundoo's shimmering blue irises as they stood silently, surrounded by the roaring fire. What she had seen in them both reassured and frightened Dinah. Mundoo was hard, resilient, and she saw a passion blazing in his eyes that was not unlike her own. She was a queen and he was a chief. They were the same. A pact had been made, a promise sealed. Dinah had never felt more alive and gave a shout to the sky, her head thrown back in glory.

After she had cleaned up, she joined the Yurkei for a celebratory feast alongside Bah-kan, Sir Gorrann, and her two Yurkei guards. It was a feast to put all others to shame, even the endless feasts she had known at Wonderland Palace. Birds of every type were paraded in on the backs of Yurkei warriors. Each bite tingled with rich spices, woodsy and full of flavor, each taste manipulated by Iu-Hora, their local medicine man. Dinah was given piles of edible mushrooms, each one producing a unique effect—some made her sad or melancholy, while others made her jubilant or silly. Some produced a feeling of intense passion that climaxed in seconds and left her breathless, clutching the table. One gave her a hallucination of the palace, filled with thumping red hearts and fluttering peacocks. Another showed her a river of blood, soaking her feet. The effects weren't lasting—most were no more than a minute—so Dinah eagerly awaited what each new mushroom would bring.

Dessert was a towering concoction of berries and edible plants, along with some hearty honey bread of which Dinah couldn't seem to get enough. When the bread was broken open, a tiny flame that somehow burned inside the loaf extinguished, leaving warm bread dripping with hot honey. It was incredible, and Dinah happily licked the honey off of her fingers, aware that perhaps a queen shouldn't engage in such behavior. She hardly cared. The Yurkei didn't care, either.

Cheshire sat beside her on one side and Sir Gorrann on the other; and while Cheshire was constantly trying to engage her with compliments or observations, she couldn't bring herself to be kind to him, not yet. She did find herself staring at him when he wasn't looking, taking in his jet-black hair and eyes, so like her own, a mirror image really. She imagined him with her mother, laughing and touching, finding every spare moment to be together, caught up in the danger of their forbidden passion. She couldn't picture it, and at times the idea made her sick. Since he had arrived, Cheshire had given her a number of gifts—a lovely diamond brooch in the shape of a cat, a heavy purple riding cloak, a new set of dark-red leather boots imprinted with a heart on each heel. She pulled on the boots immediately and shoved the other presents into her bag. He could not buy her loyalty or love, not yet, but she needed new boots and so allowed herself to slip into their rich soles, her sore feet rejoicing.

Her training with Bah-kan and Sir Gorrann continued—brutal mornings, everyday—until she was able to spar competently with Sir Gorrann, even beating him on occasion. All the mornings she had played swords with Wardley were returning to her, and her strokes became quick and hard as her body intuitively spun and leapt. Somehow, without her noticing, the blade and her body had become one. One morning, as Dinah was bathing, Cheshire approached and invited her to train with him on throwing daggers. Dinah reluctantly agreed, but to her dismay found that she thoroughly enjoyed herself. There was something about winging a dagger at a tree that released her growing anxiety about leading an army. Cheshire was extremely skilled with a dagger, and Dinah realized that he had generously allowed her to hold her dagger to his throat in the orchard that evening. He could have disarmed or killed her at any time.

As they threw the knife, Cheshire recounted for her parts of her childhood that she had almost forgotten—her fifth birthday, a certain croquet game, when she broke her leg climbing a statue. He had indeed been watching her, but she told herself that it meant nothing. It was hard enough to consider that she was of his blood, let alone to develop the daughter/father bond that she had been lacking her entire life. And so, she didn't speak. She just flung the daggers, again and again, loving the *thwunk!* against the tree bark when the knife made contact. She enjoyed their time together more and more as the days wore on.

Preparing an army took time. There were weapons to procure, horses to train, and large caravans of food to be assembled piece by piece. It was decided that Dinah would take a thousand Yurkei warriors with her as she marched south. If there was to be even the slightest hope of victory against the King's army of ten thousand Cards and growing, then they needed the support of the rogue Cards who dwelled inside the Darklands. These were men, dangerous men, who had deserted the Cards and fled south, where they could live in relative freedom outside Wonderland law. Then again, they had to live in the Darklands, which to Dinah seemed to be punishment enough.

Mundoo and his army of four thousand Yurkei would march north, gathering men from the smaller tribes that lay scattered below the Todren, and make their way down from there to Wonderland Palace. Not only would this ensure that the palace would be attacked from both the north and the south—essential when the palace was surrounded by a circular wall—but the King of Hearts would surely focus on Mundoo's large and noisy army, allowing Dinah and her small army to creep up from behind. Cheshire's hope was that Dinah's army would surprise him, or at least alarm the Cards. They would sack the palace together, independent armies working as one. He was unnervingly clever in battle strategy, and Dinah saw instantly why the King had chosen him over his peers to be his advisor. Cheshire's mind was not unlike his dagger. Razor sharp and lethal, it could be wielded completely in whatever way he chose. He explained that her small army of Yurkei would be there for her protection in the Darklands, but they also served as a symbol to the rogue Cards of her commitment to a new kind of existence, one in which Wonderlanders, Cards, and Yurkei all existed and fought together to end tyranny. In his words, seeing the Queen of Hearts leading an army of Yurkei warriors would be enough to sway even the hardest mind. "Wars," he reminded her, "are won in the mind, not in the field."

On the day of their departure, a few months' time since Dinah had descended from the mountain with her crown, the women of the Yurkei tribe silently gathered to present Dinah with a gift: a suit for battle, adorned with elements representing both Hu-Yuhar and Wonderland. As the women unfolded it before her, Dinah bit her lip to keep from bursting into tears of appreciation. Here she was taking these women's husbands and sons to fight for her—some surely to the death, and they were giving her a work of art, something that could never be repaid or replicated. *She would make them widows and they gave her gifts.* The breastplate was white—a pure, flawless white that reflected bright rays of sun. Across the front was a red painted heart, slashed through with a single broken edge—it was very similar to her father's armor, only it had been bent and shaped to a woman's body. It came down and hit her at the hip, where tiny red hearts lined the sharp edging. They gave her leg and arm guards, black and marked with the same red heart.

The armor, while meticulously crafted, was just a foretaste of their artistry and talent, shown fully in Dinah's cloak. To call it a cloak or a cape was a mistake, for it was so much more than that. It fastened around her neck and was buoyed out from her shoulders by the same remarkable light wood that held the Hu-Yuhar tents aloft. A thick collar of black-and-white checkerboard fabric fanned out from the sides of her neck and curled into two hearts just below her cheeks. The collar was lined with soft white gossamer feathers plucked from young birds and the cape was made of white crane feathers. The tip of each feather had been dipped in red paint, giving the appearance of a blood-tipped wing. The cape stretched out behind her like wings, long enough to brush the ground. Dinah let them dress her and braid her hair with ribbons. When they all stepped back, wide-eyed, she knew she was ready.

Dinah settled her ruby crown on her head and turned to face the women. Some were weeping, others looked simply afraid, their wide blue eyes open in fear. As she emerged from her tent, Cheshire put his hand over his heart and gasped. Sir Gorrann, steps behind him, raised his eyebrows.

"How do I look?" asked Dinah with a smile.

Bah-kan was sharpening a knife on a small rock nearby and looked up in her direction. "Terrifying. A thing of nightmares."

"If *you* think that," she replied, "then they have done a fine job."

She gave a thankful nod to the Yurkei women, who gathered around and laid their hands over the heart on her breastplate, giving her healing tinctures and murmuring quiet prayers for her success.

That night, Dinah had barely returned to her tent before tears of gratitude fell heavily. There was little time for tears while the gears of war were turning, and she was grateful for their release.

The sun rose and set in the sky, and before Dinah felt she could wrap her head around all the details, it was the night before their departure. All of Hu-Yuhar fell silent, and Dinah could feel the heavy desperation and fear in the air—so much was at stake in this gamble, this gamble that rested on *her*. The throne of Wonderland, the fate of a native people—it all weighed on her shoulders, heavy as the cape they had draped over her. As a dark night fell over Hu-Yuhar, so removed from those who clutched each other desperately in their tents, Dinah walked through the silent valley, making her way toward the towering stone cranes that guarded their whispered secrets. There was one more thing that she wanted.

Without the aid of her guards, Dinah climbed the ladder and entered Mundoo's tent. He was feasting with his family, and Dinah felt rude about interrupting this sacred last night at home. Still, she pushed open the flap and climbed to her feet. Mundoo's wife and seven children looked up in alarm.

"I need to speak with you before tomorrow."

Mundoo gestured with his hand, and his wife and children scampered out onto the bridges, which rocked loudly in the cool mountain air. Dinah lifted her fingers to the crown. Lately, whenever she felt the creeping doubts or the listless fear that had come with preparing for war and death, she touched her crown. It centered and reassured her. She gave a slight bow to Mundoo before she began speaking in a quiet yet forceful voice.

"You have something I want. I feel that we have given you a great deal in our negotiations. I have not asked for anything."

Mundoo laughed as he lustily licked the grease from his fingers. "You have asked for nothing. Nothing except a crown on your head and to become the most powerful person in Wonderland."

Dinah swallowed and continued. "I want him back. He is no good to you dead. We need him."

"No. YOU need him. A normal steed will fit you just fine."

"Any man who rides a Hornhoov knows that to be a lie."

Mundoo rose and sat stiffly on his throne of golden cranes. He looked at Dinah, amused. "I cannot give you the mad beast that has killed so many of my warriors. It goes against every principle of Yurkei justice that we have, even if I believe he would aid you in battle."

Dinah smiled. "I realize that, and I would never ask you to compromise your rule or reputation with your people. But what if I could offer you, and the Yurkei, something greater than death?"

Mundoo raised an eyebrow at her, his radiant blue eyes boosting what little confidence she had at that moment. "And what could that possibly be? What could possibly equal the cost of lives? Some of your Wonderland gold perhaps? A raid of your treasury once you are crowned?" He scoffed. "It is so like Wonderland to think they can buy Yurkei justice. You do not understand our way if you think gold can pay for blood."

Dinah opened her hands in a show of mercy. "Not money. I would give you life for death. It is the only thing that is greater."

Mundoo tapped his fingers above his lip. "My curiosity bids me to hear you out. Continue. But be careful that you don't insult me in my own tent, in my own kingdom. You are not my queen, Dinah, do not forget it." His eyes lingered on the hatch door that flapped open at the bottom of the tent. "It's a long flight down from the crane's wings."

Dinah bowed her head. "Chief Mundoo, in place of Morte's death, I propose to give you life. Twelve lives for the twelve that he took. Twelve Hornhooves. Once I am Queen, I will breed Morte with your Hornhoov, Keres. You will get twelve of his foals, male and female, which eventually you could breed as well. Hornhoov foals are very rare, as you know."

Mundoo darted from his throne and grabbed Dinah's chin. "Do you take me for a fool, girl? Or are you the fool? With an army of

Hornhooves, my tribe would quickly grow to be a threat to Wonderland Palace itself. How am I to believe that you will give me his offspring?"

"I will. You have my word as Queen."

"You aren't Queen yet," he snapped. "How will I know that you will hold to your promise?"

Dinah felt the crown heavy upon her head. "I swear it on my brother's life, on Charles's name."

Mundoo released her. "Then I accept. Twelve Hornhoov foals for the Yurkei, brought to us when they are a year old to begin training."

Dinah nodded. "Twelve. And not one more."

"And what if you do not become Queen? That is quite likely you know."

Dinah was already climbing down the ladder. "Then we will all be dead anyway. Good night."

And so she had been reunited with Morte. She found him in a pen as high as three men, lined with the strong white wood that held the tents of Hu-Yuhar aloft. This wood, however, was ringed with thorns, and she saw hundreds of tiny cuts along his legs and head. Morte had been so happy to see her that he only stomped around her three times as he threatened to crush her to death. Finally, once a stream of steam hissed from his nostrils, he let Dinah run a single finger down his massive nose. He lifted his knee so she could mount and jumped from the opened cage. They ran through the valley for hours, the thundering of his hooves scaring the other wild ponies into submission. Later that week, the Yurkei presented her with a saddle, built specially to ride a Hornhoov, originally built for the Chief. It straddled Morte's neck, rather than his back, but it also had a groove where Dinah could sit on her knees if she so desired. With her steed, her saddle, and her crown, she led the army of a thousand Yurkei south, navigating a secret narrow path that wound down from the Yurkei Mountains, through the middle plain and into the Darklands. The path had led her here, to this pit of wet sorrow, astride Morte, proud and exhausted. Dinah looked now, out at the tents, silent in the morning air.

The black devil gave an impatient stamp of his hooves as she pondered what she came here for. What had Sir Gorrann said? *A conflict between two Yurkei, oh yes.* She climbed down from Morte, who gave an angry snort when she attempted to tie him to a pole. His saucer-sized eyes shimmered with anger. *Would she never learn?* Instead she dropped the reins and Morte galloped off. He would return when she needed him, dragging along a bloody carcass of some poor animal to place at her feet. He would then feast on it until Dinah heaved up her supper in a bush.

Dinah ducked into Sir Gorrann's tent. The men were waiting for her—Cheshire, Sir Gorrann, and Bah-kan—all stood silently as she peered curiously at each of them. Their faces were twisted. They looked alarmingly happy.

"What are you staring at? Where are the warriors? Have they already killed each other?"

Cheshire let a devious smile creep over his face. "There are no warriors. Follow me." Without another word, he stepped out of the tent, with the two other men following.

"What?" Dinah ran to catch up with him, her sword bouncing across her hip. "Stop! I'm in no mood for a game right now! I think you have played enough with me for a lifetime."

Cheshire's grin stretched even wider, a naughty cat, caught in his deception. "I think you will much enjoy this game, Your Majesty."

They were climbing a low grassy ridge, slick and wet from the evening mist. Dinah slipped a few times as she made her way up the rise, her boots squirming in dark water that ran uphill. "Have you found more rogue Cards? Send the ambassadors to speak with them at once."

"No," replied Cheshire. "Not *rogue* Cards." He stopped Dinah and held her by the shoulders. "Listen to me now, as you didn't before. Climb to the top of the crest and see what we have brought you, a gift to our Queen from your loyal servants." He bent his head to her ear and whispered, "But mostly from me."

Sir Gorrann and Bah-kan hung back just before the crest of the hill. Dinah gave Sir Gorrann a strange look as she walked away from them. He gave a small nod and so she continued climbing. The top of the hill looked out onto a low meadow, dotted with white mossy trees and small pools of still water. She squinted, unsure of what she was seeing. Then her heart began hammering. Men. It was a line of men. Men wearing black. Thousands of them, each armed, bearing the familiar uniform, black on black. A man on a large white horse led them forward. Dinah's breath caught in her throat. *Had she been tricked? Was this her father's doing? Had Cheshire played her?* The white horse was plunging toward her now, but it didn't move like a Hornhoov—he was too slow, and the rider was smaller, with a mane of curly brown hair blowing in the....

Dinah didn't feel her body start to move, but soon she was sprinting over the meadow, screaming his name, tears falling freely down her cheeks, the opposite of a queen, a woman lost, a child coming home. There was no majesty, no decorum, only him, always him.

"WARDLEY! WARDLEY!!"

He abandoned his horse, sprinting toward her as she screamed his name.

"WARDLEY!"

They collided in the middle of the field in a tangle of limbs and a crushing embrace. Both fell to the ground, sobbing, pressed into each other with a breathtaking fierceness. Wardley was kissing her forehead, his arms wrapped tightly around her.

"I thought I would never see you again!" sobbed Dinah.

"I'm here now. I'm here. Shhh."

She raised her hands to his face, feeling his cheeks, his new beard. "It's you. You're safe." Dinah was babbling now, close to hysteria. "I'm sorry, Wardley, I'm sorry, please forgive me. Forgive me for hurting you, for stabbing you." She pressed her hand against where she knew his wound to be. "I'm so sorry!"

Wardley's eyed filled with tears. "You have nothing to be sorry for. I'm the one who is sorry. I'm a coward. I should have left with you. I should have found you sooner. You are the rightful Queen, I should have protected you." Wardley crushed her close to his chest.

"You did, Wardley. You saved my life." They leaned their foreheads together, their hearts hammering loudly in the damp wind. Dinah wiped away her tears, suddenly aware of making a scene in front of throngs of armed men. "What are you doing here?" she whispered. Wardley looked down at her, his eyes the color of warm chocolate, eyes she had loved her entire life. Her heart was captivated by him, even after all this time.

"Dinah, don't you know? I'm here to command your army."

He grabbed her arm and pulled her to her feet. Dinah looked out at the sea of soldiers in black, all standing motionless: warriors, murderers, and prisoners. The Spades had arrived.

A smile crept across her face.

With these men, she could crush the King.

CHAPTER FOURTEEN

Sleep was of paramount importance, yet Dinah couldn't think of anything she needed more than to let her eyes feast on Wardley's slumbering face. She watched silently, mesmerized by the way his lips parted slightly with each deep breath, with each rise and fall of his chest.

After their joyous reunion, once they returned to camp, Dinah had seen how exhausted Wardley was. His lips were cracked and bleeding, and dark circles shadowed his eyes. He was thin, thinner than Dinah had ever seen him, and there was a tortured ache present in his face that broke her heart. The Spades, eight hundred and seventy-two in number, had marched for a week under his leadership and arrived hungry, weak, and irritable. They possessed a begrudging respect for Wardley, but the Spades as a group were independent and unruly, and he held onto his command by the skin of his teeth and the ferocity of his blade. After he made sure that the men were settled into their makeshift tents, he promptly collapsed into Dinah's open cot and fell asleep within minutes. Dinah perched on a stool nearby, her hands folded together, her sword across her lap, her black eyes drinking in every breath of him. *He's here*, she thought, *he came for me. I wasn't wrong to believe he'd find me.* Wave after wave of relief washed over her, a flood of penetrating joy. It wasn't just that he was alive and unhurt—not on the surface, anyway—but that she had someone here she trusted without hesitation. Sir Gorrann was a fine companion, but Wardley had known Dinah her entire life, in the intimate way that only a childhood friend could.

She continued to watch him sleep until her own weariness closed her eyes. She curled up beside him and they slept. She awoke to Morte's impatient, thundering steps outside the tent. He was hungry; he was always hungry. So Dinah found a live chicken and gave it to Morte, who enjoyed chasing his prey around, toying with it, before he mercilessly speared it through the middle with one of the bone shards encircling his hooves. He then settled into the dirt to feast on its still-flailing body, and Dinah returned to the tent with a distaste for breakfast. Wardley, however, awoke starving and Dinah couldn't feed him fast enough. She knelt by his bedside as he devoured dried bird meat, loaves of bread, and apples. Crumbs drifted down onto his long legs. His brown eyes bore into hers, overjoyed to see her, and yet filled with a terrible guilt. Wardley insisted that Dinah tell him everything, down to every last detail. She took a deep breath and recounted her story, alarmed at how dangerous everything seemed in retrospect. She started when she was awakened in her bed by a hand over her mouth and continued on through the details of Cheshire's affair with her mother. The night on the mountain with the cranes and the shadows she kept to herself. That moment was hers alone, concealed close to her heart, next to the place where she held Wardley. He watched her with amazement as she told her tale, his face reacting boldly to each turn. When she finished, he sat quietly for a few minutes before speaking.

"So Cheshire is your father?"

"So it would seem."

"And you believe him?"

"I don't have to believe him. I know it to be true. Look at him, and look at me. I looked nothing like my father—" Dinah corrected herself, something she was starting to do more often. "I'm sorry, the King of Hearts. I look nothing like the King. And I believe that my mother had an affair. When I was young I heard them arguing about it. There are so many things that fell together when he told me, so many disparate pieces that fit perfectly into place. My life makes sense now, even though the whole thing is a bit alarming."

Wardley was quick to see through her easy cadence. "A bit alarming?" he scoffed. "That's how you feel about Cheshire being your father?"

Dinah walked over to the tent flap and looked through the narrow sheaf of light. Thousands of tents littered the damp ground as far as she could see. "He's clever. He's organized this entire war, all to put me on the throne. He saved my life and probably will again. The King never even looked me in the eye. He hated me. He murdered Charles, Wardley."

His voice softened. "I know. But be wary that your gratitude turns into blind trust."

Dinah shook her head. "I won't. I promise." Cheshire was the least of her concerns. Right now there were a thousand Yurkei warriors, three hundred rogue Cards, and almost nine hundred Spades all gathered in one wet field. The Spades were the most loathed of all Cards among the Yurkei. If they all weren't careful, the war could start and end right here.

Wardley looked past her, casually resting a hand on her shoulder. "It's good to see you, Dinah."

Dinah's skin tingled at his touch, at being near to him. A smile crept across her face, and she forced herself to take a few quiet steps back into the tent.

"Sit down. You are exhausted and in no shape to be moving around. But tell me all that's happened in the palace since I've been gone."

"I'll tell you later, but right now I have to get ready to meet with the war council. Do you mind if I clean up?"

Dinah rolled her eyes. "I've seen you bathe a thousand times."

"That is true." Wardley crouched next to a small bowl of water and pulled his shirt over his head. Dinah struggled to keep her face motionless as her eyes raked over his tan, taut skin and she watched with pleasure as he scrubbed the grime off his lean chest. As he lathered a bar of soap through his hair and scraped the dirt from under his fingernails, he repeated most of what she already knew: after she had stabbed him (way too deep!, he was kind enough to remind her) he was transported to the infirmary, where the King of Hearts had found him and demanded his head. Wardley had assumed that he would die right there and then.

"He was mad with rage, Dinah, furious and insane. You've seen him drunk—well, this was a thousand times worse. He began striking the midwives and the nurses, screaming, 'Off with his head! Off with his head!'" Wardley shook his head. "I was terrified. I couldn't move, I couldn't fight. I could barely stay conscious, for gods' sake. Luckily, one brave doctor convinced him that my blood on the table was price enough. No man would let himself be injured that deeply on purpose. The King stuck his fingers deep into my wound to make sure."

"Oh, Wardley. I'm so sorry."

Wardley let the wet rag linger over the jagged, ugly scar on his shoulder, four inches long and barely healed. Dinah felt tears flood her eyes as she looked at the hideous wound she had inflicted. "I'll get you some Yurkei medicine for that. Their potions possess incredible healing powers, surprisingly much more advanced than ours." She let her fingers softly trace the scar before stepping away.

Wardley nodded as he mopped at the back of his neck. "As I healed in the infirmary, I heard rumors of my fate. The King wanted my head, but had been dissuaded by his *council.*" Wardley pronounced the word sharply, making it clear that he meant Cheshire. "I was stripped of all my titles and duties. I was still technically a member of the Heart Cards, but I was no longer the future Knave of Hearts. Xavier Juflee dismissed me from being his apprentice." Dinah winced. Wardley practically worshipped Xavier. "The King ordered me into service before I was completely healed. All I did after that was labor in the stables, forced to rebuild each wooden gate by hand with inadequate tools. It was my punishment." He puffed up his chest and gave her a sad smile. "I have a new title, I'll have you know: Wardley the Weak, the Card who was bested by a princess. A title fit for a king, don't you think? Most days I was unable to work in the stables because of my wound, so I would just lie in the hay, dreaming of an escape from the pain."

He paused. "Many times I woke up in the stables, not remembering that I had fallen asleep. The days seemed never ending, and the nights...." Wardley had a faraway look in his eyes, a look that Dinah had seen before—it was a place she could never reach him. His mind was elsewhere and for a second she saw a flicker of *something* pass in front of them.

"Wardley." At the sound of her voice, he snapped back to attention, his eyes filled with tears. "And then...?"

"After a while Cheshire found me. He told me bits of his plan, each week a bit more information—never enough that I could act on it alone, and never enough that I could ever accuse him of treason. He's crafty, Dinah."

So am I, she thought, *because he is my father.*

"Finally, the man told me what he wanted. He wanted me to lead an army of Spades south to meet you, here in the Darklands. To fight for the rightful Queen, to fight for you." He smiled. "But I did not need convincing. You are the rightful Queen of Wonderland, and like a sister to me. I wondered: how do you convince an army of Spades to fight against their fellow Cards? What would make a single Spade drop their loyalty to one crown to fight for another?"

Dinah had no idea. Wardley leaned forward, a drop of water falling off a curly lock of brown hair. "*Rights,* Dinah. The Spades long for their own rights. As it turns out, I didn't have to convince anyone. They have been waiting for this for a long time. Combine that with the King growing madder every day and it was an easy sell. Our departure date was set, in the middle of a long night. I stole away from the stables and came to the place that Cheshire had told me, half-convinced that this was some sort of insane game that the King was playing to test my loyalty. But there they were in the darkness, a silent army of Spades just waiting in the courtyard, with their commander Starey Belft at the helm. Here's what I've learned, and what you should remember: the Spades' loyalty is not to the King. It has never been to the King. It is to Starey Belft, for he lives the depraved life of a Spade, and so they respect him. They would follow him into hell, and they did. We marched for two weeks' time and lost more than twenty men. We only have a few horses. The things I've heard from these men, you wouldn't believe...."

Sir Gorrann poked his head into the tent and looked surprised to see Wardley soaking wet and Dinah watching silently.

She smiled. "It's not what it looks like."

"I couldn't care less. The council is waiting for yeh both."

Dinah gave a slight nod. "We'll be there shortly. Thank you, Sir Gorrann."

He left and Wardley eyed the door skeptically. "What about him? Do you trust him? You know he was in Cheshire's pocket, don't you?"

"Aside from you, I'm not sure there is anyone I fully trust, or ever will again. The man I thought was my father tried to kill me. My mother lied to me my whole life. And yet, I believe that Sir Gorrann has my best interests at heart. I consider him a dear, eternally grumpy friend."

Wardley pulled a ripped tunic over his head. He softly took Dinah's face in his hands and her heart stopped. "You do know what you are doing, don't you? You're planning a war, Dinah. A war in which many people will die, perhaps even yourself. This isn't playing swords in front of the stable. This isn't a game."

Dinah pulled back from him, her face flushed. Wardley always knew how to get under her skin. "Of course I know! I'm the rightful Queen. Shouldn't I fight for my throne?"

Wardley shook his head. "You are, but I worry for you. You've never seen a battle, you've never seen a man...."

Dinah slapped him hard, across the face. "What? I've never seen a man die? I've seen my brother's body crumpled on a stone slab. I've seen a farmer with an arrow buried in his back just because he happened to be near my path. I killed more than a few Cards on my way out of the palace, and I see their bloody faces in my dreams! So don't tell me that I haven't seen death or war, or that I don't know what I'm doing. I've been at war with the King of Hearts since the day that I was born."

"You slapped me!" Wardley laughed a bit before stepping back and shaking his head, his eyes searching her furious face. "You are not the same girl that I kissed under the Julla Tree. That hurt!"

"Don't forget that again," she snapped, resentful that Wardley had riled her up, as he always did.

"Let's go, they are waiting for us."

"Don't be mad. I'm sorry I doubted you." He reached out and tugged playfully on her braid, and Dinah's fierce heart melted.

CHAPTER FIFTEEN

The war council met in a circular black tent that sat squarely in the middle of all the other tents, a dark spot in a sea of clouds. Long onyx flags with the symbol of the Spades stitched haphazardly across their front panels snapped in the wind, blowing out from the tent pillars. Before the Spades had arrived, the war council's conversations had taken place over fires, or in regular tents. This tent was new, large, and intimidating. It carried a message: the Spades were not to be trifled with. As Dinah walked toward the tent with Wardley, several Spades bowed before her. It had been a long time since Cards knelt before her, and Dinah felt a rush of pride as their heads tipped to the ground. *I will be their Queen, someday.* Dinah ducked inside the tent flaps, Wardley behind her. A large circular table made of light wood filled up the room, forcing them to stand pressed against the soft black fabric of the tent. Rising up from the table stood a model of Wonderland Palace. Dinah marveled at its construction—every window, gate, and turret was present, each tiny shutter accounted for. She ran her fingers over the model of the stables, the rose garden, the Black Towers, and the iron walls that surrounded the city in a perfect circle. The hardened tips of her fingers rested on the Great Hall and she looked up in amazement.

"How did you get this?"

"Allow me to answer that, Your Highness." Starey Belft crept out of the corner, darkness hiding half of his scarred face. Dinah recognized him by his face, which she'd seen at various palace events, but also by his commander's brooch—it was black like all the Spades' insignias, but a single white diamond sparkled from the middle, denoting a higher rank. Half of his face had been badly slashed during a battle with the Yurkei, but the other half remained ruggedly handsome. He looked tired and worn, with deep plum circles underneath his eyes. Starey Belft was famous for his fierce loyalty to his troops and his love for loose women. He gave Dinah a wink with his good eye.

"You look well, Princess. You've lost your round baby cheeks."

"And you, sir."

"Eh, I look like I got slashed in the face with a knife."

There was a painful silence in the tent until Bah-kan burst out laughing. "AYE! You did!" Starey glowered at him.

Dinah motioned for him to sit. Each member of the council took his seat around the massive wooden castle. "Again, I will ask, how did you come across such a masterpiece?"

Starey Belft cleared his throat. "Ah, I took it, Your Highness. When I knew we were leaving the palace and turning our loyalty to you, I broke into the King's chambers and took his model, piece by small piece." He demonstrated by breaking off half of the kitchen, folding it flat, and then putting it back into place.

"It's a puzzle!" exclaimed Dinah.

"It made it a bit easier to transport. Still, I don't think my Spades relished carrying it through the Darklands."

Dinah rested her hands on her lap. She didn't want to appear too pushy, and yet she could already feel the rising tension in the room as the Spades' demands went unmentioned. The Spade commander was playing a game with her, waiting to see how long she would go before addressing them. She would play her own game then. "How is it, Starey Belft, that you came to be in this tent today bearing the weight of the palace on your shoulders? It must be an incredible load to bear alone."

"It is, my Lady." Starey took a long sip of the ale the Spades had brought with them. After all, who went to war without libations? She stared unflinchingly at him until he shrugged sheepishly. "What do you know about the life of a Spade, my Lady?"

"I know that living the life of a Spade is an honor."

Starey jumped to his feet, his face flushed with anger and inches from hers. Everyone in the tent held their breath until he seemed to think better of his actions and turned away. When Dinah opened her mouth to speak, Starey Belft turned and spit, spraying the ale from his mouth all over Dinah. She coughed and wiped her eyes, willing the churning rage inside of her to dissipate. *He should not have done that.* Sir Gorrann stepped in front of her, his sword drawn and trembling as he pointed it at his old commander, a man Dinah knew he deeply respected.

"Yeh forget yerself, Commander! Sir, this is the future Queen of Wonderland and yeh will respect her as such."

Starey Belft laughed. "Sit back down, Gorrann. I could skin you for treason you know, you traitorous letch."

The men stared at each other as Dinah wiped the ale off of her chest with her sleeve. Finally, Cheshire's voice boomed out from behind the wooden Black Towers, the height of the spires amplifying his disembodied voice over the tiny palace. "Both of you sit down. There will be no fighting in this tent, no skinning of anyone. Starey, tell us your story. But if you are here, you must respect the Queen. She understands that you've had a very long journey and that you weren't in your right mind when you happened to spill your ale near her feet."

"Spilled it out of his mouth," mumbled Wardley.

"It's fine," murmured Dinah, patting her hair with her sleeve. "I've had much worse."

Starey Belft's anger turned quickly to shame. "I'm sorry, Your Highness. It's just that, if you think the Spades live a life of honor, you are mistaken. I should have expected that the daughter of the King of Hearts would never know the truth of our lives." Starey collapsed back into his chair. "In between birth and death, the life of a Spade is one of misery and sacrifice. We are considered the lowest ranking of the Cards, and are treated with disdain by the rest." He gave Wardley an accusatory glance. Spades had no love for Heart Cards. "As you know, Spades are not allowed to marry or bear children. When we take our oaths, we are sworn to live for Wonderland Palace, so why would we have a need for women, love, or comfort? Spades live in the freezing barracks that lie just behind the Black Towers, stacked one on top of the other, so that you never know whose piss you'll be standing in when you wake up. We have a place to sleep and food to eat, but nothing more. When Hearts, Clubs, or Diamonds go home, what do they return to? A room in the palace? A wife, a son? We return to nothing but the cold and the darkness." Starey gave a shiver.

"And I don't care what the official stance of the Palace is, but there is something that permeates the ground near the Black Towers. The black roots run through our sleeping quarters. It makes men angry, makes men mad. And just when we seem to have unity, the prisoners come. Straight from the Black Towers, released to the Spades to serve the realm. Murderers, thieves, liars, rapists—that's who the King sends to make up his army. How are we ever to rise above our rank, when our barracks are constantly being filled with the dregs of society? We cannot, which is just how the King likes it."

He took a breath and sat back on his wooden stool, taking a long sip of the swirling golden ale. "The life of the Spade, my Lady, is *not* 'honorable' as you say; no, it's filled with fighting and bickering amongst ourselves, for we have nothing to do but the King of Hearts's dirty work. It is a miserable existence. We are asked to live in this constantly changing darkness, and yet, if the King needs someone assassinated, who does he come to?" Starey beat his breast with a gloved fist. "He comes to me, comes to me to murder his enemies, to seek out Yurkei spies, to dispose of his mistresses when he grows tired of them. I have thrown men in prison that simply looked at the man in a way he did not like. I do these things, and for what? To see my men treated like sewage, discarded like day-old tarts?"

He brought his fist down onto the wooden palace and the stables crumpled beneath his hand. "Tell me, Your Highness, what will my legacy be? A legacy of death and sorrow, a life of cold waste, praying that war will come, just so we may take leave of our sorry quarters? I tell you, no! If it is the last thing I do in this sorry world, I will leave the Spades in a better position than they are in now. My men deserve better than this excuse for an existence, for we are the ones who fight and die for this kingdom."

Bah-kan spoke up from the corner of the room, where he softly ran a dagger across his giant cheek. "You fight and die for unjust wars. The Yurkei have done nothing to deserve your raids. Your men are brutish and cruel—they are monsters."

"I will not listen to a coward speak," replied Starey Belft, his face stoic.

Bah-kan leapt up with a roar and Dinah barely had enough time to fling herself between the two men.

"STOP! As your queen, I order you to STEP BACK!" The men pressed on both sides of her.

"SIT DOWN! Obey your queen!" cried Sir Gorrann. The men, their chests heaving against Dinah, took a single step back, more out of self-preservation than respect, Dinah suspected.

Bah-kan eyed Dinah as he spoke in clipped Yurkei. "You are not my queen; the Yurkei have never submitted to Wonderland domination. But I am sworn to protect you, as Mundoo commanded. Do not forget, little girl, that is why I obey you now."

Dinah nodded and waited until Starey and Bah-Kan sat back down, her patience gone. "Sir Starey, what can we do for you? What demands have you brought on behalf of the Spades? What price will I pay to have them fight for me?"

Starey handed Wardley a rolled piece of paper, which he then gave to Dinah. "It's all written there for you, made up of the voices of a thousand Spade warriors, voices that have been oppressed and enslaved for centuries. We have five demands. First, a Spade shall be allowed to marry and bear children. Second, a Spade can choose to live with his family in a private household within the kingdom, as do all of the other Cards." He paused. Dinah nodded. These seemed reasonable. "Third, we would ask that you move our barracks away from the Black Towers, to the south side of the kingdom, as the first major project once you are crowned Queen. Fourth, we ask that the Queen would meet with a small group of established Spades before declaring war or ordering raids on any group of people. We would like to have a say in the matter before we are asked to sharpen our axes for battle. Our final demand is that the Spades will take new rank just under the Heart Cards, and be paid accordingly. This will allow us to afford more for training and feeding, so that we may build a strong army, inside and out."

Dinah faced him across the wooden structure. "If this war works, Sir Starey, there will be no need for raids, or battles. We seek peace with the Yurkei."

"A strong queen needs a strong army."

"He is right, Your Grace," spoke Cheshire. "Though you will not war any longer with the Yurkei, you will still need an army to police the city and to protect you. Especially once you have established your rule, there will be parties who seek to harm you." *Like the Diamonds and the Clubs,* thought Dinah, *who will have just been usurped by the Spades. I will elevate one group to make two others angry.*

Perhaps this was the game that Wardley had spoken of. War was, at its most basic, the great reassigning of positions—a king who could become a prisoner, a princess who could become a casualty of war. It occurred to Dinah that her war might not be over once the King was dead. There would be many sacrifices made in order to win, and many of them would make the pillars of Wonderland society very unhappy. Dinah tucked the scroll into her tunic.

"I will think on your demands, Sir Starey. For now I would encourage you to take a much-needed rest and sober up. We have much planning to do. We will meet back here this evening, just after dinner is served."

The war council rose to its feet and bowed before Dinah exited the tent. Cheshire trailed behind her. Dinah handed the scroll to him. "Please look over these and make sure there are no tricky loopholes. Return it to me so that I may look over it again by tonight."

Cheshire rested his hand on her shoulder. "You did well in there, my Queen. I am so proud of you, as both your humble servant and your father."

Dinah felt unsure of how to respond and so she strode away from him, toward Morte, who stood waiting for her beside her long white tent, which someone had haphazardly painted with a red, slashed heart. "I'm going for a short ride to clear my head. Please have it read when I return."

Cheshire bowed, a feline smile stretching across his thin face. "Nothing would please me more, Your Majesty."

"Sir Gorrann!"

"Yes?"

"Please join me for a short ride."

Cheshire's smile disappeared, but he turned away before Dinah could see it. Sir Gorrann gave her a half salute with his hand. "With pleasure. I need to fetch Cyndy."

Morte was pawing the ground impatiently and beginning to nip at the tent. His hooves brought ripples up from the grassy surface, where the water underneath sloshed and bubbled. "I'll meet you at the blighted ponds. He cannot wait."

Dinah bowed her head with reverence once she reached Morte, and he lifted his leg for her to vault onto his back. Morte ran with abandon for the blighted ponds. Dinah relished the damp wind on her face as they flew across the wet valley. The ponds were not far, which was convenient, for it was where the army drew their water from seemingly endless pools of refreshment. Alongside the clear, delicious pools of perfectly cool water, there were other ponds, the blighted ponds. She had seen them almost every day for the past few weeks, and even now stared at them with amazement. The murky pinkish waters were topped with a foamy froth that looked delicious, but smelled and tasted atrocious. Every now and then a creamy, shimmering bubble would rise up from the fathoms below. Bordering on the edge of the moss, the bubble would creep a few feet over the ground and then begin to float slowly toward the nearest living creature. They were easy to avoid if one watched out for them, for they drifted at a snail's pace; but if they touched the skin, as one unfortunate Yurkei warrior had found out, they burst open, bathing the unfortunate victim in a warm splash of effervescent pink. Seconds later, skin, blood, and veins would begin to turn white and harden. The warrior was left petrified within minutes, a creamy pink bubble formed over his lips. The Yurkei had been afraid to touch him to give him a proper burial, and so they had left his body behind in the blighted ponds. The next day when they had returned to gather water, the warrior's body was gone, and in its place was a new rosy pocket of water. It had consumed him, and he had become whatever had eaten him from the inside.

Dinah watched with caution as Morte drank mightily from one of the clear pools. There were no roaming bubbles so far, but she could see the blighted ponds rippling in the distance, a sea of foamy pink bubbles against the green moss.

"I hate this place." Sir Gorrann rode up beside her, his mare panting with exhaustion. He looked over at Morte. "Gods, he's fast. Cyndy here was galloping her fastest, and we were still at least a half mile behind you."

Dinah smiled and rested her hand on Morte's chest. He shot her an annoyed look and stepped away. "He wasn't even truly running. When the King chased us, he was running so fast I could barely make out the landscape."

"Mmmm. He's an incredible monster, isn't he?" They both glanced over at Morte as he happily stomped a toad to death.

Dinah trained her eyes on the ever-shifting ponds. "Tell me, Sir Gorrann, what do you think of the Spades' demands? This is why you agreed to find me, right? Why you said you would work with Cheshire? *This* was your agenda. You wanted to make sure that I survived and made it to the right people so that I could advance the cause of the Spades. Is that correct?"

He looked out into the distance. "Yeh would be correct. I never hid that I had an agenda, not from yeh. If I can't bring back Ioney and my Amabel, at least I can better the lives of those men that I would call brothers. But I will fight for yeh, Dinah. I believe that yeh will be a great queen, and I will fight even if yeh don't agree to the Spades' demands. They are fair demands. There was nothing that seemed... in excess." He paused and took a sip of water from one of the clear ponds. "Of course," he continued as he wiped his mouth, "If yeh don't accept the Spades' demands, yeh will not have an army. Yeh will have a thousand Yurkei warriors, three hundred Rogue Cards—who are useless if yeh ask me—and the King will wipe all of yeh from Wonderland like the dirt under his feet."

"Can we win?" Dinah asked.

Sir Gorrann watched with a wary eye as two champagne bubbles began drifting toward them, so light and friendly on the wind. "Perhaps. But we will surely not win without the Spades. Mundoo was counting on them joining us when he marched north. Without them, we haven't a prayer. The Cards don't fear the Yurkei near as much as they should, but they will fear a line of Spades."

"Then it is done." Dinah watched a pretty pink bubble burst across a low rock. Within seconds, the moss covering its surface shriveled and turned white. "And when you are allowed to marry, will you marry again, Sir Gorrann?"

He looked out at the low valley, now filled with several hundred floating pink bubbles, all very slowly making their way toward them. "For many of us, there is only one person who can fill the spaces of our heart."

Dinah thought of Wardley, the way his breath had washed across her face, the way the scar on his shoulder had stretched when he raised his arms to wash his body. She loved every part of him. For her, there was no other. "Yes."

His gold eyes rested on her face, the crinkles in his eyes showing the first signs of a smile. She snapped her fingers for Morte, who didn't come, so she began walking quickly toward him.

"Thank you for your input, Sir Gorrann. I think we should head back to camp."

He watched a shimmering bubble that rolled slowly toward his feet. "Couldn't agree more. I hate this wretched place."

Dinah looked out over the landscape, so enchanting, a world of soft pink bubbles and warm light. She shrugged. "It feels like love."

"And that's why it'll kill yeh," replied Sir Gorrann, nudging her toward Morte.

CHAPTER SIXTEEN

When she wasn't meeting with the council, Dinah continued to train with Bah-kan and Sir Gorrann, but now Wardley brought his own special expertise into the bouts. Crowds of Spades and Yurkei swarmed their training circle to watch the epic battles of sword and strength, blatantly ignoring Starey Belft's shouted orders that they should return to their own sparring circles. Dinah was usually the first one out of the ring, followed by Sir Gorrann, and then Wardley. Bah-kan was unstoppable, with the exception of one warm afternoon when his sword swung a little too close to Dinah's neck. Silver flashed in the sunlight, followed by a loud metallic thump and Bah-kan looked down in amazement at the dagger lodged deeply in his breastplate, just above his heart. He leveled his furious gaze upon Cheshire, who was perched calmly on a horse a hundred yards away, his purple cloak billowing out behind him.

"Bah-kan." He shook his head sadly. "Remember who you spar with, sir, and slow your blade." Then he turned and rode calmly away, leaving the crowd stunned and impressed.

Bah-kan yanked the blade out of his chest with a scowl. "He's overly protective of you," he snapped in Yurkei. Dinah allowed herself to boast, if even for just a minute.

"He's my father." *And he is dangerous from even a distance.*

She instantly regretted saying it out loud and soon retired to her tent, her mind sloshing with conflicting emotion. Preparations for war continued at a frantic pace, and most nights Dinah fell into bed exhausted to the core. Her body ached, her mind was spent, and she wished she had insisted on bringing the heavenly grass mattress from Hu-Yuhar instead of this makeshift cot. Usually, a deep sleep took her immediately, but not this night, just a few days before their departure for the palace. *Fall asleep!* she commanded herself. *You have much to do tomorrow; SLEEP!* The more aggravated she became the less likely sleep was, and she found herself tossing needlessly on her cot. *Something* was keeping her awake. There was a voice trailing on the edge of the warm wind. *Come to me.* Dinah tossed and turned. Sleep was a white rabbit on quick feet, and no matter how much she tried, she could not follow it into the blissful dark.

Exasperated, Dinah sat up and pulled on her tunic and boots. The damp air of the Darklands was growing warmer each day as summer neared and she had no need for heavy wool or feather pants. She grabbed a handful of sugar cubes from an open bag and ducked out of her white tent. Her two guards were, of course, wide awake when she passed them outside.

"Your Highness?" Ki-ershan was the only Yurkei warrior who addressed her as his queen. Dinah had grown quite fond of him.

"I'm just going for a short walk through the tents."

"You may not go alone."

"I won't. I'll have Morte with me."

The guard glanced up at the massive beast that had trotted over to greedily consume the sugar cubes. The bone spikes that protruded from his hooves were white as the moon in the flickering torch light.

"Are you sure, my Lady?"

Dinah touched his shoulder. "It's just a walk, I promise. I'll be back in half an hour."

Normally the guards would not let her out of their sight unless she had a protector—Sir Gorrann or Wardley or Cheshire would do, but the truth of the situation was obvious: what could they do that Morte could not? Morte had killed a white bear, something that five of the best Yurkei warriors could not do. He would protect her. Dinah began strolling up and down the rows of tents, first the black Spade tents, which reeked strongly of men, ripe sweat, and ale. Loud snores filled the narrow grassy corridors between tents, and Dinah smiled at each resonating snort. She lightly touched the tent flaps as she walked by, lingering on how close she felt to these soldiers when they weren't looking her up and down with doubt. These men, they would fight and die for her, even if they weren't sure about her ability as queen. They believed in her, in her claim for the throne, but most importantly they believed she would acknowledge their rights. Whatever the reason, she would appreciate every sleepy sound that came from their filthy mouths. After the battle, there would be far fewer voices to hear.

A large field separated the Yurkei tents from the Spades. Morte galloped across it with abandon and waited impatiently for her on the other side. The Yurkei tents were vastly different from the Spade tents. The Spade tents were black and shaped in the typical triangular tent form with black flags flapping from their posts. The Yurkei tents were circular and white, utterly without color or flags. They hovered above the ground, buoyed up by thin wooden reeds. Dinah knew from her time in Hu-Yuhar that they were also much more spacious, comfortable, and portable. She wandered the line of Yurkei tents, up and down their endless aisles. There were no sounds here of sleep. The Yurkei were silent sleepers—there was nary a breath to be heard. The same held true for anytime they moved. The King and his vast resources and armies had failed to wipe them from Wonderland for one reason: they were stealthy warriors and could launch an attack without making a sound. Many villagers didn't even know that their town was being sacked by the Yurkei until it was over and an arrow protruded from each of their chests. Compared to the Yurkei, the Spades were hulking and clumsy, with their only talent being the swing of a sword and the cruelty with which they inflicted injuries upon their enemies. *No wonder they hate us so*, Dinah thought, *we are like ungainly giants, stomping across their land on big feet.* She stopped to take a breath.

The night was still and damp, the stars clustered in one small corner of the sky. Just out of the corner of her vision, Dinah caught the slightest flickering of purple light. She blinked. It was still there, a flash in the dark, a blue glow where there shouldn't be, pulsating from between two tents. Taking a few steps back, Dinah walked close to the line of white, round, cloudlike structures and peered between two that were situated abnormally close together. Between the two tents sat another, only this tent was almost perfectly round—a sphere with a wide bottom, balancing precariously on two long wooden poles. The shape would have been abnormal enough if it wasn't for the strange, hazy lapis light that pushed out from the tent. A trail of bluish lavender smoke exited through a hole in the top of the tent, winding and curling in on itself. Morte gave a loud snort and began bucking unhappily. The ground shook when his massive hooves met it and she feared he would wake the entire army. Dinah reached for him.

"Shhh… shhhh… it's okay." Morte yanked back from her touch and galloped a few feet before he knelt to the ground. He stared at her accusingly for not following him. Dinah turned back to the tent, her curiosity piqued. This was the tent of Iu-Hora, the

Caterpillar—the witch doctor who had traveled south with the Yurkei. Iu-Hora was the alchemist who created the incredible medicines that healed the Yurkei so quickly. He had potions and herbs for every ailment, several of which Dinah had used in her time at Hu-Yuhar. He was said to be many things—mad, a genius, an evil incarnation of the Yurkei's power and myth. Some said he hatched from a cocoon, others that he was brought down to the tribe by cranes. Each Yurkei either loved or feared him, dependent upon whether or not his medicines had been used to save their lives. Either way, he was guarded fiercely from the rest of Wonderland by the Yurkei. It was said that he held the secrets to the world within the confines of his pipe.

Recently, Dinah had heard whispers that Mundoo had sent Iu-Hora south with Dinah so that his potions might be used to sway the opinions of the Spades if needed. It hadn't been, but the idea that one could drug an army into doing one's bidding was disturbing. Dinah blinked in the hypnotic light, unsure of how long she had been staring at the tent. It reminded her of a glistening, opulent blueberry, and she found herself drifting toward it, not unlike her reaction in the mushroom field. *Stop it!* she told herself. *Be wise!* She spun on her heels to leave when a soft voice beckoned from the darkness, sweet like honey and heavy like wool.

"Come to me. Dinah, my child, come in, come in! Let me know who you are."

Morte gave a snort of unhappiness from across the field. The tent pulsed again with the light and Dinah found herself taking the few steps up the wooden platform and stepping into the tent. It took a few seconds for her eyes to adjust to the strange light, which she realized was coming from a large hookah pipe in the middle of the room. It was almost as tall as Dinah herself, blue light flickering out from the bottom of the pipe. The glass of the hookah was transparent and inside, silver-and-blue-veined leaves flickered and glowed. A thick smoke filled her eyes and lungs, and she instantly began to cough and choke as a voice filled the room.

"Take a deep breath, little Queen. Let it fill you. Only then will you be able to see and hear your future. Or answer the question *who are you?*"

Her eyes cloudy, Dinah was barely able to make out the outline of the massively fat Yurkei man who sat perched on a pile of bright pillows. His girth hung over the sides of the cushions, and only a yellow feather loin cloth stood between her and his complete nakedness. His skin was dark and shiny and, unlike most Yurkei, completely unmarked by white lines. On the side of the tent, hundreds of clay pots and hanging scales all clamored for space. The walls of the tent were adorned with hanging herbs, potted plants, and a style of finger painting that Dinah had never seen. Iu-Hora noticed her staring with interest at his work.

"The Darklands have provided a most bountiful crop on which to experiment. I have already made three new potions since we've been here! One for rashes, one for aging eyes, and one for... well, you don't need to know that. You'll see."

She looked over at him again, but was unable to make out his face. It kept shifting and changing, but that was just the hazy light, wasn't it? *Wasn't it?* She was very confused. Dinah felt the smoke make its way into her lungs, and a pleasant warm sensation began to stir under her rib cage. She was feeling very light, very free, very happy.

"Here. Take a drag." Out of nowhere, a chubby hand extended the end of the hookah pipe to her. "Just one taste, Princess. Just one taste and hear what Iu-Hora has to tell you."

Impulsively, Dinah took the pipe and inhaled deeply, before she could think about the decision. Then she heard Sir Gorrann's words. "Impulsive, like your father." But that man wasn't her father. Or was he? She couldn't remember, and didn't seem to care. The smoke went down sweet and tingly, and she immediately felt like she was bursting with joy. Her head was clear, and her ears were open. She collapsed with a giggle onto a pile of pillows nearby.

"Did you get these from Wonderland? The Yurkei don't have pillows like this."

"They came to me how they came to me. You did not come here to ask questions about the pillows. You came here to ask much more difficult questions. And I am here to ask you... who are you?"

"I'm Dinah," she answered. "And I do not know why I came here."

"You are here because I brought you here. I have been waiting a long time to meet the Queen of Hearts."

"I'm not Queen yet."

He seemed to slither around her. "Ah, yes, war. The coming war, the great war. A war that will change the fate of Wonderland. Battle. Blood, smoke, and birds. A deck of cards, falling... falling. I see a hiding girl, a bloody sword, a fractured heart."

His words made no sense to Dinah. She laughed and then felt suddenly somber. "Can you see the outcome? I hear the Caterpillar is a predictor of fortunes."

For no clear reason, Dinah started laughing at the word *fortune*. It was so amusing, that word.

"I cannot see the outcome of the war, because it involves the fate of too many. My visions are blurry with so many souls to see. I see much death and unhappiness. I see a beautiful woman weeping at a window, a skilled arrow, blue stars in the sky. I see you riding a black devil, with great wings stretched behind you."

"That would be Morte," Dinah laughed until she wept. Then she looked around. How long had she been laughing? A minute? Three hours? Three weeks? The Caterpillar emerged from the hazy light, his features still unreadable, aside from his glowing blue eyes. It was all she could see. Dinah was suddenly terrified.

"What are you doing? Get back. Don't touch me!" She thought the words, but for some reason could not make her mouth form the sounds. Slowly, his fingers reached inside her tunic, and then he spun her around. For a moment Dinah was afraid of what was happening, but then she felt the hot caress of his fingers against the scar on her shoulder.

"This was my work. A scar left on a queen by a chief. Something that she will never forget, but a sting that healed quickly." Something was seeping through her skin from his fingers. She could feel it alternating hot and cold, tingling against her shoulder. It was inside of her, whatever it was, passing through her skin like water. Iu-Hora spun her back around and suddenly Dinah felt like she was floating with him, up and up, up through the tent into the stars that looked down on dead Charles. They were flying through the sky now, over the Darklands, over the fields; they flew up, up, and away until they hovered above Wonderland Palace. The Black Towers shimmered with wickedness below. She blinked. No. She wasn't in the sky. *Was she?* She was in the tent, and his blurry face was inches from her own, his hands on her face. Iu-Hora's voice changed as he leaned forward as if to kiss her, and she felt the thick smoke from his mouth wash over her face. All the smoke was suddenly sucked out of the circular tent and there was nothing but darkness, nothing but the heat of his forehead against hers and the sharp blue of his eyes. A low, terrible voice boomed out from the blackness. It belonged to Iu-Hora, but it didn't sound like him. Dinah found herself very afraid, more afraid than she had ever been.

"Queen of Hearts, the daughter of two fathers, heed my words. To wear the crown upon your head, you must pierce the heart of one man and cut out the heart of the one you love most. Cat will not keep his promise to crane, and your head shall roll to a rest in the grass."

Iu-Hora gave a silent gasp and suddenly blue smoke trailed out of his lips. His voice returned to normal and a silly giggle filled the tent as the light also returned to normal.

"Would you like more, my Queen?" Dinah pushed him backward into the pots and scales, which went crashing down under his massive weight. She wasn't sure what was happening. Blue smoke was pouring out of her mouth, changing colors as she breathed. Red morphed into a fiery orange, which curled into a pale blue, then a misty gray. Coughing, she crawled toward the tent flap.

"Come back!" he cried, laughing. "I have so much more to show you!"

She was running now, away from the tent, smoke pouring from her eyes, ears, and throat. It steamed out of her skin. She stumbled and fell to the ground. His voice returned and whispered in her ear, although she was nowhere near him.

"Keep your temper, Queen of Hearts."

Morte was beside her now, and she weakly pulled herself up to step upon his hoof, a bone shard giving her a thin cut on her ankle. She flopped over his back, lying face down across him as she continued to choke on the colored smoke pouring from her mouth and nose. Morte began running back to her tent. Dinah's body began to shudder as if it had forgotten how to function. She was alternately freezing and stifling hot, and her mind was racing, making jumps of illogical means. Was she up or down? Where was she? After what seemed like years, Morte arrived in the Spades' camp and came to a violent stop in front of her tent. Yur-Jee and Ki-ershan leapt to their feet and gathered a shaking Dinah from his back. They babbled frantically in Yurkei, their voices so loud to Dinah's ears. She heard pieces of their conversation.

"Iu-Hora! No Wonderlander has ever been in his presence! What did he give her? Witch doctor! Pure evil!"

Wild hallucinations ran through Dinah's mind, and she heard pieces of Iu-Hora's words again: *"Queen of Hearts, the daughter of two fathers... wear the crown upon your head... pierce the heart of one man... cut out the heart of the one you love most. Cat will not keep his promise to crane... head shall roll to a rest in the grass."*

As the guards babbled in rapid Yurkei, Dinah heard Wardley's voice ringing above the commotion. "What the hell happened? Give her to me! Bring Cheshire NOW!"

Wardley cradled her against his chest, and she was aware that he was carrying her inside her tent. A thin trail of maroon smoke curled out of her lips and Dinah blew it lovingly at his face. She struggled to stay awake. Wardley leaned his face over hers. "You can close your eyes, Dinah. I'm here." Sleepiness overtook her, and she was happy to fall asleep in his strong arms, the arms of the one she loved the most.

CHAPTER SEVENTEEN

It took two days to completely get the smoke out of her system. She slept all of that first day, with the most vivid and bizarre dreams she had ever had. She would wake drenched in a sweat that pushed itself out of her skin in a swirl of vibrant colors, to find Cheshire and Wardley staring down at her, discussing things that she could barely understand.

"When will she be fully aware?"

"Hopefully the tea will draw out the hallucinatory effects of the smoke."

"Did they find him?"

"The Yurkei are guarding him day and night. We will not strike. Actually, I think he might be of great use to us."

"Has Mundoo been notified of what his witch doctor did to the Queen?"

"We sent two riders this morning with the message. They also carried our finalized plans for the battle. God help us if they are caught."

"They won't be. They're Yurkei."

Dinah would listen for what could have been hours or seconds before drifting back into her dazzling sleep. The next day, she woke to a cool cloth being pressed against her forehead.

"Your Highness?" She looked up, expecting to see Sir Gorrann, but instead found herself uncomfortably close to Cheshire's face. "How are you feeling?"

Alarmed, Dinah pushed herself up faster than she should have and was rewarded with a bout of nausea. "Oh. Oh." She allowed herself to sink back into the cot. "What happened?"

Cheshire resumed lightly patting her head with the cloth. "What do you remember?"

"I was out walking, because I couldn't sleep... and I found Iu-Hora's tent." She frowned. "And then... then...." She should have remembered, but there was a gaping hole in her memory; it was puzzling and unnerving. She could see bits and pieces, but the knowledge of what had happened was missing. "I'm sorry...," she sputtered. "I don't really remember. There was smoke and light and...."

Cheshire made a disgusted sound, yet his face showed a certain delight and fascination. "The Yurkei witch doctor has more powers than Wonderland has ever bothered to fathom. I highly doubt that you wandered there *entirely* on your own accord. He's been known to call those to him when he feels the need, whether by injury or trance. There is evil in that tent that might be of use to us yet. He has a mastery of alchemy that Wonderland has yet to discover." He stroked Dinah's head softly, attempting to soothe her. It made her uncomfortable. "We almost lost you to the fever. If you had died, Iu-Hora's head would have been sucked down into the shadow ponds by now. You have caused a great stir, daughter."

Heads... *something about heads...* Dinah couldn't remember. There was only the unclear memory of smoke and light, and a burning deep in her lungs.

"Do you feel well enough to sit up now?"

"Yes." Dinah hated depending on him for anything, but she let him help her up and hold her hand as she gently made her way to a small wooden table. Soup steamed in a small mug and, somehow, there was a pile of warm sweets waiting for her. She looked up at Cheshire with amazement. "How does one make *warm pies* in the wilderness?"

He shrugged nonchalantly. "There is nothing I can't get for you." Cheshire raised a spoon to her lips.

"I can do it myself, thank you." Dinah clutched the spoon with determination and shakily brought it to her dry lips. "How did you get the—was it poison?—out?"

Cheshire leaned back on his chair and folded his long hands under his chin. "Wild lavender rice tea. Rice attracts moisture, and the smoke, when inhaled, became a form of liquid hallucination. It's quite fascinating. I visited the witch doctor myself after I saw you, and he explained its full effects. My dagger at his throat helped a bit, I think. After that, the Yurkei wouldn't let anyone come near his tent." He paused. "I hate to be the one to tell you, but this incident only served to fan the flames of anger between the Spades and the Yurkei."

"We're on the same side for gods' sake," snapped Dinah. "Either way, many of these men will die, all for me."

His smile faded. "That's where you are mistaken. These men do not fight and die for you. No man fights or dies for a leader. He dies for an ideal. That ideal is embodied in your person. The Spades will die fighting for their rights, for the rights of the men that they stand beside. They fight for the right to bear children, for a chance to live forever through their heirs. The Yurkei fight to reclaim the land of their forefathers." Distracted by a sweet on the little table, Cheshire summed it up, "Don't delude yourself, these men fight for themselves."

Cheshire selected a slice of plum pie and took a small bite. Dinah had never noticed how small and sharp his teeth were. His bites were half the size of hers. "Fathers and sons, my dear. That is what these men fight for, even if they believe they are fighting for you. Part of becoming a leader is learning how to manipulate that belief. It's the way power works. Your face and dress and crown represent these things for them, but it wouldn't matter if it was you, or another. Your task now is to become a queen for whom they'd be willing to die."

Dinah stared at the ground. She had behaved so foolishly by going to Iu-Hora's tent, and yet, she was furious at him for pointing out the truth. "Ironic how you can speak of sacrifice with such ease when you only looked after your own interests while the King beat my mother and treated me with contempt."

Cheshire flashed a pitying grin at her. "Poor girl. Is that what you believe? I simply see it as keeping your best interest at heart. I would have loved nothing more than to steal you and your mother away in the dead of night and start over in a new place, a new town, away from the King, where I could love you both proudly. And yet, by doing that, I would deny you the crown, a chance to become the most esteemed person in Wonderland. Instead, I suffered in silence, watching the love of my life be touched by a man who disgusted me, and watching my daughter be raised by a man who hated her."

Cheshire slowly folded his napkin, taking care with each corner. When he was done, a tiny paper mouse remained. He set it inside of her empty tea cup before standing to leave. He calmly tucked in his purple tunic before suddenly leaning over her menacingly. His sweet breath swept over her face. "Do not presume to know me, daughter. I have sacrificed *everything* to get you where you are. And instead of being grateful for my sacrifice, and the sacrifice of all of the men here, you repay us by wandering right into the arms of a mad witch doctor so that we might have watched you die slowly. You are not a child anymore. You are a queen, so behave like one!"

He stood up and took a deep breath, adjusting his brooch as he transformed himself back into the smooth, unruffled Cheshire. "Make sure that you don't do anything strenuous today. No sparring. No fighting. Wardley or Sir Gorrann is to be with you at all times. I don't trust your Yurkei guards anymore."

Dinah watched in simmering silence as Cheshire whisked himself out of the tent. Her appetite had disappeared. *He was right.* It was time to quit playing these risky games to satisfy her childish curiosity. She was no longer a girl sneaking into the Black Towers with Wardley. Her kingdom was at war, and she was too indulgent of her own whims. The consequences of her actions would be real and severe. For gods' sake, she had almost started a war here in their camp.

A true leader would create allies out of enemies, but her actions had only served to create division. *I will remember that,* she thought. *I will remember that what the queen does matters. I will listen to Cheshire's wisdom, no matter how strange he makes me feel.* Deep in thought, she munched quietly on a blueberry tart. As she went to take another bite, she looked down in shock at the tips of her fingernails. They were a deep orange, stained with the poison that was slowly seeping out of her body, a real reminder of how close she had come to ruining the lives of thousands. She didn't believe that Iu-Hora, the witch doctor, had intended to kill her, and yet, he was dangerous just the same. Alone in the tent, Dinah closed her eyes and vowed that she would no longer make impulsive decisions on whatever whim came over her at the time. The cause and the crown came first. *I will be the queen they deserve.* She would work harder to remember that these were her people here, both the Spades and the Yurkei. It was her job to lead and protect them. Her foolishness prior to war was inexcusable.

She guzzled cool water from a nearby bucket and lay down for a few more hours before she felt ready to stand and walk. When she finally left the tent, bright sunlight blazed down on her through the mist of the Darklands. Wardley was waiting for her, his long legs folded beneath him as he balanced his sword on one finger. "You're up!" His long arms wrapped around her shoulders, and Dinah gladly let him pull her against his body. "Come here, you idiot! I was so worried. Why did you go to Iu-Hora? Haven't you heard the rumors about him? They say he grinds up the bones of his people to fertilize their mushroom fields. What were you thinking??"

"I don't know. It was foolish and it won't happen again," replied Dinah calmly. "And no, I hadn't heard that." She pressed her face against his shoulder. "Though I do not doubt it."

"What happened in there? What did you see?"

"I can't remember."

Wardley made a doubtful face.

Dinah sighed. "It's hard to explain—it's like someone has pulled a black cloth over that memory. I know he told me something important, but I cannot remember what it was, only traces of words." *Cat. Heart. Grass.* "It's there, I just can't reach it."

Wardley stepped back and took stock of her body. "How well do you feel? Are you sure you shouldn't be lying down?"

Dinah shook her head. "No. I've been sleeping most of the day. I don't deserve any more rest, especially when my men are so busy." All around the camp was a flurry of activity. Horses were being fitted for breast plates. Swords were being sharpened, and the sound of metal on metal was deafening. During the day the camp was usually filled with the raised voices of men, but today there were no voices to be heard, only the sound of work and progress. All of these sounds fell under an eerie quiet that permeated the air.

"Why is no one speaking?" Dinah saw several Spades cast fascinated looks in her direction and then drop their eyes when she looked back. "What's going on?"

Wardley gave her a quizzical look before pushing her hair aside to whisper in her ear. Dinah's heart beat rapidly as his breath brushed her cheek. "Tomorrow we begin our march north, Dinah. The war is upon us."

Dinah quickly counted the days on her fingers. Missing an entire day had left her confused. He was right—they would march out the following day, headed for Wonderland Palace. How had it arrived so suddenly? The Spades continued to stare at her.

"Move along!" Wardley snapped, and they begrudgingly obeyed.

"Why were they staring at me like that?"

"Probably because you are the only woman in this camp." He fidgeted awkwardly.

"Tell me the truth," snapped Dinah. She had known Wardley long enough that it was painfully obvious when he was lying.

He sighed. "Cheshire has been telling everyone how you survived the encounter with the Yurkei witch doctor, how in return he gave you a vision of our victory."

Dinah looked at Wardley and gasped. "THAT is a lie!"

He clamped his hand over her mouth. "Shh. It doesn't matter. It gives the men hope, letting them believe that you have some special knowledge of a victorious battle. Who knows, it might even be true. The men will have less fear when they go into battle if they believe fate is on their side."

Dinah grabbed Wardley's arm. "That is a false hope. There was no word of our victory. Although...."

Cat. Heart. Grass.

"There might have been," Dinah admitted. "I can't remember. Still, I want the men to believe in themselves, not some false prophecy. They need to have faith that we can win."

"And why exactly will we win?" asked Wardley.

"Because we are on the right side," answered Dinah, unconvinced. "Because we have to. Because it is right." Dinah looked out over the camp. She knew the odds. Her men were outnumbered and perhaps outmatched. The Yurkei and the Spades would fight with a certain fervor, but did fervor and righteousness matter when the numbers were not in their favor? Dinah felt a fresh stab of fear. "Do you believe we can win? As the once future Knave of Hearts, do you think we will win?"

Wardley glanced down at Dinah, his face a book of weariness as a lock of curly brown hair fell over his eyes. Dinah felt her heartbeat quicken. "Take a walk with me, Dinah. There's something I want to show you."

CHAPTER EIGHTEEN

Morte dutifully followed Corning, Wardley's obedient white steed, out of the camp and into the wilds of the Darklands. They walked in silence for about an hour, through hot swamps and over a field of strange rubbery plants that produced in Dinah an uneasy feeling of being watched. The plants seemed to be alive—unfurling themselves toward Morte's hooves as they passed before recoiling, rejected and hungry. As the valleys seemed to grow wetter and wetter, Wardley turned them slightly east, and the horses began a laborious climb up slick grassy hills, their hooves slipping on the slimy moisture that permeated the ground. Before long, the rolling peaks ended at a tangled bramble patch that defended itself from invaders with wicked-looking black thorns, each the size of a hand. They dismounted their steeds. Wardley staked Corning and Dinah laughed at the idea that she would try that with Morte. The best she could hope for is that he would be here when she came back. Wardley slashed at the bramble in front of her as they pushed through its sharp tangle. The bramble grew thicker; the light dimmer. Dinah thought she heard water. Dinah pricked her hand on one of the thorns and watched her blood pool in her palm.

"Wardley…."

"We're almost there. It's just around here." Wardley stepped to the left and disappeared behind a wall of thorns. Her hands out in front of her, Dinah pressed on. She followed Wardley's footprints until they led her out to a small, magical clearing. Behind them was a silent blue pool of water, so still and clear that the light reflecting from it cast turquoise waves across Wardley's handsome face. At the center of the pool, unattached to any rock or other structure, a waterfall flowed UP from the middle of the perfectly still pool, its stream turning into mist once it hit a certain height. The mist then spiraled and disappeared into the sky. They stood in silence for a few minutes before Wardley spoke softly as Dinah stared in fascination.

"Incredible, isn't it?" Wardley pulled off his boots and soaked his feet in the shallow pool. "I've never felt water this clean. It's the perfect temperature—not too hot, not too cold. I found this while you were sleeping off the hallucinations. Cheshire was watching you, and I couldn't just sit there wondering if you would ever wake up, so I wandered. Found this place." He shook his head. "I prayed that I could take you here one day; that you would wake up. Dinah, think about it—where does the water come from? There is no visible spring under the surface and yet—the water keeps rising. It's a miracle."

A smile crept over his face, so lovely that it hurt her heart. "Wonderland is a pretty wondrous place, wouldn't you say? I had no idea that so much lay outside the palace walls. It makes me want to climb on Corning and just disappear. I understand why those rogue Cards fled the palace. There is so much raw beauty out here in the wild."

His eyes followed Dinah as she pushed herself into the pool and wandered toward the middle until she stood right before the waterfall. She reached out her hand. Streams of warm water flowed upward through her fingers, as if Dinah herself was the source of this wonder. The water seemed to have a mind of its own between her fingertips, and tiny droplets crawled from the bottom of her wrist to her fingers before lifting off into the sky. She walked back to the edge of the water and climbed out, the hem of her tunic soaked. Smiling, she sat beside Wardley and dipped her wiggling toes into the pool. She glanced over at him, lounging easily beside her on the bank. This was how it always was: Dinah and Wardley. Together. She poked him.

"Remember that summer you stole the tarts from the kitchen, when Harris chased us down the hallway screaming? I've never laughed so hard. You had flour all over your face, and yet when he saw you, the first thing you did was scream 'I didn't do it!'" She laughed at the memory—Wardley, a lanky young boy, his face covered with jam and powder, stuffing as many tarts as he could into his pockets. The sun had filtered through the red heart windows as his thin body tore through the castle, Heart Cards and Harris bellowing behind him, and Dinah too, always a few steps behind, watching him with adoration. Together they hid in the courtyard behind her mother's white rose bushes that snaked over the walls, stuffing their faces with the tarts and giggling uncontrollably.

"It wasn't like you were starving. You just wanted to steal something."

"I did. I was a good kid, but at that moment, stealing tarts seemed dangerous, like a crime punishable in the Black Towers." He grinned. "It was infinitely exciting."

Dinah shuddered at the memory of the towers and looked down at the pool. "When I'm Queen, I will tear them down, until nothing but the roots remain."

"You have always been fond of making grand queenly statements." Wardley smiled as he tucked her black braid behind her ear before a profound sadness pierced his gaze. "It will never be good like this again, will it? War is coming, and somehow you and I are right in the thick of it."

Dinah nodded and stared at the waterfall, completely aware of Wardley's hand resting mere inches away from hers on the bank. She watched a tiny pink fish swim up the waterfall, its tiny fins flapping in the upward-flowing stream. Suddenly realizing what was happening, the fish reversed course and struggled to swim against the current. It was no use. The fish was sucked up into the sky with the water that turned into a pinkish mist. Seconds later, we heard a plop and saw the little fish swim away. Wardley continued on, unfazed.

"You know what I keep thinking about? How I hope that my parents have the good sense to stay out of the fight. My mother will stay huddled inside with the rest of the court, holed up in the Great Hall, but my father might just decide to be a hero and don his Card armor for one last battle."

Dinah gave his hand a squeeze. "He won't. He'll know it's you coming."

Wardley swallowed. "Yes, but… what if he doesn't? What if he puts on a helmet and I don't recognize him in the battlefield? What if I…?" His words faded on his tongue. A few moments passed as they both remained silent. "What are you afraid of?" he whispered.

Dinah swallowed before lowering her voice to a murmur. "Everything. I'm afraid that the men will see that I am just a girl who was rejected by the King. I'm afraid I'll die silently and quietly, like the flame blown from a match, and I'll be nothing more than a child who played at war. I'm afraid of losing you, or Sir Gorrann, or even Cheshire. I'm afraid of letting down the

Yurkei people." Dinah lifted her foot and watched droplets of water roll off her muscular calf. "Mostly I'm afraid that I'll die, and it won't matter if I have a crown on my head or not. I'll die the same as other men, with a bloody sword through my chest, one final breath lost in the madness."

A sword. What had the Caterpillar said to her? "You will pierce the heart of one man and..."

Her memory was there, but then it was gone again, the way a butterfly would land on her hand but leave the moment she glanced at it. "I'm even afraid of what happens if we are victorious. I'll be Queen. Can I rule? Will I be a good ruler, or a terrible one, like my...?" She stopped. "Like the King of Hearts. If that even happens. If we can get through the gates."

Wardley absently clasped her hand in his, their palms slick with comingled sweat.

"Do you believe we can win, Wardley?"

He stared out at the small pond. His face was ruddy and flushed from the walk, and for a moment he reminded Dinah of the boy with the stolen tarts. But then she saw the stubble creeping up his cheeks and the way his sculpted muscles tensed under his shirt. He had become a man since she had seen him last. He sighed and rubbed his face with his other hand.

"We can win, but it's not in our favor as it stands right now. The King has us outnumbered almost two to one and that means the odds are against us. The iron walls are perfectly round, which means that to surround them, we will be stretched thin in all places. We have the Spades, which will help, for they are ruthless in battle, but he has the Heart Cards, who are the most-skilled fighters in Wonderland. He has Xavier Juflee." He gave a laugh. "We have an exiled princess, the King's horse, an army of wild natives, and the Spades. And even if we win, once we are inside the gates, the people of Wonderland Palace will not welcome us with open arms. They loathe you, do you realize that? The people fear you, Dinah, and for good reason. You are bringing death and war upon this city, a city that has never seen a battle. Almost every man in the kingdom is a Card, and the King will deploy all of them to his defense."

"Yes, but we have the Yurkei...."

"The Yurkei have never attacked a city. What do they know of walls and iron gates and a palace made of stone and glass? The mounted Heart Cards will smash against the Yurkei on the north side, while we battle our way through a sea of Hearts, Clubs, and Diamonds, all while the Fergals rain arrows down around us." Wardley shook his head. "If we are captured, our fate will be much more terrible than dying quickly on the battlefield. They will throw us into the Black Towers to rot, until we become one with the tree, or worse. The King of Hearts is a hateful man." He looked over at Dinah, his brown eyes gazing with adoration and sadness over her drawn face. "I swear to you this day, here in this place, that I will kill you before I let the King torture you. And I hope you will do the same for me."

Dinah smiled back at him, knowing that she would never be able to take Wardley's life. No, not even to save him. Love had made her impassively hard and needlessly soft at the same time.

"I keep thinking," he muttered, "that this might be the last time I do anything. The last time I eat bread. The last time I dip my foot in a pool. The last time that I get to speak with you as a friend, and not as a commander to his queen."

Dinah felt her heart start to gallop within her chest. It raced so fast she felt it might explode. Despite all the oxygen running through her veins, she was frozen in place. Wardley seemed oblivious to her discomfort. He leaned back onto the mossy ground, stretching his arms above his head.

"Tonight could be the last night that I watch the stars simply to remember my place in this world. Everything that we have can be taken away. It will be taken away for many men that rest in those tents, maybe from you, maybe from me."

Dinah felt the fury climbing up through her chest, only this time it was different. This was a longing, a need, something that felt like falling, like a string was yanking her heart out of her chest. *Toward him, only him, always him.* She was no longer in control—all she could feel was the needing, the wanting to touch him. The passion crawled up through her until she became its puppet. It moved her limbs, her mind, her lips. She wanted him. She had waited long enough, and had almost lost him once. He was still speaking when Dinah leaned over him, her arms on either side of his body.

"If this is the last then there is something…. Dinah, what are you doing?"

Tenderly, she bent over him, her lips brushing his, as gentle and soft as dew drops on a petal. His lips were warm and moist, and tipped with everything good Dinah had ever tasted. Her red lips dusted across his, feeling his mouth staying painfully still. He lay motionless, frozen. *What am I doing?* Dinah yanked her head back and looked down at him with confusion and hesitation.

Wardley gave a painful grimace, and then he grabbed the back of her head roughly, pressing his lips hard against hers. Dinah gasped at the force with which he kissed her. It was the opposite of gentle—it was a forceful, hungry kiss with more than a hint of anger beneath it. With a grunt, he flipped Dinah over onto her back and leveled his body over hers before he started kissing her again, ever harder and harder, until Dinah felt her lips going numb.

It was delicious and full of pleasure, and yet, something wasn't right. Wardley's hands were pressed against her shoulders as if he was holding her down, or holding himself back. It was a defensive pose and his body was tensed in anger. As he kissed her furiously, Dinah felt a wet tear drip down his face onto her cheek. She pushed his face back. It took her a minute to catch her breath. This was not how she dreamed their first true kiss would be—aggressive and slightly violent.

"What? Wardley, what is wrong? *What are you doing*??" Her eyes traveled over the face she knew so well, and she could feel her heart wrench painfully when she recognized his grim determination. Her face, in turn, displayed a new emotion as she looked up at the man she loved so much: rejection.

"I'm sorry, Dinah." He turned away from her, his voice shaking. "I can't do this."

Dinah's hands clenched. "What do you mean, you can't do this?"

Wardley sat back and extended his hand to help her up. Dinah slapped it away. "Please don't touch me." She sat up, her limbs trembling with unfulfilled passion.

"Dinah, please!" Wardley grabbed her roughly, his hands on the sides of her neck, his forehead pressed up against hers. His voice was filled with desperation. "Don't you understand? I WANT to love you this way. I've never wanted anything as much as I want to love you in this way, the way you love me. I've begged and pleaded with the gods to give me those feelings for you! I want to be your king, your husband, your lover. But I cannot...," he struggled with the words. "I can't force myself to feel those things for you, no matter how much I wish it, no matter how much I long to be the man you deserve." He kissed her trembling forehead. "You are my best friend, a part of me! I love you, Dinah, and I will fight for your right to rule to my death! Does that mean anything? That I would die for you, gladly?" His face was contorted in agony as he looked into her black eyes. "Dinah, please! Please say something. I can't bear the silence. Please!"

They were both breathing heavily now. Dinah stared at him, her heart shattering into heavy pieces. The world seemed to be cracking and breaking under her feet. Wardley opened his mouth again, his words broken and tender.

"You have no idea what I left behind to come and fight for you...."

"Do not speak to me."

It was like being plunged into icy waters when you were burning hot—Dinah felt a ripping that was both parts of her soul and her vision of their future. She was left empty, drained— without her love, without him.... *He would never be hers.*

"Please leave." She turned away from him, her voice flat and dead. "Please leave, Sir Wardley. You have done your duty here."

He grabbed her arm and tugged it. "Stop it, Dinah! Don't talk to me like that. Don't turn away from me. I won't leave you, not in this state. Please, look at me."

She turned to him, her face a mask of stone. "You kissed me once. Is this all a game, Wardley? One more secret of my twisted upbringing? Did someone hire you to make me love you? Do you remember that day under the Julla Tree, when you kissed me? Was that part of the plan?"

Wardley grabbed her hands. "What are you talking about? Of course I remember. I kissed you because I *wanted* to. Because you were the first girl that I ever cared for. But even then, I knew that my feelings for you were not of that nature, no matter how much I tried to force them."

"Force them? Did you force yourself to play with me when we were children? Or to seek me out when we were older? Were you forced to train me on the sword or to follow me here?"

Wardley shook his head angrily. "No. Never! You're not listening. You don't understand—Dinah, I would do anything for you!"

"Except truly love me in the way a man should love a woman," she replied coldly. "Except kiss me."

"Does that even matter? I am yours in every other way. I have chosen you, and I would again. If only I could make my heart obey what my brain knows so clearly. I have tried and tried. I don't want to lie to you. I care about you too much. Dinah... please understand... you are my best friend. My Queen."

There was a deep truth to his words, and yet, Dinah felt she couldn't stand to look at his face anymore. Tears were flooding her vision, and a retching sob was making its way up her throat. She took a deep breath. "I need you to leave. Now. Please, Wardley."

"Dinah, no—"

"I COMMAND it. Please, leave me." She gave him a pleading look, a tear dripping down her face. Her voice was barely a whisper. "Please, Wardley, please do me this kindness."

Wardley's face contorted with a misery almost as terrible as the heartache she felt. He gave her the softest of kisses on her cheek and turned away from her, making his way to the edge of the clearing. "I'll be waiting for you tomorrow morning as we ride north." He stared at her, his face wrenched with guilt, before disappearing into the bramble.

Dinah waited until she couldn't hear his footsteps before collapsing into tears. An empty hopelessness overtook her, and she lay beside the pool, barely breathing through the ache. The thought of being with Wardley had kept her alive all those cold nights in the Twisted Wood, all those warm afternoons in Hu-Yuhar. She had always envisioned him sitting on the throne beside her, his hand in hers as they led Wonderland into a glorious and peaceful future. Now, there was nothing, only blackness and despair. She gladly gave herself over to the sorrow. It washed over her, a wave of anguish and rejection, and she let herself drown in the feeling, glad to feel anything.

For hours, she lay beside the pool, her heart throbbing over each word he had said. She sobbed and screaed, she raked the dirt with her fingers and let her dagger tremble over her neck for a few seconds before flinging it away. When the night finally settled around her, she heard someone calling her name. *Wardley?* She listened again. *No. Sir Gorrann.* With trembling hands, Dinah pushed herself to her knees and splashed the clear water of the pool on her face. Opening her black eyes, she stared at herself, hardly recognizing the face in the reflection. The girl she had been was gone. She had left Wonderland Palace an idealist, a naive girl who dreamed of an easy crown and ruling beside a man who would understand and love her heart. Their days would be filled with praise and their nights with perpetual passion, wrapped inside each other.

Now a jilted woman stared back at her, a forgotten child, a bitter warrior. The ends of her black braid dripped in the pool, the remnant of her childhood, this long black hair, her mother's hair. And yet, even when her mother had everything—a crown, a husband, children, and all the riches of Wonderland Palace—she had been unhappy. She could never truly be with the man she loved. Just like Dinah. But unlike her mother, Dinah would not lie down and die. Unlike Davianna, Dinah would have to fight for her crown. Hands trembling, Dinah picked up her dagger where it lay buried in a nearby log and walked over to the pool. With two short tugs, she was able to cut off most of her hair, so that it hit her right at the chin. Without a second thought, Dinah tossed her braid into the pool and turned to meet Sir Gorrann, who ran up to her, his eyes filled with concern, his voice raining curses down on her that she didn't hear. The pain was still alive inside of her, consuming and insatiable. She was rejected and desperate, filled with a new fury, this one dangerously ferocious. She was filled with a longing for destruction, a need to empty herself of all this sadness. He gave her a hard shake, and Dinah's glossy eyes finally connected with his.

"Yer Highness! Dinah! What's happened?"

Her lips trembled into an ironic smile. "He doesn't want me. After all this time."

Sir Gorrann's eyes filled with empathy and he let Dinah lean against him. "I'm sorry, Yer Grace. Come on, let's get you back to your tent."

She felt raw inside, stripped, and she followed without thought. Only the anger was left behind, and it was a raging current, Dinah helpless in its flow. She let Sir Gorrann help her through the bramble back to where Morte waited for her. He pawed the ground impatiently until she mounted him. With a click of her tongue, they were flying over the landscape, leaving Sir Gorrann trailing far behind. She felt something shift inside of her. With each pound of Morte's hooves, she felt her sadness turning to anger. Her rage was boiling over, spilling out until she seethed with fury. If she could not have him, she would at least have a crown.

If she could not quench the fire burning within her, she would set Wonderland ablaze.

The Fury, the final volume in the *Queen of Hearts* trilogy, coming soon.

ACKNOWLEDGEMENTS

Many thanks to the wondrous people who made this novel possible:

Ryan Oakes: for his endless feedback, support, and the sheer power of his belief in this novel, which propelled it from a vague idea into a tangible reality. Thank you for your unflagging love, your creative thinking, and your amusing knowledge about fantasy and fight training. Thank you for giving me the strength to stay true to my instincts and story.

For Maine: you are my wonder.

For Ron McCulley and Tricia McCulley, who are a model of patience, support, and just the right amount of parental devotion: thank you.

My elegant sister, Cynthia McCulley: thanks for always putting a smile on my face, and for agreeing to be a horse. Your shared love for dramatic music helped write this novel's most exciting scenes. The next one is for you.

Beloved friends who helped this process by just being their superb selves as the story unfolded—Kimberly Stein, Sarah Glover, Emily Kiebel, Cassandra Splittgerber, Elizabeth Wagner, Jordan Powers, Terri Miller, Nicole London, and Karen Groves: thanks for listening when I described something in my head for *hours*.

My intimidating test readers—Katie Hall, Michelle Rehme, Erika Bates, Jen Lehmann, Denise McCulley, Patty and Sarah Jones, Angela Turner, Holly Cameron, and Stefanie Feustel: thank you for helping sculpt this novel into something I am very proud of.

This book passed through the hands of more than a few skilled editors: Erin Armknecht, a story and formatting editor whose input is so great that it simply cannot be calculated, Jeni Miller, whose skill and editing eye were both completely terrifying and completely accurate, Jess Riley and Wayne Parrish, the *Queen of Hearts* blazes so much brighter because of you.

Crystal Patriarche, Heidi Hurst, Sara DiVello, and the entire SparkPress/BookSparksPR team: you're an amazing bunch.

To Erin Chan, equal parts charming and talented: thank you for being the striking silhouette that graces the cover.

Mae Whitman: thank you for being the inspiration behind my Dinah. You are a fierce little thing, and I admire every minute of your work.

Finally, the man, Lewis Carroll: *Alice's Adventures in Wonderland* is the most delightful, cavernous thing I have ever read. Thank you for being the true genius behind these characters, and for letting me wander, pen out, in this magnificent place.

ABOUT THE AUTHOR:

Colleen Oakes is the author of the *Queen of Hearts* saga and the *Elly in Bloom* series. Though relatively new to publishing, her work has garnered the Next Generation Indie Book Award in the young-adult category. She received her BA in creative writing at Concordia College in Bronxville, New York. A proud member of the Rocky Mountain Fiction Writers, Oakes lives in Denver with her husband and son, where she reads, swims, and writes.

Connect with her at www.colleenoakes.com, at Facebook.com/authorcolleenoakes, or on Twitter @colleenblooms.

Look for her next fairy-tale trilogy, *Wendy Darling,* to land in 2015.

ABOUT SPARKPRESS

SparkPress is an independent boutique publisher delivering high-quality, entertaining, and engaging content that enhances readers' lives. We are proud of our catalog of both fiction and non-fiction titles, featuring authors who represent a wide array of genres, as well as our established, industry-wide reputation for innovative, creative, results-driven success in working with authors. SparkPress, a BookSparks imprint, is a division of SparkPoint Studio, LLC.

To learn more, visit us at www.sparkpointstudio.com.

CPSIA information can be obtained at www.ICGtesting.com
Printed in the USA
LVOW06s1728100315

429949LV00006B/861/P